BECOMING GRACE DIVINE

NIKOLE CAROL JALBERT

Copyright 2016 Nikole Jalbert Houser

This work is licensed under a Creative Commons Attribution-Noncommercial-No Derivative Works 3.0 Unported License.

Attribution — You must attribute the work in the manner specified by the author or licensor (but not in any way that suggests that they endorse you or your use of the work).
Noncommercial — You may not use this work for commercial purposes.
No Derivative Works — You may not alter, transform, or build upon this work.

Inquiries about additional permissions should be directed to: info@booktrope.com

Cover Design by Greg Simanson
Edited by Steve Trinward

This is a work of fiction. Names, characters, places, brands, media, and incidents are either the product of the author's imagination or are used fictitiously. Any resemblance to similarly named places or to persons living or deceased is unintentional.

Print ISBN 978-1-5334-5237-5
Library of Congress Control Number: 2016905918

For my father, David
I will always be your girl

Chapter 1

I WAS CONCEIVED at the top of a broken Ferris wheel on the night my parents met. If I didn't know my mother, I could have been fooled into thinking it was romantic. But there was nothing romantic about my vicious, emotionally damaged Irish-gypsy mother. She had picked up an easy mark with intentions to swindle him out of money, and gotten bored when the Ferris wheel broke. I didn't know anything more about my father than his name, Ray Tivens. Mama told me he was no good, and that he never wanted me. She told me this so often I was positive it wasn't true. Maybe that was just the hope of a little girl who wanted at least one parent to love her.

My mother, Wanda Therese Shayler, was Irish born and likely in the US illegally. I have no idea if that was her real name. I doubt she even remembers what it was. Every place we went she was someone new, adjusting her personality to the situation. She was five feet of curvy seduction, with hip-length sable hair and deep brown eyes. Men were helpless to resist her, and she made a good living off that. Her favorite cons always involved married men and blackmail. Luckily, she never involved me in those.

We rarely stayed anywhere for longer than it took to con someone out of enough money to move on. Mama always acted as if something were coming to get her. I did my best to stay out of her way. She taught me to pick pockets and play simple cons. No one suspects cute little girls. I did what she wanted to avoid getting slapped around, and learned early on never to ask for anything.

I think my life might have been better if I hadn't so closely resembled my dad. I've never seen him, so I'm guessing, but I look nothing like my mother. I'm five-ten to her five feet, and my body has always been slender and athletic, not voluptuous. I've made the best of my B-cups with push-up bras, and have a nicely rounded ass. My hair is a much lighter brown than Mama's, and I've since cut it off to avoid any resemblance. My eyes are sky blue, and my skin much darker than her pale Irish. If we were standing next to each other, no one would have thought we were mother and daughter. Most of my life I've wished we weren't.

I left Mama when I was sixteen. I was determined to prove to her that I wasn't anything like her. She told me that gypsy was in my blood and I'd never be able to settle anywhere, that living the legitimate life wasn't something I could do. She hit me, then gave me five grand, along with a phone number where I could reach her when I came to my senses.

She was partly right: I wasn't able to stay in one place, but I didn't call my mother. Even if she had me pegged as a drifter, that didn't mean I couldn't live legitimately. I got my GED, and then found work wherever I could. It wasn't easy, and I was often tempted to use my con skills, but I mostly resisted that urge. (I might have run a small con on a landlord once, but he'd deserved it.)

I started doing caricature art and face painting at street festivals to make extra money. I'd always loved to draw, but had never thought I was talented enough to make a living out of it. I couldn't afford to take classes, but I met a college art professor who wasn't too old, and he traded sex for art lessons. It wasn't my finest hour, but I learned a lot from him, and he always treated me well. I ended up living with him for six months; turned out to be the longest relationship of my life. But he started to get too close—telling me he loved me—so I left. I'd never loved him. I liked him, and enjoyed him as a person. But I'd grown up being told that love was a disease, and despite telling myself I didn't believe it, I still ran from that.

When I was twenty-four, I found the courage to try and get a small gallery in Maryland to show my work. The owner was an older woman who took pity on me and allowed me to hang a few pictures in her place. I was shocked when all of them sold. I put in a few more, but after the initial interest, it petered off, so I continued waitressing to pay the rent. I hadn't expected my art to lead to anything, anyway.

A month after I first sold a sketch, a man walked into the restaurant where I worked. He was about six feet tall, with a familiar color of brown hair, starting to gray at the temples, and sky-blue eyes. Sorrow was embedded in his expression, and his shoulders were slumped as if perpetually ashamed of something. It wasn't the fact that I was looking at an older male version of myself that convinced me I was looking at my father, but the way he wrung his hands anxiously. I did the same thing, and Mama had always smacked me for it, saying, "Your damn loser daddy did that all the time. Cut it out!"

He wrung his hands through our entire first conversation, as he told me he was my dad, and that he'd found me through a private investigator, using my artwork. He cried and apologized so much it was as if he were trying to give me a Sorry for each day of my life that he'd missed.

Two weeks later I found myself sitting on my blue Harley-Davidson Heritage Softail Classic, in the driveway of a worn-down house in Eastham, Massachusetts. The engine was still ticking as I steadied the bike with my leather boots on the dirt driveway. The house was two stories, the brick walkway and front step so decrepit that plywood had been placed over it. With some new windows, fresh paint, a lot of landscaping and love, though, that house could have been beautiful.

There was a detached garage that had been converted to an art gallery. It had been closed for years; the studio above it was still stuffed with the artist's abandoned tools. The area was dotted with scrub pine and locust trees, with a smattering of crabgrass fighting for dominance with the dirt and sand. The house was on a quiet dirt road, a fifteen-minute walk from the ocean. It was the kind of place I wished I'd grown up in. And it was my new home. My first home. It belonged to Ray Tivens; it was still too weird to think of him as Dad.

I stood beside my Harley, looking at the house Ray had just bought. He'd been shocked when I immediately accepted his offer to move in with him. He didn't know me that well, but I was hoping to change that. I didn't know how to be a daughter, any more than he knew how to be a father, but we both wanted a chance to figure it out. So this ramshackle old house was to become my first home. We'd restore it together, building a family and a house at the same time. That was the hope, anyway.

I had been standing in that driveway for five minutes. Because of the Harley's penchant for roaring, I knew Ray was aware I had arrived. I appreciated him giving me a few minutes to collect myself. I needed to come to him. I thought about the man who'd named his baby girl Grace Divine, in a naïve hope that it would keep her safe. I sighed. His baby girl was a damaged half gypsy, cruising through life with a Harley and a bad attitude. I had been Divvy since I'd been old enough to introduce myself. Maybe here, in this place, I could learn to become Grace Divine.

Chapter 2

I WALKED UP the stone path, more of a suggestion than a path at this point. I set my black-heeled boots on the plywood covering the crumbling brick steps and knocked on the door.

Ray opened it with a tentative smile. "Hey, Divvy," he said. There was a long moment where we stood looking at each other. "Well, welcome home."

I could tell he wanted to hug me, but he didn't try. He'd admitted to me that his years as a drunk had left him feeling like he didn't deserve happiness. He was still afraid of it, and wasn't sure how to reach out to me. He let out a sigh of contented relief when I stepped in and hugged him. He helped me carry my bags inside.

I fell in love with the house immediately. The front door opened into a small entryway, with the stairs to the second floor opposite it. A large living room was to the right, with an old fireplace in need of some TLC. The dining room was on the left, and Ray was halfway done ripping down the wall that had separated the kitchen from it. There was a small half bathroom off the kitchen and a slider leading onto the rotted back deck.

I sat down at the kitchen table, pushing aside dust and construction tools.

"So," he said, sliding a pizza box over to me. "What do you think of the place?"

I looked around the room, at the half-torn wall. "With a lot of work this place will be beautiful."

"It needs an artist's eye. That's why I wanted you to help me."

I smiled at him, but it made me sad that he was searching for reasons to want me around. He didn't seem to understand: I already trusted him. He was a man who wore his emotions in his eyes. I believed him when he told me my mother had stolen me away from him, and that he'd always wanted me. I just had to convince him somehow that I believed him.

But I didn't know how to say all that, so I just played along. "I'd love to help with the house. I've never done anything like this before, but I love new things. You're right about that wall, it has to go. And these floors? They'll be absolutely beautiful once they're refinished. You just can't find these old wide planks anymore."

He played with his pizza. "I'm glad you like it. I've been doing all the work myself, but I've been thinking of asking some friends to come in on the project. Trace has finished fixing up his son Axel's place, and he needs something new to do."

"Trace is your boss, right?" If he was the man I thought, he was a lot more than that. He was the man who'd found my father drunk and hopeless, gotten him sober, and given him a life. Ray spoke of him with an emotion most men would be uncomfortable expressing.

He smiled. "Yes. The best friend a man could ask for. He's got a great family: four kids, three boys and a girl. You'll meet them all soon. The younger two are about your age. I think Gage is twenty-one now."

"Axel and Gage?" I raised an eyebrow. "Is the other one named Driveshaft?"

He laughed. "Mason, and the girl is Bodel. They've kind of adopted me. I hope you like them."

"I'm sure I will. But for now, I want to eat some pizza and watch a movie with my . . ." I choked on the word "dad." Ray and I had talked for hours, both in person in Maryland and on the phone during my two-week drive up the coast, but we were still basically strangers. I saw a flash of hurt in his eyes, so I reached across the table and took his hand. "With you," I soothed.

The couch had seen better days but we sat on it, drank soda, and watched *Roadhouse* on the heavy old TV that sat on the floor. I wasn't sure if this was what a father and daughter were supposed to do, but it felt right.

I spent the next few days setting up my room and going through the gallery. I didn't own much, but Ray had found a bed, a dresser, and a wobbly nightstand for my room. I'd spent all my life in hotels or dingy one-room apartments, so having a whole house was disconcerting.

There were three bedrooms upstairs and a small bath at the top of the stairs. Ray's room was to one side of the bathroom, and the two smaller bedrooms were crammed on the other. My room was connected to the spare bedroom by a small window in the wall. I imagined children having Nerf-gun wars through it by day, and whispering secrets by night.

I was more interested in the gallery than the house. The old owner had been a painter, and had left some of her supplies behind in the former garage, which had been converted into a gallery. I didn't paint, but maybe I'd give it a try now that I had something to play with. I set up my easel and sketchbooks, charcoal, pencils, and pens.

Ray was a decent cook and we ate amid the dust of construction at the dining room table. We walked through the house and debated over removing walls, paint colors, tile versus linoleum, lighting, and what kind of sound could be considered music. We didn't talk about my mother, my childhood, or his years as a drunk.

I learned that my father loved classic rock and country music, and cheesy B-movies from the eighties. He left wet towels draped over the toilet, snored like a thunderstorm, and walked around in his tighty-whiteys between the hours of four and seven in the morning. Ray carefully asked me questions and I dodged most of them. I didn't think the details of my childhood were things he needed to know. He couldn't erase the past, so knowing about it would only give him something else to take the blame for.

Protecting him aside, I wasn't good at talking about myself. Opening up to people was not in my skill set. I was great if you just got a quick glimpse. Right below the surface, though, there was a swirling mess of psychosis. It was better for everyone if I was just a flash on my Harley as I passed by.

On Saturday I woke up late as usual, to the sound of Ray ripping down the kitchen wall. It was a beautiful day for early May and I decided I'd go for a ride down to Provincetown. I put on my black leather pants, a bright pink bra, and a white tank top with a black skull and crossbones across the boobs. I spent a few minutes on my makeup and hair, knowing the hair would be a waste because of my helmet. But due to its shortness, if I didn't take a moment styling it, it tended to get scary.

When he saw me, Ray paused with his crowbar and raised an eyebrow. "You look, ah, nice," he said. I imagine an experienced father would have thrown a fit over the outfit. Luckily, he was new to the whole parenting thing.

"I figured I'd head up to Provincetown for the day, see what's at the end of this sand bar."

He fidgeted with the crowbar and looked down at his feet.

"What?"

"Well, I was going to ask you to do me a favor, but you're busy. I can . . ." he began.

"What's the favor?" I interrupted.

"I want to get the front steps fixed. Especially with you jumping on them in those heeled boots. I'm afraid you're going to slip and break your neck." He blushed, as if embarrassed to be worried about me, then continued, "I have a mason in mind to do the work. He's at a family barbeque down the street. Would you mind stopping in there and asking him to come check out the job?"

"No problem. Which house?"

"It's the third one down heading back to the main road. There'll be a bunch of trucks parked out front. Everyone will be around the side of the house."

"I'll swing by. Anything I can pick up while I'm out?"

"Just a mason."

"I'm on it." I grabbed my tasseled black leather jacket and headed out to my Harley.

Chapter 3

THE HOUSE WASN'T hard to find, with four pickup trucks, a restored old-school Mustang, and a spray-painted, metallic-blue car—a mongrel created from at least three different models. I pulled past the row of trucks and cars to the last spot in the sandy driveway. A mass of people were in the side yard of the house, congregating around a grill and an old picnic table.

The Harley commanded attention, and every eye turned to me. I killed the engine and slung my leg over the bike as I took off my helmet. I ran a hand quickly through my hair and turned to the family. My eyes went to the guy at the grill, probably because he was shirtless. He had the kind of body I considered it a crime to clothe. He was tall and broad, and had muscles that made my fingers itch to touch them. He had short brown hair and sunglasses covering his eyes. His jeans hugged his hips; I saw the flash of a tattoo on the back of his right shoulder, just before he turned to face me.

I scanned the rest of the people as I walked closer. There were two other men who looked enough like the shirtless wonder to be his brothers. A pregnant brunette was looking at me suspiciously, leaning against a gigantic bearded man. A smaller non-bearded version of the giant stood beside him, grinning at me. A pretty blond, also pregnant, was walking out from inside the house, along with an older version of the three brothers and a beautiful woman who was obviously the pregnant brunette's mother. A toddler was wrapped around the medium-sized brother's leg. They all watched me walking toward them in my leather.

To my immense pleasure, the shirtless guy stepped around the grill to meet me.

"Hi," I said, throwing on my best smile and using my "from nowhere" accent. "Sorry to interrupt your party. I need a mason."

The man grinned at me, which took me completely off guard. He exuded confident alpha male, but the grin had a hint of the playful bad boy. He held out his hand. "If you're looking for Mason, you've found me," he said as his hand enveloped mine. "If you're looking for someone to lug some bricks around, you're looking for my brother, Axel."

"I might be in the market for both," I said, realizing I'd just let my natural Irish accent slide out.

He laughed and let go of my hand. "You must be Ray's daughter," he said, taking off his sunglasses. He pinned me with stunning dark-blue eyes. "I'm Mason Tavish."

"Grace Divine Shayler, but you can call me Divvy. Ray sent me over to find Axel. He wanted to get the front step looked at."

Mason smoothly took my arm and led me to the others.

"This is Ray's daughter," he told them. "Grace Divine, but she prefers Divvy. That's my brother Axel, and my nephew Danny on his leg. The blond is Axel's wife, Maxine. That's my sister Bodel and the idiot she married, Zach. That's Zach's brother James. Stay away from that one."

"Hey," James protested.

Mason ignored him. "My parents, Trace and Nancy. And that is my baby brother, Gage."

"I'm not a baby," Gage groused.

I shook hands and filed away the names and connections. I had always been really good at remembering names. My mother had trained me as a small child. It was important as a con artist to remember everything.

"Grace Divine?" Bodel said, her tone doubtful. "That's quite a name."

I bit back the sarcastic comment about her own peculiar name, saying more diplomatically, "Blame Ray. He's the one who chose the name. I just go by Divvy."

The little boy still coiled around his father's leg looked up at me and said, "Talk pretty."

"Thank you," I said, wondering what had made me forget myself and not hide my accent. Then I felt Mason brush up against my arm and remembered. "My mother was born in Ireland," I continued, surprising myself. I never volunteered information.

"It's a beautiful accent," Nancy said. "You look just like Ray."

"I don't think I've ever seen Ray in leather pants," Gage said.

"Let's hope we never do," I said. Everyone laughed; I could see why Ray liked the family so much. They were good people. But Mason was too close to me and Gage was edging closer. I turned my attention to Axel.

"So, do you think you have time to run over to Ray's and check out the steps?" I asked.

"'Course he does," Trace cut in, slapping his son on the back. "And as soon as you're done, drag Ray over here. Burgers'll be done soon and I know he's planning on skipping lunch. Divvy, why don't you sit down with me?"

I knew I was trapped, and that Ray had known sending me to this house was going to make escaping to Provincetown impossible. Trace took my arm with the same gentle command as his son. I found myself sitting at the picnic table.

"I was going to head up to Provincetown, actually," I said.

"You can go up anytime. Mason makes great barbeque, and I want a chance to talk with my friend's daughter." He grinned at me and I gave up. The family was too charming and welcoming to trigger my normal flight reflex. I was relieved when Mason returned to the grill. Gage sat down next to me but kept a respectful distance. I forced my eyes away from Mason's body to look at Trace.

"Ray's been so excited the last few weeks," Nancy said from beside her husband. "He had me pick out the sheets and comforter for your room. I hope they are to your liking."

"Those sheets are wonderful," I said. "I'm used to cheap hotel-room ones, and those horrible lumpy pillows."

"You travel a lot?" Nancy asked.

"I never stay in one place for long," I said, stripping off my leather jacket. Nancy reached across the table for my arm.

"That is beautiful. Can I take a closer look?" she asked.

I stood up and leaned across the table so she could see my tattooed arm. The lush green vine started at the bottom of my wrist and wrapped around to a large half-open rose on the back of my shoulder. I had designed it myself and spent painful hours to have the detailed leaves. I turned and pulled my tank top aside to show her the blond faerie sitting on the leaf on the back of my shoulder, as her face raised to smell the rose.

"She is beautiful," Nancy said. "Ray said you are an artist. Did you design this?"

"Yes."

"You do beautiful work."

"This is the only tattoo I designed. I don't do tattoos." I shrugged and sat back down. "I don't like my canvas to flinch and bleed."

"Can't blame you," Nancy said. "What do you like?"

"Pencil sketches, charcoal, some pen cross-hatching. I tried to sell some of my work in Maryland. It was the first place that was willing to take my stuff."

"Congratulations."

"Thanks, but I didn't sell enough to pay the rent, so I had to start waitressing again. That was why I jumped on the opportunity to come here. I get a chance to get to know my father, and I'll have plenty of time to work on my art." I wasn't entirely comfortable with Ray footing all the bills during my stay, but I didn't say this thought aloud.

Gage moved closer to me on the bench. I glanced over at him. He was a handful of inches shorter than Mason and much more slender. He had a dancer's body and the grace to go with it. His eyes were Trace's deep brown. He would be fun. He promised a good time, the kind with no strings attached. But my attention went back to Mason at the grill. His back was to me and I took a moment to inspect his tattoo. It was a beautifully drawn masculine angel with the words, *RIP Michael* under it. Mason turned his head and caught me looking. He smiled, but his eyes went to Gage, who was now only two inches away from me.

"Gage," he said, causing Gage to jump like he'd been struck. "Go get me a fresh shirt, will you?"

"Go get it yourself," Gage said in that patented put-out-younger-sibling tone.

"I'm cooking. And you're the one who gave Danny the barbeque sauce."

"How was I supposed to know he'd use it as a weapon against you?" Gage asked, but he got up and headed into the house.

When I turned back to Nancy and Trace, they were both watching me with interested looks on their faces. It made me nervous.

"So you were saying you don't stay in one place long?" Nancy asked.

I shrugged. "It's the way I grew up. My mother would say it's in our blood. Irish gypsies. And I like to travel, see new places."

"What's the longest you've ever lived somewhere?" Trace asked.

"Nine months."

"Were you homeschooled?"

"Sometimes. I patched together an education. I have a GED. I never really liked school. I got in trouble for drawing all over my tests."

Nancy sat back a little. "I've lived in this town all of my life. I hadn't been out of New England until last year. My son-in-law Zach sent us to Italy. My daughter might have had a problem with marrying a rich man, but I sure as shit didn't."

"Love you too, Nancy," Zach said from where he stood talking to Mason and Bodel.

"It must be so wonderful to have seen so many places," she continued.

I shrugged. "Don't take having a home for granted."

Gage returned and tossed Mason a black T-shirt. I was sad to see all that tan skin and muscle disappear.

"Food's ready," Mason said. His eyes caught on something down the driveway and I looked to see Axel and Ray, with Danny swinging around Ray's neck. Ray waved at me and unhitched the child to hand him to Axel.

"I'm sorry, Divvy," Ray said. "I should have known Trace would never let you leave."

"It's fine. I never walk away from good free food." I turned toward Mason. "It better be good."

He grinned at me and licked some barbeque sauce from his thumb. I had an intense detailed image of him licking barbeque sauce off me. I tore my eyes away and focused on Ray to kill the sexual heat that was rising. It was going to be a long afternoon.

Chapter 4

I WANDERED DOWNSTAIRS with my sketchbook, ignoring the sounds of construction. I was drawing each of the rooms as they were, then adding furniture in different positions to see what it would look like. I preferred drawing people, but I wanted to challenge myself. I felt my fuzzy black pants slipping down and pulled them back up over my butt. My shirt wasn't long enough to reach my pants, but few of my shirts were. I'd worked hard for my abs and I liked showing them off. I was barefoot as usual, despite the debris the construction had left on the floors. I curled up on the floor in the corner of the living room and began to draw.

Commotion and male laughter in the kitchen drew me away from my work. I found Ray sharing coffee and donuts with Axel, Mason, and Gage. I had spent all of last night trying not to think about Mason, and failed. It wasn't like me to fixate on a man. I plastered a smile on my face as the four men turned to me.

"Morning, Divvy," Ray said. "We didn't wake you, did we?"

"I was up already. Mornin' guys. Is there a coffee for me?"

Mason held out a cup. I took it, trying not to notice the heat of his fingers as I searched through the bag of donuts for something good. "These look great!" I selected a gigantic chocolate glazed.

"The place is close by," Gage said. "I can show you where."

I took a bite of the donut and my eyes nearly rolled back in my head. I sat on the edge of the dusty table and closed my eyes to enjoy my breakfast. I noticed the men had gone quiet, but I was too blissfully happy with my culinary masterpiece to care.

"You act like you've never seen a woman eat before," I muttered as the silence continued.

"Not like that," Gage said. There was a grunt, and the conversation I had interrupted continued around me. They were discussing the steps and other work on the house.

"I'm surprised your brothers talked you into coming," Ray said to Gage.

"I have to be careful with this masterpiece, but that doesn't mean I can't help," Gage said. I opened my eyes to realize he was talking about his body. Confidence and arrogance were apparently in healthy supply in the Tavish family.

"Our poor delicate baby brother," Axel said.

Gage glanced at me and blushed. "Stop calling me that."

"Stop being a delicate flower."

"Your hands could use some calluses," Mason said. The comment made me think of Mason's strong hands stroking over my skin.

Shocked at myself and irritated, I turned my attention to Gage. "It'll be good for you. Some scrapes and scratches, maybe even a sprained ankle would build character."

He went pale, and all four men stared at me like I had said something evil. I searched through the information I had learned during the party the day before, and realized my mistake.

"Oh, I'm sorry, Gage. I didn't think," I smiled apologetically. "No more jokes about sprained ankles when the professional dancer is around. I promise."

Gage recovered quickly and smiled back at me. "I'm not a professional dancer yet."

"You will be," I said confidently. "You'll be touring with some dance group before you know it."

I saw the hope and fear in his eyes. He wasn't like his older brothers. Mason and Axel were solid men who liked working with their hands and sitting on the back deck drinking beer with family. I recognized in Gage the eagerness to travel. Unlike the rest of his family, he wanted to get away from the Cape, to travel and see the world. I could understand him completely, and I could see how his deeply rooted family might not.

"Have you been to Cali?" he asked.

"I've been everywhere."

"I'd love to hear about it."

"I've kept a scrapbook," I said. "I'll show it to you sometime."

"But not right now," Axel cut in. "Trust me, Divvy, I'd love to see and hear about some of the places you've been, but we've got a step to build."

"Don't let me keep you," I said.

Axel and Gage started for the front door.

"You be careful with that masterpiece, Twinkletoes," Mason said. Gage turned back to him, stepping close to glare up at his bigger brother. My fingers curled around an imaginary pencil, as I started sketching the two of them in my mind. Despite the bravado, the love they had for each other was obvious. I wanted to catch the look in their eyes as they grinned at each other.

"Divvy?"

I realized now Ray was talking to me. "What?"

"Mason and I are going to be working in the living room replacing the windows in there and framing in the window seat."

"Oh, let me go get my work."

"Work?" Mason asked.

"I've been sketching the house," I said. "Before-and-after stuff. Trying out different designs and colors."

"I'd love to see it," Mason said.

I looked into his eyes to determine if he was genuinely interested. That was a mistake; I couldn't tell if he was interested in my art, but he was obviously interested in me. I retreated a few steps, hating it. What was it about Mason that threw me so off balance?

"Maybe if you play your cards right," I said, and went into the living room to get my sketchbook. I ran upstairs to avoid him, refusing to consider it a retreat. I settled in the empty bedroom on the floor and stared angrily at the blank page. I was a confident, independent woman. I did not let men intimidate me. He wasn't trying to intimidate me. He wasn't doing anything but subtly flirting. Yet there was something in his eyes that scared me.

I looked down at the sketchbook and began to sketch Gage and Mason, glaring at each other with brotherly affection. I relaxed as I worked. I still preferred drawing people. I spent time on their faces, closing my eyes to bring them into focus. I looked at the finished product and grinned. I had captured the look in their eyes. It made me think of Stacey, and I ran my fingers over the faerie tattooed on my shoulder.

I sketched Ray to distract myself, letting my mind go into my work. I wasn't going to dig through old, painful memories that morning. I was going to spend my time in the present. I slipped into the deep calmness that drawing always gave me. I stopped paying attention to what I was doing.

"Hey, there." Mason's voice made me squeak indignantly. I started like a rabbit and pulled my legs up against my chest. He laughed at me, looking huge from my seat on the floor. "Didn't mean to startle you."

"Don't sneak up on me when I'm working," I gasped, feeling ridiculous. My sketchbook was pressed against my chest where my up-drawn knees had plastered it. I tipped it back and realized what I'd been sketching. I'd drawn Mason as he'd looked the first time I saw him: standing in his jeans with his back to me, his strong body twisted as he looked at me over his bare shoulder. I slapped the sketchbook closed quickly.

"Lunchtime," he said. "Ray sent me up for you."

I blinked and checked my watch. It was 12:30. I had been sitting on the floor in the empty bedroom for hours. I stretched out my legs and winced.

"Need a hand up?" He was holding his hand down for me.

"Thanks, I lose track of time when I work." His hand wrapped around mine; I felt the shock of heat through my entire body. He pulled me to my feet, then caught me when I lost my balance due to the pins and needles. His chest under my hands felt insanely good, and I knew I had to get away from him. I quickly stepped away, bracing myself against the wall and rubbing at my leg. I looked down at my hands and blinked. Now where was my sketchbook?

I looked up to see the book in Mason's hand. He had taken it so smoothly I hadn't noticed.

"You okay?" he asked.

"I'm fine, just pins and needles," I said, trying to get my rebellious brain to work properly. He made me clumsy and tongue-tied, and I was the daughter of a very successful con artist. My mother would have died of shame if she could see me now.

Mason had opened the book while I rubbed at my leg. I figured it was stupid to protest. Besides, he was looking at the first sketches: generic depictions of the rooms. As long as I could stop him before he saw the last drawing . . .

I watched his eyes as he turned the pages. I couldn't decide what he thought, and it irritated me that I cared. I made art because I loved it, not to please other people. But I wanted Mason to like it, to think I was talented. I really needed to get away from him.

"So?" I prompted.

He grunted in a noncommittal way. Then he turned to the drawing of him and Gage, and the look on his face changed.

"That's more like it," he said.

"What?"

"Well . . ." He ran a hand through his hair and I started trying to figure out how to get the sketchbook back before he saw the last picture. He continued, "I'm no art critic or anything. In fact, if you repeat anything I'm about to say to my brothers, I will have to kill you."

I laughed.

"Just had to warn you. I have an image to uphold," he grinned at me. "Anyway, the first ones are okay. But this," he indicated the sketch of him and Gage, "this is beautiful. I've always loved art that catches emotion. I look at this, and I can see how I feel about my brother. You caught that. The first sketches show you have talent, but this shows you have a gift."

I stared at him, completely speechless. That was by far the best compliment I had ever received. He seemed oblivious to my shocked state, and turned the page. I realized he was looking at the sketch of himself, half-naked and looking over the top of his sunglasses. That picture caught emotion, but it wasn't brotherly love in his eyes, it was lust. He looked at the picture for a long time, his face unreadable. Then he grinned and looked down at me.

"Damn, I have a nice ass. Let's go get some lunch."

I snatched the sketchbook from his hands and rushed past him down the stairs. He followed me, laughing softly.

Chapter 5

I WAS GLAD it was Monday. Mason worked, and wouldn't be around the house making me lose my mind. I spent most of my day peeling wallpaper in the spare bedroom and the bathroom. I was grateful I'd been born after the seventies when that pastel floral pattern had been in vogue. I took a ride over to the paint store to get some samples, then spent an hour lying in the sun on the rotted back deck. Not having to go to work was wonderful, but the arrangement was still making me uncomfortable. Ray said he was happy to pay for everything. My only bills consisted of my cell phone and the insurance for my Harley. I was relieved he had never asked how I had afforded to buy the brand-new motorcycle without payments. I didn't think he would have approved of my winning it in a card game, especially since I had cheated.

I decided to make dinner for my father. Seeing as I didn't cook, dinner was going to consist of boxed pizza, but I knew Ray would love it anyway. Maybe he could teach me how to cook. I settled on the new window seat in the living room he and Mason had finished the night before. It overlooked the front yard and a little overgrown garden to the right of the crumbled stone path Axel was planning on replacing.

I sketched idly in my sketchbook, realizing it was almost full. I'd had so much time and inspiration since coming to the Cape. The sun lulled me to sleep.

I woke up with a shriek and slapped at whatever was crawling on my face.

Mason's, "Whoa, sorry," made it through my sleep-addled brain and I stopped myself from breaking his fingers. I let go of his hand and sat up.

"Don't fucking do that to me, dammit!" I snapped.

"Sorry," he said again. "I didn't mean to scare you."

I stood up and adjusted my tank top.

"Is that a faerie?" he asked, his hand catching the bottom of my shirt and pulling it back up over my belly button. I had switched my normal belly-button ring to the small metal faerie that Stacey had given me. I tried to pull my shirt back down, but he didn't let it go. "You have a thing for faeries."

"My friend Stacey did. She gave it to me. Let go of my shirt, Mason."

He grinned at me but stepped back. "You looked really cute curled up in the window."

I chose to ignore his flirting. "Where's Ray? And what are you doing here?"

"Ray's getting some things out of the truck. We're gonna do the last window in here."

"Didn't you just get off work?"

"Yeah, but I don't have anything better to do today."

Frustrated beyond words, I threw up my hands and headed upstairs.

"Come on, Divvy," Mason called, coming after me. "What did I do?"

I turned on the stairs to be face to face with him. "I'm in a bad mood. Just leave me alone."

"Whatever I did, I'm sorry."

"You didn't do anything, you jackass. I am a psychotic bitch, okay? Now piss off."

I spent a few hours brooding in my room, making angry sketches that all ended up being of Mason. It was so unlike me that I was starting to worry. I didn't do relationships. I slept with men I found attractive and moved on. It should have been that simple with Mason, but it wasn't. If and when it happened, as it almost certainly would, it wouldn't be just sex with him. There was some crazy connection between us, but I sure as shit wasn't going to let it tie me down. I was a gypsy by choice. I loved moving from place to place.

I should just sleep with Gage. He'd be a fun, no-strings sex experience. But I knew I couldn't. If Gage was stupid enough to go for it, it would just ruin his relationship with Mason. I wasn't about to avoid a messy relationship with Mason by sleeping with his brother and ruining their relationship. Whatever did happen, I'd end up hurting someone, and I hated it.

A knock on the open door frame got my attention. I looked up to see Ray in the doorway, looking uncomfortable.

"Hey, Ray," I said.

"Hey. So, are you gonna tell me what's going on?"

"What?"

"Mason was happy as a pig in shit until he talked to you. He barely said a word while we did the window, then he refused to stay for dinner."

I bit my lip. "I may have snarled at him."

"What did he do? If he's bothering you, I won't have him come around." He was trying on that protective-dad role, and it made me smile. It was nice to have someone who would protect me, even if it was unnecessary.

"He's not doing anything. Don't get mad at Mason. I'm just in a bad mood."

"I don't entirely believe Mason doesn't have something to do with your mood." He wrung his hands and stepped back. "I'm sorry, Divvy. I'm overstepping boundaries again. This isn't my business."

I smiled at him. "You're my father, Ray. You want to protect me. I love that, really I do. You're not overstepping. I'm attracted to Mason, but I just got here. Hell, I just met you, and I've got too much going on to deal with him too. Mason has been nothing but politely flirtatious. I'm just not up to figuring out how I feel about that right now."

He put an arm around me. "Mason's a good man, Divvy. Tell him what you just told me and I know he'll back off."

"I'm not sure I want him to. That's my problem. So let's go have some pizza and forget about it for tonight. Why don't you tell me if you've got any potential girlfriends?"

He looked at me like I had suggested he wrestle a tiger. "I haven't been on a date in years," he admitted as we went downstairs to the kitchen.

"Why not? You're a handsome guy. You're only forty-two. You've got a good job, a house that will be beautiful." I pulled the boxed pizza out of the freezer and preheated the oven.

"That's now. I spent over a decade as a drunk," he reminded me, "sleeping in my car."

"But that was the past. You've been sober for what, seven years now?"

"Seven years, June 21. The first couple were hard for me. I even had to call Trace a few times to stop me from going into a bar. He always came, no matter where I was or what time I called. He'd bring me to his house and we'd play poker."

"What about now?" I asked, putting the pizza in the oven before the timer told me it had preheated. "You still struggle with wanting a drink now?"

"Rarely. I can even go into a bar now. I've gone a few times with Trace and Mason after work. I can be around alcohol without wanting it. I have my bad days when I get lost in my past, but I just call Trace and have him and Nancy over for dinner. And now I've found you. I haven't wanted a drink since I saw you."

I smiled. "That's great. I normally push people to drink, not the other way around."

"I'm just happy you didn't slam the door in my face. I'd about given up ever having a relationship with you. And now you're here. And you don't seem to hate me. You don't seem angry at all."

I saw tears in his eyes and hugged him. "It's not your fault you weren't there. My crazy mother stole me away from you. So you were a drunk. You're not now. And you've given me this great opportunity to work on my art." I looked into his eyes, the same pale blue as my own. "More importantly, you've given me a chance to be a daughter. To have a family."

He hugged me tighter and I relaxed against him. The stove beeped and made us both jump and laugh. We wiped the tears from our eyes and I checked the pizza.

"Do you have Mason's number?" I asked.

"It's on the fridge. Why?"

"Just have to make a quick call."

I went out to sit on the new front steps with my cell phone. Mason picked up on the third ring.

"Hello?"

"Hi, Mason. It's Divvy."

There was a pause. "Oh. Ah, what do you, ah . . ."

"I called to apologize . . . and to thank you."

"What?"

"I was a complete bitch to you, for no reason. I'm going through a lot right now. I just met my father for the first time a month ago. This is the first time I've had family, at least family that wants me around. I think I hide it well, but I'm pretty screwed up about everything right now. So I snapped at you."

"It's okay. I shouldn't intrude on this time you have with Ray."

Now I felt even worse for snapping at him. "I don't want you to feel that way. I don't want you to avoid me. I'm not very good at having friends. I don't stay in one place for long. I never have. I don't make friends, because I hate losing them. But Ray is going to be here, and he's my father, and always will be. So I think it's safe for me to have friends, I just don't know how to go about it. So if I snap at you, call me a bitch and tell me to stop."

He laughed. "Okay. I was gonna come by after work on Wednesday. You promise not to snap at me then?"

"It's a promise. I'm gonna go have dinner with Ray."

"I'm glad you called me, Divvy. I'll see you later."

I hung up and sighed. I was going to regret telling him not to avoid me, but I was so happy about realizing I loved my dad that I didn't care.

Chapter 6

THE NEXT DAY I met Ray at the door after he got out of work.

"Hey, Divvy," he said. He always seemed surprised to find me still there when he got home.

"Let's go for a walk," I said.

He looked at me a moment in his worn, dirty jeans and sweaty T-shirt. I realized he was probably tired after a long day of work, but he smiled and the shadows left his eyes. "A walk sounds great. Then I can make some dinner."

"I was hoping *we* could make dinner," I suggested, hoping to find more common ground. "I mean, if you don't mind teaching me. Something easy; hardest thing I've ever tried is scrambled eggs, and I burned them."

Ray slowly put an arm around my shoulders and we walked toward his truck. He still touched me as if afraid I was made of smoke and would diffuse with the slightest touch. I had to find a way to reassure him that I wasn't going to leave him. He kept his head tilted up and I could see the tears in his eyes but they didn't fall.

We drove down to the beach and watched as a man threw a ball into the high tide for a big, shaggy dog. The sun was sinking down toward the water.

"I'd have thought we'd see more dogs down here," I commented.

"It's not allowed," he said, indicating a sign. "No dogs between Memorial Day and Labor Day. We've got another few days before it's officially closed to dogs. After that, it's possible to sneak in either really early or really late, but during the day it's impossible. I used to walk my dog before work in the morning, but he died last year."

"Oh, I'm sorry."

Ray smiled, looking out at the water. "He was a good dog. I rescued him when he was fourteen. His owner died, and no one wanted to adopt such an old guy. We had a good three years. I'd do it again in a heartbeat. His name was Henry."

"Wish I'd gotten a chance to meet him."

"He helped keep me sober."

I wanted to lighten the mood, so I asked, "Why aren't dogs allowed here?"

"Tourists. Us locals get shoved aside until they go back where they belong in September. No dogs on the beach, the seashore, anywhere for the next three months." Ray shook his head and grinned at me. "I don't really qualify as a local. I'm a fresh Washashore."

"A what?"

"It's the term for people who move to the Cape. If I stay long enough, some might consider me a local, but not all. The real hardcore Cape Codders are an odd bunch. Many of them haven't been over the bridge in years." I almost tripped in the sand, trying to imagine never leaving a place as secluded as Cape Cod.

"I wanted to talk to you about some things," I said, keeping my eyes on the waves.

"Anything."

"I only want to say this once, then I don't want to talk about it again. I just think you should know what my life was like, so you understand me a little."

"Okay."

I wasn't sure why I was going to tell him any of it, but it felt right. I began, "I don't need to tell you how crazy Mama was; you know that. She had her good days. I'm not gonna lie and say she didn't hit me. I *can* tell you honestly that it wasn't that often."

Ray opened his mouth to say something but I shushed him.

"Don't say anything. It wasn't your fault. You would have been there if you could. I'm not telling you so you can feel bad about it. I'm just telling you so you know."

We walked in silence for a minute. I thought about all the lies my mother had told. I realized I had no idea what had happened between Ray and her. The only thing I knew was that Ray had been eighteen when I was born. And I only knew that because I could do basic math.

"How did you lose me?" I asked.

"What?"

"I mean, did Mama just pack up and leave while you were at work? Or sleeping?"

Ray stopped walking and turned to face the ocean. "You were four months old. She was having one of her crazy spells. She was screaming at me; accusing me of wanting to hurt you. She grabbed a knife off the kitchen counter and chased me out of the house. I stayed out for a few hours to give her time to calm down. When I got back, you were both gone."

He didn't say it, but I knew that wasn't all that was gone. Knowing Mama, she'd emptied his bank account and stolen his car, knowing he'd never report her. It didn't surprise me at all that she'd gone at him with a knife. She kept one woven into the braid in her hair at all times. What surprised me was that she had taken me with her when she ran.

"I'm sorry she stole me," I said.

"So am I."

We let the waves do the talking for a minute. I hadn't wanted to have this conversation, but I knew we had to. We had to share this pain so we could move past it.

"She used me for her cons," I said. "Not her sexual ones, but she had me picking pockets by the time I was four. I was good at it. Still am, actually. Not that I do anything like that," I clarified as his head snapped in my direction in shock. "I just practice. It's habit."

"Practice?"

"I've stolen and replaced your wallet a few times in the past week," I admitted.

He reached into his back pocket and felt for his wallet. I handed it to him.

"I don't think I like that habit."

I shrugged. "Conditioning. I accept certain personality flaws about myself. I keep the skills honed, but never use them. I think that's good enough."

He grunted, obviously not pleased, but willing to let it go.

"We moved around a lot," I said, forcing myself to stop wringing my hands. "When I was fifteen we moved to Jamestown, Rhode Island. Mama loves tourist towns; plenty of marks just passing through. I met Stacey when I enrolled in the high school there. I started spending nights at her house. Her mother was great, made me feel like family. So when Mama decided to move on, I stayed. It wasn't pretty. There was a big fight. I'll spare you the details."

I sighed, remembering the horrible things Mama had said to me and Stacey's family. "Anyway," I continued, "Mama bought me a car and gave me five grand. She told me how to find her when I got over my snit, and then she was gone. I stayed with Stacey and her mother for a while. But Mama had been right. I couldn't stay. Stacey was furious with me when I left." I paused again, my mind attempting to go to the darkest place of my memories. I shook my head. He didn't need to know about that. I was never going to tell anyone about that. I was going to forget it. It didn't happen.

"I got my GED in the next town I stopped in," I said. "I didn't look for Mama. I'd been trying to get away from her since I was old enough to crawl. I never wanted to see her again!" I wasn't sure if I should tell him the last part, but I did anyway. "She's tracked me down twice. Once when I was twenty, again when I was twenty-two. I saw her coming both times, and managed to get away before having to talk to her. I packed up and left town each time."

He had taken my hand as I talked. His grip now tightened and he let out a long sigh. "I wish I could have been there for you, baby. I should have looked harder. I shouldn't have given up."

I stopped walking and turned to face him. "You found me now. And I don't care about the past. I don't see the point in dragging around resentment and anger, at least not at you. You have shown me more love and kindness in the past month than Mama ever showed me. I've always dove into things headfirst, and I'm not going to pussy out on this. I love you, Dad."

Ray started crying as he pulled me against his chest. I cried too and held him back. I had been raised to hate this man, and raised to see everyone around me as a mark, as an opportunity to steal and cheat. But I wasn't my mother. I was me. And now I had a great father who loved me, and I wasn't going to waste a moment I had with him.

Chapter 7

THE NEXT TWO WEEKS passed quickly. I spent most of my days working on the house and in my studio. I selected a few of my rough sketches and expanded on them. I went for rides on my bike and found a few places that begged for my attention. Despite my pension for drawing people, I was attracted to the scenery of the Cape. One day I stopped on the side of the highway in Wellfleet to sketch the marsh. I went to the beach and sketched a father and daughter flying a kite, and a little boy building a sand castle.

Ray and I made dinner together every night, except for Wednesdays and Saturdays. Wednesday was fried-fish night; Saturday was pizza. Mason and Gage found their way over many nights, either to help work on the house or just visit. Gage had latched onto me as a source of information about traveling. I showed him my scrapbook and told him about some of the places I had been. I used him as a way to avoid being alone with Mason.

My traitorous brain refused to stop thinking about the big, dependable, sexy man who kept accidentally brushing against me and grinning. I had started working on a full-size portrait of him from that first day I'd met him. I was playing with the paints I found in the gallery. I added lines of color to my pencil-and-pen drawings. The result was stunning, as the paint drew the eye to what I wanted to emphasize.

When I wasn't in the studio, I was with Ray. I had missed out on having a dad for long enough. We finished removing the wall separating the kitchen and dining room, making it one large, comfortable room full of sawdust, broken plaster chunks, and two different color schemes. I loved working on the house with him. I even managed to work beside Mason without imagining him naked, most of the time.

I waited for the nagging feeling to grow in my chest, the one that always pushed me to move on, but it didn't come. I knew it would at some point. I had lived with Stacey and her family for over a year and felt similar to how I did now, but I'd left them. I didn't stick anywhere.

"Hey, Divvy," Ray said, coming into the living room and disturbing my daydreaming.

"Hey, Dad. How was work?" I asked.

He still looked startled when I called him Dad, but he was growing used to it. "Great day to work outside," he said, indicating the cool early summer evening. "Mason's having a big Memorial Day party this weekend."

"Sounds fun," I said, hiding my worry.

"I'm not feeling up to makin' dinner tonight. Want to get some takeout?"

"No. I'll cook something. You go take a shower."

"You sure?"

"Have some faith," I said, patting his arm. "I have a great teacher."

I thought about the coming party as I fried some chicken and mashed potatoes. Because I was distracted, the potatoes came out a bit watery with some chunks, but I added butter and salt and ignored the consistency.

Mason had done nothing to hide his interest in me. I had a feeling he and Ray had talked about me on more than one occasion. From what I could determine, Ray was unfortunately on Mason's side. Mason was smart enough not to push me, but the tension between us was growing. I was dreaming about him every night, dreams so carnal and aggressive I'd wake up gasping.

I burned one piece of chicken to a blackened crisp that not even a dog would eat. I saved the rest and heated some frozen broccoli in the microwave. I was irrationally proud of myself for making dinner, despite the simple fare and its imperfections. Ray sat down at the table in his sweatpants and T-shirt and complimented me between bites.

I liked having someone to cook for. I liked having someone to sit on the lumpy couch with to watch bad movies. I liked having a dad, even if I was old enough not to need one. I shook my head at the thought. Everyone needed a dad; there wasn't an age when they became superfluous. I hadn't had one for twenty-four years, but I had learned how essential he was in a month. I'd never had anyone I could count on before. Mama hadn't been the kind of woman who inspired trust. She had treated me as a possession, one she loved when I was useful, then hated once the job was done. Ray had never treated me like that. He looked at me like I was his entire world. I thought this should have scared me, but it hadn't. I had settled into this new part of my life as a daughter.

My mind wandered to Mason again, and I wrung my hands. I still didn't like the way he looked at me.

Chapter 8

RAY AND I WALKED over to Mason and Gage's house for the party. We were met at the front door by the biggest dog I had ever seen. He came up to my hip and was a mass of shaggy white and gray fur. He let out an explosion of barking, but his tail was wagging so I wasn't worried.

"Dammit, Mop!" Bodel appeared behind the dog in the doorway. "Don't be so dramatic." She looked up at Ray and smiled. Her smile dimmed when her eyes met mine.

"Hey Bo," Ray said.

"Good to see you, Ray. How goes work on the house?"

"Your brothers haven't told you?"

"I haven't seen much of them since you recruited them." She didn't look at me, but I heard the real words beneath the polite ones. Bodel didn't like her brothers spending so much time with me. I respected her protective instinct, but she should at least have had the guts to call me out on it directly.

"I'm getting old," Ray said, rubbing at the messy fur on Mop's head. "I need all the help I can get."

"You're forty-two, hardly an invalid. Well, come on in." She stood to the side as we walked past her. I gave her a long, challenging look before following Ray through the house.

It wasn't much of a house. An attempt had been made to clean, but it was a bachelor pad and disorder reigned supreme. The front door opened to the large living room. A small kitchen with a slider leading to the side yard was to the left of the door. The stairs to the second floor were on the far side of the room. I noted a tiny half bathroom in the kitchen as I followed Ray outside through the slider.

The Tavish family was all there, along with Bodel's husband and his brother. I was greeted warmly by everyone despite Bodel's initial chilly hello; apparently she was the only person who had a problem with me. Gage latched onto me immediately and began asking me about New Orleans. I settled at the picnic table.

I found myself the center of conversation. Everyone wanted to know about the places I'd been. I kept to the happy stories. I didn't tell them about my numerous close calls with muggers and other unsavory people. I didn't mention my mother or the cons she'd forced me to participate in. I didn't talk about the rat-infested apartment, with roaches big enough to carry off the mini-fridge.

Mason stayed close to me, despite supposedly being responsible for the grill. He kept innocently brushing against me and it was driving me to distraction. His covert move of choice was to pet Mop, who was settled at my feet, always rubbing against my leather-clad calves in the process. I decided that wearing the knee-high boots, black jeans, and leather corset had been a bad idea. The corset laced up the front and had a low back, but it was on the sexy side of slutty. Mason liked it a little too much.

"Do you ever get tired of moving from place to place?" Bodel asked. There was enough edge to her tone that Mason stiffened and gave her a look. Gage was oblivious, but Axel also noticed and frowned.

"I like seeing new places, meeting new people," I said carefully.

"And when will you be moving on from here?"

The other conversations that had been going on around us quieted, and I knew everyone was listening. Ray was standing beside Trace, trying too hard to pretend he hadn't heard. I looked pointedly at Bodel, flicking my eyes over toward my dad. She glanced at Ray and had the grace to look apologetic.

"I've never had a family before, Bo. I'm liking having a father, and I'm in no rush to move on."

"Ray was telling me about your art," Zach said, putting a hand on his wife's shoulder and smoothly shifting her away from me. "He says you're quite talented. It's my mama's birthday in a few weeks, and she has a love of artwork. Maybe you have something she'd like that I could purchase for her?"

"I've had a lot of time to work," I said, grateful that he had so nicely disarmed the situation. "I've completed a few pieces. I could do something special for her. I love a challenge."

Zach and I settled in to talk about my work and when he could come by and see it. He had an easy, confident way about him that I admired. The relaxed Georgia drawl was pleasant to listen to. I could see how his personality complemented Bodel. She had lowered her hostility to a slight simmer, and when Zach looked over at her she couldn't help but smile at him. I envied them that connection.

"I'm sorry if Bo is a bit snarly," Zach told me quietly. "I'd say it's hormones, but she's overprotective of her brothers, and it's her nature to be pushy."

"It's fine, Zach. She's just looking out for her siblings." I thought about Stacey for a brief moment, but pushed the memory aside.

"Food's done," Mason announced. "Someone want to grab the plates and stuff from the kitchen?"

"I'll get it," I said, needing to be away from the frivolity for a minute. Thinking of Stacey had unsettled me and I needed a moment alone.

I headed back into the kitchen to find plates, napkins, buns, and condiments on the counter. I took a moment to figure out how to get everything outside in one trip. Mop lumbered into the room, ramming his head into my crotch with so much enthusiasm that I lost my balance in the three-inch heels and fell onto the floor. I landed on my butt, laughing. He began licking my face. I put my arms around his big neck to haul myself to a sitting position.

"Mop, you big dumbass." Bo pulled him off me, with surprising strength. She rubbed at her rounded belly a moment, before offering me a hand up. "Sorry about that, he's going blind and his depth perception is off." The hostility was gone from her tone, so I took her offered hand and stood up.

"It's okay. He's a great dog," I said.

There was a moment of awkward silence. Bo's hand traveled to her belly again.

"When are you due?" I asked, desperate for conversation.

She smiled and it made her look startlingly like Mason. "Late August, maybe first week in September."

"Is it a boy or a girl?"

"It's a boy." Her pleasure was obvious. "It's a damn good thing, 'cause I wouldn't know what to do with some whiny little girl." We shared a laugh, and I imagined that we could become friends.

"Have you picked a name?" I asked.

There was a flash in her eyes I couldn't put an emotion to. "We're naming him after Zach's first wife. She died when she was very young."

I bit my lip at the genuine sadness I saw in Bo's eyes. "I'm sorry."

She smiled and rubbed her belly. "Her name was Alice, so we're calling our son Alex. Alex Walter Cutter."

"Strong name," I said.

She nodded. When her eyes met mine again they had sobered. "I need to say something to you," she said.

I leaned against the counter and nodded at her to continue. I knew I wasn't going to like what she had to say, but I respected her directness.

"I'm sorry I've been a bitch," she began. "I want you to know that I like you, I really do. And under other circumstances I think we could be friends."

I nodded, unsurprised by her words. "But you don't want me hanging around with your brothers."

She shook her head. "Not exactly. In fact, I think it's great that Gage has someone like you to talk to. He's wanted to get away from here since he was a little kid and none of us really get it. You're great for him. You can teach him the things he needs to know to be on his own, moving from place to place."

"I'm glad I can help him," I said.

"But Mason's another story," she continued. "Mason has always insisted on loving being a bachelor, but it's bullshit. Since he was a kid he's had simple goals. He wanted to work for my dad and eventually take over the business, get married, and have kids. I'd say a house with a white picket fence, but that cliché isn't quite right." She bit her lip and looked out the slider.

"He got burned once, romantically, and he's been dating stupid, noncommittal summer girls ever since. But now you're here. He has never been like this before. He barely takes his eyes off of you."

She looked me straight in the eyes now. "Divvy, if you were going to stay, I'd say you were perfect for him. But you're not going to stay. You're going to leave. And you're going to rip out his heart when you go."

The truth of her words hit me hard. I had been thinking the same thing since I met him. Her tone was gentle as she continued. "Look, I know I don't know you that well. At all, really. But I can tell you don't want to hurt him. You won't do it on purpose. But Mason isn't the kind of man to do anything halfway. It'll break him when you go, and it'll hurt you too. I don't want that. I just don't want anyone to get hurt."

I looked at her. She wasn't accusing me or condemning. I saw only concern and regret. I wished I had a brother or sister who cared so much about me. Stacey rose unwelcome in my mind, and I blinked back sudden tears. I couldn't survive hurting someone else the way I'd hurt her.

I looked out the window at Mason, standing confident and relaxed at the grill. She was right, I'd destroy him. Just like I had every person who'd come to care about me. "I've hurt people before," I heard myself say. "I don't want to hurt him. I don't want to hurt anyone. It's just the way I am. I don't stick anywhere." *I don't belong anywhere,* I added in my head.

Bo touched my shoulder. "I said that all wrong," she began.

I held up a hand to silence her. "Hey, tell everyone I got sick and headed back home."

"Divvy, I'm sorry," she began. I ignored her and headed out the front door before she could see my tears.

Chapter 9

I WALKED BACK to the house in the growing darkness. I'd been crazy to have gone to the party in the first place. I should have found an excuse not to. I was breaking all my rules: I didn't make friends. I didn't insinuate myself into other people's lives. I stayed aloof but friendly, and everyone stayed safe that way.

I closed the front door behind me and sat on the steps to unzip my boots. I pulled off my socks and rubbed absently at my feet. Bo's words echoed in my head. Yes, I was going to hurt everyone. I had done it before, over and over again. I was always the one who left. No matter how happy I was somewhere, something deep inside would force me to move on. I had learned my lesson with Stacey. I'd tried to belong to a family once, and had ruined it. I ripped apart the lives of so many people, just by being what I was.

But this time was different. This time there was Ray, not some generous man willing to take me in. He was my father. I could leave, and he would still be my father. I would have someone to come back to here. I would have a home here. But Mason couldn't be a part of that. If I let myself get involved with him, he wouldn't let me walk away. He might even try and follow me, like Stacey had. I shook my head at the horrible memories, blinking back tears. I was *not* going to hurt anyone else. I was going to stay away from the entire Tavish family.

The front door burst open, so hard that it hit the wall. I jumped to my feet as Mason entered the room like an enraged bear. I backed up as he came at me without slowing down. I ended up with my back against the wall. His hands slapped against the wall above my shoulders, caging me in. He kept his body a few inches away from mine, but I knew I was trapped. I looked up into his eyes and lost my breath. His body shook with contained violence, but I wasn't afraid. I knew instinctively that he wouldn't hurt me. I stayed very still and looked into the passionate blue of his eyes.

"What did my sister say to you?" he growled. It wasn't a question, but a demand.

"Don't be mad at her," I began. There was a flicker of true fury in his eyes and I decided that telling him what to do was a bad idea. I switched tactics. "She didn't say anything but the truth."

His body moved an inch closer to me, but stopped before we touched. "Answer the fucking question, Divine."

A shiver of lust went through me and I tried to hide it. "I can't do this, Mason. I know I'm not going to stay. I'll move on. And when I go, I'll hurt you. I'll rip your heart out and drag it with me. I won't do that."

He watched me for a few breaths. His big body was so close, capturing me against the wall. I wasn't afraid. I wanted to be afraid. Instead, I was more turned on than I had ever been in my life.

"So you were just going to make the decision for me?" he asked. "I don't get a say?"

I opened my mouth to speak, but he pressed his body fully against me and I lost my voice as pleasure sang through my veins. His mouth lowered until he was speaking against my lips. "I'm not going to let you walk away from this. I sure as hell can't. I can't get you out of my head. I think about you all the time. I dream about you every night. I need to touch you all the time, be with you all the time. I don't know what this is between us, but I know you feel it."

I searched for my voice as his chest pressed against my sensitive breasts. "Mason, it doesn't change anything."

"Bullshit. You may be a coward, but I'm not. Whatever this is that pulls me to you, it scares the hell out of me. But I'm not gonna chicken out and run away from it."

"I'll hurt you," I gasped as he pressed his hips into me.

"I don't care." He rocked against me and I reached for his chest. He caught my wrists and pinned them against the wall over my head. A moan escaped my throat as he stretched my body and claimed it.

"I don't care," he repeated, his breaths coming in pants. "If you're going to hurt me when you leave, it'll be worth it. I need you, Divine." His grip on my wrists tightened and a whimper of pain escaped my lips. His eyes lost their intensity as I saw a flicker of fear in them. His grip on my wrists relaxed and he took one slow, deliberate step back from me. I almost cried out at the loss of all that heat and pressure. He looked into my eyes and I was shocked at the vulnerability I saw. I wanted him to come back to me, needed him to slam that magnificent body against me, into me.

He took a deep, long breath. "If you tell me to go, right now, I will. I'll walk away."

I stared at him, trying to get my mind to work.

He pressed a gentle kiss against my lips, feather-light. "It's all or nothing with me, Divine. So take me, or tell me to go."

I wanted him more than I had ever wanted anything. Need burned through me so fiercely it was almost painful. I couldn't tell him to go. I didn't want to. I tilted my head and kissed him.

He slammed me back into the wall, his body hard against mine, his tongue forcing itself into my mouth. There was nothing gentle in him, and I loved it. I wanted to drown in his harsh, aggressive power. His hands released my wrists to close over my breasts. The tight leather of my corset rubbed against my erect nipples and I moaned into his mouth.

He forced a knee between my legs, pulling my hips up so I was riding his thigh. The friction had my insides erupting with shocks of near-orgasm. His hands grasped my hips and he stroked his thigh back and forth against me. His mouth stayed on mine the entire time, his kiss overpowering teeth and tongue. If I had been able, I would have been screaming.

Without any warning he dropped me to the floor. Before I could realize what was happening, he tossed me over his shoulder. The air left my lungs in a whoosh as he ran up the stairs with my stomach slamming into his powerful shoulder. He dropped me onto the bed so hard I bounced.

"Take that fucking thing off," he ordered, pointing to my corset. "I liked it, till I realized I have no idea how to get it off."

I laughed, delighted with the barely controlled violence of his desire. I started working on the complicated crisscross of leather that held the corset together. I heard him moving but couldn't look up from the laces. When I did look my mouth went dry. He towered over me, completely naked. I needed to draw him like that. There was so much power in that dominant, muscular body. I wanted all that power to slam into me, to break me and make me his.

He looked at my bare breasts and grinned wolfishly. "Take off your pants. Let me see all of you."

I unbuttoned my jeans and started on the zipper, but he pounced on me before I had a chance to start wriggling out of them. His hands gripped the material and wrenched it down my legs. He didn't even glance at my lacy black panties before stripping them off me. He ended up kneeling by my feet to pull the panties free. I took my only opportunity and caught his knee with my foot. He lost his balance and fell onto the bed beside me. I jumped on top of him, needing to try and capture some of that strength.

His laugh was rough and dangerous. He easily rolled on top, his hard length pressed firmly between my legs. His hands caught my wrists and held them down. His mouth burned a path down my neck to my breasts. I twisted my hips, needing him inside me. He muttered a curse and shook his head.

"What?" I gasped.

"I don't have a condom." His body was shaking with need.

"I'm on the pill," I said, wrapping my legs around his hips. I felt the tip of him against my slick heat. He hesitated a moment longer.

"I'm safe," I assured him.

He looked into my eyes. "We'll see about that," he said. Then he slammed into me so hard my body slid up the bed and my head hit the wall. He swallowed my scream of pleasure in a kiss that was all teeth. I never got a chance to catch my breath as he began pounding into me. I pushed uselessly against his hands pinning my wrists to the bed. He invaded every inch of me with possessive finality, leaving me completely vulnerable. I screamed as the orgasm exploded through my body. He didn't slow down. His body rammed into mine, harsh and demanding. I gave him everything he wanted. I begged for more.

He let go of my wrists to grasp my hips and pull me harder against him as he came. His mouth closed on my shoulder, teeth nipping into my skin. I bit him back, pulling him as deep inside as I could as I wrapped my legs around his back. He collapsed on top of me, his body shaking with the force of his release.

I lay beneath him, paralyzed with pleasure. Nothing had ever felt so good, so right. I let my fingers stroke his hair while his ragged breaths grazed over my breasts.

He moved so suddenly that it made me gasp. He rolled off me and moved away, sitting on the end of the bed. I stared as his massive shoulders sagged and he caught his head in his hands. Panic bit into my skin.

"Mason?" I moved toward him, becoming aware of a pleasant soreness in many places.

His voice was so shaky that I couldn't understand what he said. I reached him but didn't touch. I said his name again and he lowered one hand to look at me over his shoulder. He looked devastated and terrified.

"How badly did I hurt you?" he asked.

The reason for his retreat became clear and I grabbed his face in my hands. My touch shocked him and he turned his body toward me.

"You didn't hurt me at all," I said, looking into his eyes so he could see the truth. "That was by far the best sex I've ever had. You were perfect. Wonderful."

He looked confused.

"Seriously? I didn't scare you?"

"Not at all." I kissed him, needing to chase the worry from his eyes. When I drew back he was smiling.

"I was so rough with you," he said, his hands finding my wrists, his grip gentle. He brought my wrists to his lips and kissed them. "I lost control, Divine. I don't do that. Or I haven't. Not in a long time."

"I like you out of control. I'm not a china doll, Mason. I like it hard and rough. I love it. Come here." I pulled him down on the bed, settling against his side. His arm wrapped around me, pulling me snugly against him. I nuzzled his neck, loving the scratch of his five o'clock shadow. He let out a sigh of contentment and my body rose and fell with his chest.

"I meant what I said before," he said. "It's all or nothing for me. I know you're going to leave. I'm not going to say it won't hurt. It will. But I'm not going to miss having you while I can."

I shifted around so I was propped on his chest, looking into his eyes.

"I wish I could promise not to hurt you," I said.

"No one can promise that. And this thing we have, it's worth whatever pain I end up having to carry."

I kissed him. The kiss was gentle, a slide of lips and tongue. His arms wrapped possessively around me and I felt safe. I was his for as long as he could hold me. Maybe he was strong enough to keep me, strong enough to root me. I ignored my fears and let myself drift off to sleep in his arms.

Chapter 10

I WOKE UP suddenly, barely stopping myself from a scream as I felt arms around me. The arms were gentle, though, and the night before came back. I opened my eyes to see Mason watching me.

"Good morning," he said.

"Mornin'." I stretched, letting the blanket fall down my body. His eyes went to my bare breasts and he grinned.

"My morning just got better."

A noise down the hall drew my attention to the open bedroom door. I squeaked as Ray sauntered down the hallway. I snatched the blanket up and dragged it over my head.

"Oh, grow up," he said as he passed.

Stunned, I let the blanket fall away from my face. Ray stopped at the top of the stairs. He grinned at me. "Come on, Divvy. I knew he was there." He laughed at the look on my face. "I might be your father, but I didn't raise you. I don't see you as a little girl. You're a grown woman. That's how I met you. It saves me a lot of grief."

I searched for words and battled with my embarrassment. Mason was propped beside me, the sheet down to his waist. If he was at all uncomfortable being found naked in a bed with his friend's daughter, it didn't show.

"Seriously," Ray continued. "Stop looking at me like that."

"This doesn't bother you?" I finally managed to ask.

"Mason talked to me about you weeks ago," Ray said. "He's my friend. He's from a good family. He'll treat you right. I told him to go for it." When I only stared at him, he just shrugged. "I'm going to go make breakfast. You two want pancakes?"

"That'd be great," Mason said.

I was still too stunned to speak, so Ray rolled his eyes at me and went downstairs. I turned to Mason.

"You talked to my dad about me?" I latched onto that piece of information.

He ran a hand through his hair. "Yes. I wanted his approval."

"For what, exactly?"

He shifted around so he was sitting. I sat up beside him, but his eyes went to my breasts as the sheet fell down. I could tell the blood was draining from his brain, so I picked up the sheet and held it over my breasts in order to get intelligent sentences from him.

"What were we talking about?" he asked.

"Typical male." I rolled my eyes. "You talked to Ray?"

"I'm not sure how to say this." He ran a hand through his hair.

"Say what? Did you just walk up and say, hey Ray, mind if I fuck your daughter?"

He frowned. "Of course not. I just wanted him to know that I wasn't going to come between you and him."

"What do you mean?"

"He just got his daughter back. I knew I wanted you. I knew I had to have you. But I wasn't going to endanger your relationship with your dad. If things do go badly between us, I'll walk away. I'll keep my distance and stay out of your way. I won't have you run from me—and leave him, too."

I stared at him as understanding dawned.

"Look, I know you're going to leave." He reached out to trace my jaw. "I get that. But I couldn't be the reason you left early. I've known Ray for seven years, Divine. All he talked about for most of those years was the daughter he had lost. And now he's found you. I can't take that away from him."

I leaned forward and pressed a kiss against his lips. "You can't take that away. I grew up with the mother from hell, who hated me. But I wanted a family. Someone to love me no matter what. I won't give up Ray. Not for anything. No matter what happens with us, he's my dad. And I can't tell you how much it means to me that you talked to him, and that you understand the way I am."

"I don't understand, not yet." His thumb stroked my cheek. "But I want to." He pulled me against him, kissing me hard. I was reminded of his strength, his overpowering desire from the night before. He pulled me so that I was straddling his lap, and gave me proof that the desire was still going strong.

I glanced over my shoulder at the open bedroom door.

"Do you have discovery fantasies?" I asked.

He frowned at the door, and I could see by the look on his face that he didn't. I was glad. The biggest turn-off I could think of was the idea of my newly discovered father walking back upstairs to see me riding Mason.

"I'll get the door." I sprang away from him before he could stop me, dashed to the door, naked and giddy, and shut it. I turned back and then took a moment to look at the beautiful naked man in my bed.

"Don't keep me waiting," he ordered.

I didn't.

Chapter 11

SUNDAY WAS A WONDERFUL DAY. Ray, Mason, and I painted the living room a warm yellow, ordered pizza, and talked. We argued over music, movies, and family. Mason asked a handful of leading questions about my childhood, but he didn't press when I dodged them. It was easy to be around him. That was a new experience for me. My previous lovers had always made me jumpy and uncertain once the sex was over. Mason was too relaxed to put my guard up.

I spent my Monday in the studio. I worked on the large portrait of him, based on the first time I had seen him. I knew the lines of his body and face more now, and I added the details. I glared at the dark pen lines and wanted to add color. I needed to capture the blue of his eyes. I glanced at the paints and decided to experiment.

At first the only color I added was the eyes. It took me a long time to get the color just right. But the two small pools of color weren't enough. I added sweeps of color to the jeans, some lines of tan on his cheekbones and along his strong jaw. I stepped back from it and smiled in contentment. The splashes of color brought the entire portrait together beautifully.

"I never considered the danger in dating an artist," Mason said, making me jump and squeak loudly. He laughed, obviously loving that he could get that reaction out of me.

"Don't sneak up on me like that," I yelled, trying to get my heart to stop pounding.

"Divine, I made enough noise on those creaky old stairs to wake the dead." He closed the distance between us and kissed me. I hated how easily I fell into him. He looked over my head at the portrait.

"Am I really that good looking?" he asked.

"No," I lied.

I looked from him to the portrait. I really had captured the energy of the man. There was an ingrained confidence in the way he moved that intrigued me. He was solid, capable, and sexy, yet understated at the same time.

"Does it bother you?" I asked.

"What?"

"That I used you as a model? If it really makes you uncomfortable I won't do it. Or at least I won't show anyone."

He looked at the portrait for a while. I could see the working mind I had quickly come to respect. He ran a hand through his hair. "Honestly, it's embarrassing," he admitted. "My brothers will give me hell for the rest of my life. But I love your work. I love how you capture emotion. I wanted you the moment I saw you, and you drew that without making me look creepy."

He kissed me again.

"I want to draw you naked," I said.

He shifted uncomfortably, looking into my eyes. "I think I have to draw the line there, honey."

The *honey* threw me completely off balance. He misunderstood the stunned look on my face.

"I don't have a problem with you drawing me naked," he said, rushing his words. "I'll die of embarrassment posing for you, but I'd do it. You just have to promise you'd never show them publicly, or to my family." He was blushing an adorable shade of red and shifting his feet. It made me laugh and I threw my arms around him.

"I wouldn't do that, Mason. I want to draw you for us. I wouldn't sell or show anything that personal. Especially not to your family. Your sister would kill me."

His eyes narrowed. "Bo is just a bitch sometimes when it comes to protecting me. Not that I need protecting. I am the oldest, after all. I'll talk to her. She'll back off."

"I don't want to start trouble between you two."

"I respected her choice of Zach, and she needs to respect mine."

"It must be nice to have family that cares so much," I said before I could stop myself.

He caught my chin in his large hand. "I know you don't want to talk about your childhood. I just need to say that I'm sorry it wasn't what it should have been."

I smiled up at him. He'd grown up with everything I had ever wanted. That confidence I loved so much about him was a result of his family. I had my own brand of confidence, but it was a bitchy, defensive kind. I was confident because I had been on my own my whole life. Mason was confident because he had never been alone. The contrast fascinated me.

"Have you given any more thought into opening the gallery?" he asked.

I looked through my work. I needed to do a lot more of it if I was going to open the downstairs. "I'm not sure it's a good idea," I admitted.

"Why not?"

"Because, you know, I'm not staying. It would be a lot of work and money to invest in a summer project."

I saw a flash of something in his eyes, but he hid it well with his charming smile. Before he could speak I heard a knock on the door downstairs. Shrugging, I headed down to see who it was. Zach wasn't the last person I expected to see, but it was close.

"Zach, hi," I said, ushering him inside. The bearded man moved with a grace akin to Mason's. Big men like them weren't supposed to be graceful.

"Afternoon, ma'am. I take it you forgot you invited me today," he said in his deep Southern drawl.

"I totally forgot," I admitted. "But I'm glad you're here. You said you're looking for something for your mother?"

Mason came down the stairs and greeted Zach warmly. Zach didn't seem surprised to see Mason in my studio. I didn't sense any tension between the two men. I wished I could say the same about me and Bo. I was still nervous about running into her again, despite our recent hatchet-burial at the party.

"I'll leave you two alone," Mason said. "Ray probably needs help with something."

I should have known he'd kiss me before leaving. He wasn't the kind of man to be subtle or deceiving. Zach watched him go, then looked back at me and smiled.

"So, yeah." I looked down at my bare feet.

Zach laughed and the sound took me by surprise. There was a seldom-used beautiful quality to his laugh that was enchanting. He took my arm smoothly.

"Mason and Bo had a big fight Saturday night. Mason stormed out after you. I'm not an idiot, Miss Shayler."

I shivered at the name as we walked up the stairs to the studio. "Call me Divvy, please."

"I'll indulge you in that," he said. "I called Bo Miss Tavish and ma'am for months. Nearly drove her mad."

I laughed at the idea of him antagonizing his opinionated, bossy wife. Zach's eyes went right to the portrait of Mason, and I barely suppressed a groan. It wasn't a naked picture, but it was close. But Zach didn't laugh or tease me. He studied the portrait like a man who knew art.

"This is a very unique style. Very striking . . ." He trailed off, then wandered around the room, inspecting my other work.

"All excellent," he said. "But the one of Mason is your best. The addition of the sweeps of color is unique, and really brings the details in the ink to light."

"Thank you."

"I would love for you to do a portrait for me, two if you could."

"What are you looking for?"

He turned to me. "My family is in Georgia. My mother and my mama don't get to see us very much."

"You have two?"

He grinned. "My mother isn't very maternal. She's a surgeon. Her best friend helped raise me. I married her daughter, my first wife, Alice."

"Bo mentioned her. She said you're naming the baby after her."

I saw the flash of pain in his eyes but it didn't last long. "Yes, our Alex should be arriving in three months. I know you aren't planning on staying permanently, but do you think you'll still be here then?"

"I'm not sure, " I admitted. "This is the first home I've ever had. Ray's here. I've never had anyone to leave behind before. I'm in no hurry to go. But if I am gone, I'll definitely be back. I'm not giving up my dad now that I've found him, even if I do have the heart of a gypsy."

He nodded. "You're a very honest woman, Divvy. Upfront. It's refreshing."

"Thank you . . . I think."

"It was a compliment. What I really want is a portrait of Bo and me with Alex. I want to send the portraits home to my mothers. Photos are okay, but this would be more."

"I'd love to. It might be hard to get Bo to smile at me rather than give me the finger, though."

Zach laughed again and set a hand on my shoulder. "My wife is a bit snarly at the moment. She'll calm down. I think you two will become friends, actually."

I snorted. "Yeah."

"Give her time. Mason and she are very close. Whenever I do something wrong, she runs to him and complains till she calms down. She doesn't like to share."

"Well, tough!"

He grinned at me. "This will be interesting to watch," he said. "Now, I do have to get Charlotte something for her birthday. Let me look through some of your work more closely."

He spent a few minutes searching for the right piece for his mama. He set one aside and continued browsing. I didn't have too much, but he took so long on each piece that it made me uncomfortable. I could sense his mind working, and I had no idea where it was going. He turned to me.

"I have a business proposition for you," he said.

"What?"

"I don't know if you are aware, but I have large sums of money I am fond of throwing into projects and business ventures that pique my interest." I stared as the laid-back Southern man suddenly transformed into a polished businessman. I couldn't say exactly what had changed, it was too subtle. He continued, "One of my clients is an avid art collector, and I've learned to have an eye for it myself. I'd like to finance a show for your work."

For a long time I stared at him, too stunned to find coherent words. He waited patiently for me to start acting human again. I finally did. "Are you out of your mind?" I gasped.

He smiled. "Not in the least. You have talent. I'm positive a show would be profitable for me. And personally, I'd like to help support a friend's daughter."

"You're serious."

"Very. We can work out the details later, but I'd handle all of the publicity and advertising, and pay for any materials needed to get the gallery in presentable condition."

Fear ate at me. I realized I was wringing my hands. "I don't know if I'm up for a huge thing," I admitted. "You have a lot more faith in my art than I do."

"I can work with that. I can keep it small if you'd rather."

"Why do I get the feeling that I can't say no to you?"

He grinned then, and I could easily see why he was such a successful businessman. "You can fight me for a while, true," he said. "But let's save us both the tap dance; why don't you just say yes now?"

I laughed. "What do you get out of this?"

"Other than the satisfaction of helping a new artist and friend start her career? I'll take a percentage of the profits, of course. Barely more than I need to cover the costs. I don't need the money, Divvy. I love projects. I would love to arrange this for you. As big or as small as you like."

I sighed. "I don't see how I can say no to the offer," I admitted.

"Good. We'll sort out the details later." He offered his hand. I shook it, wondering what I had just gotten myself into.

Chapter 12

I NEARLY SCREAMED when Mason's hands covered my eyes. He laughed at me while I jerked violently under his gentle touch. I would have slapped his hands away but his teeth nipped at the back of my neck.

"Hey, honey," he said, adding a lick of his tongue where his teeth had scraped.

I opened my mouth to yell at him, but he bit the spot where my neck met my shoulder and I moaned instead. The pencil dropped out of my hand. His hands were still over my eyes. I tried to shift my head but he held me still, keeping my head against him. *I need to start working in chairs instead of on a stool, so he can't come up behind me.* His lips trailed around my shoulder and I decided the stool was perfect.

"Mason, I'm working," I said, although I couldn't keep the passion out of my tone.

"You've been working all day. You're done."

"Don't tell me what to do."

"You like it." He accompanied the statement with another bite to the back of my neck. And he was right. Having him boss me around turned me on, and more than it should have.

Having nothing to say, I decided to stop playing passive. I reached behind me in an attempt to get at certain anatomy to give me control of the situation. He laughed against my skin and stepped back from my hand.

"Greedy girl," he said into my ear.

"You like it," I countered.

His hands dropped from my eyes to my breasts with no preamble. That's the way it always was with Mason. He never asked. His idea of foreplay was walking into a room and pinning me against the most convenient surface. It was the only approach that worked on me. If he hadn't been so possessive and demanding, I would have turned him down. It was never good to give me the option of saying no to sex. The more I slept with him the more I cared, and it was an unconscious reflex to avoid caring about people. Mason didn't realize it, but his forceful nature was the only thing that had kept him in my bed. It didn't matter how I felt about him as a man. I had run from other men I was fond of. Mason had knocked my feet out from under me before I'd had a chance to run.

I tried to get off the stool but he pinned me against his body. "I've been thinking about you all day," he said, his voice a caress. I would have said something in response but when I opened my mouth he slid his thumb inside. I nipped him and he growled. "You know what happens to bad little girls who bite?" he whispered in my ear.

"Why don't you show me?"

I found myself thrown across the room. I landed with a bounce on the mattress I had set up in the studio. Mason stripped off his shirt and pounced on me, his hands pinning my wrists to the bed. He caught the bottom of my shirt with his teeth and exposed my stomach. He took a moment to inspect the faerie ring on my belly button before exploring the rest of my exposed skin with his tongue. I tried to wrap my legs around him but he was too wide and I couldn't hook my ankles and get a good grip. He looked down at me with his dark blue eyes. The passion in his gaze sent a shiver through my body.

He never seemed to tire of me. He had barely left my side since the night he had stormed into the house and rammed me against the wall. It had been an intense and recreational six days since then. The man was insatiable and I seemed unable to say no to him.

He released my hands to pull off my shirt. I took the opportunity to unbuckle his belt and start working on the button of his jeans. I was only wearing cotton shorts and I knew as soon as he had them off I didn't have a chance of control. I worked fast and managed to slide my hand inside his opened jeans as he threw my bra across the room. He groaned as I stroked him. I loved the way his body froze. I never gained the upper hand for long, but when I had it, the power was intoxicating.

"You're pushing your luck, little girl," he said in a shaky exhale.

"Am I?" I pushed his jeans down his thighs. He stayed motionless and I wondered how long it would take for his control to snap. I pushed his boxers down and stroked him again. I caught his knee with my leg and flipped him onto his back. For the first time he didn't take control back from me. He lay passively on his back.

It made me pause. Too much control wasn't a good thing for me. I started to remember that getting close to people was dangerous. Letting Mason matter to me was against the rules I had lived by. His hand touched my face, his long fingers tracing my cheekbone. I looked into his eyes and nearly panicked. The gesture was too tender, too close to loving. I could handle the harsh animal roughness of his usual desire. But this softer side, this vulnerable side, I couldn't be with that. The man who threw me against walls wasn't going to be hurt when I left. I couldn't look into his eyes when he looked at me like he was now, and pretend I wasn't going to hurt him.

"What?" he asked. "What did I do?"

I absolutely wasn't going to answer that question. I wanted the animal back in his eyes. I could handle the animal. I pulled my face away from his gentle touch. He would have said something, but his thoughts died when I took him in my mouth. His hands sank into my short hair and the words he had planned came out as a moan. I pushed aside the thoughts that threatened my sanity, and focused on the man at my mercy. I watched the muscles of his arms and chest while I ran my tongue along his length. He swore when I took him deep. I loved the harsh words and the guttural tone that delivered them.

I gasped when he grabbed me by the shoulders and pulled me up his body. He released my shoulders to catch at the band of my shorts, shoving them down my legs with my help. He lifted my hips and pulled me down over him. I bit back a scream at the sensation. He paused a moment, holding me still against him. I opened my eyes to see a flash of concern on his face and bounced my hips to reassure him my scream had been from pleasure and not pain. He grinned and started moving me.

I had thought that being on top meant I was in control. I should have known better. Mason might have let me play with him for short periods, but he never let me lead for long. I loved being helpless and he knew it. His hands on my hips set the rhythm and pace. I was as out of control as I always was with him. His mouth closed over my breast as he pulled me hard against him. I lost myself in him, in his power, his animal side. I closed my eyes so I wouldn't have to see the emotion in his. I buried myself in the harsh pleasure of his body and let myself explode.

I woke later, wondering what time it was. The sky was just starting to hint at sunset. I wasn't sure when Mason had interrupted my work, but I was fairly certain it had been more than ten hours since I'd eaten anything. Mason was snoring quietly beside me. It wasn't really snoring, more of a steady, heavy breathing. It was a calming sound and I was growing too used to it. I hadn't slept alone in days, and I wasn't used to sharing so much. If I hadn't had the days to myself I probably would have killed him by now.

I extracted myself from his arms and searched for my clothes. He was a heavy sleeper and didn't wake when I left. I pulled on my shorts, bra, and tank top. The light from the coming sunset painted the room in a warm glow. I turned back to the bed and caught my breath.

The simple mattress on the floor was bathed in a stream of light from the window. The sheets I had tucked around it were white. Mason lay on his stomach, his face turned to me. One arm was out and trailed onto the floor. The top-sheet was thrown back, exposing his upper body right down to the firm curve of his ass. The sheet left a length of thigh exposed. I needed to draw him like that.

I grabbed my camera and took a few pictures, amazed that the sound and movement didn't wake him. I wanted this to be a large portrait, and I needed the colors the sunset was painting on him. I tossed the camera aside and selected my largest sketchbook. I pulled up my stool and began to work.

I loved drawing Mason. His body was truly beautiful. He was all strong lines, contrasts, depth, and character. I had fallen in love with his hands, his large, long-fingered hands. They were strong and graceful. I had drawn them many times. The way he was lying on the bed now, it appeared he was reaching for someone. He smiled faintly while he slept.

I ditched my sketchbook and selected a large canvas instead. I loved that Mason hadn't moved. I was losing the light, but I had the camera pictures for the color. I just needed him to stay still. I worked fast, so enthralled with the beauty of the scene I barely noticed what my hands were doing. I lost track of time as I captured him on the canvas.

A knock on the door made me jump, and woke Mason.

"You guys want dinner?" Ray called. "I was gonna order pizza."

It normally took Mason a good three minutes before he could form coherent thoughts after being woken up, so I answered, "Pizza sounds great. We'll be over in a few."

I watched Mason as I listened to Ray retreat down the stairs. I had been so absorbed in my work I hadn't heard him coming up the stairs. I was lucky he hadn't opened the door.

Mason blinked sleep from his eyes, running a hand through his hair. He looked at the canvas and frowned.

"What are you doing?" he asked.

"Ah, working."

His eyes narrowed. He stood and I watched him while he gathered his clothes and pulled them on. I loved watching him move. He really was an artist's dream.

"You keep looking at me like that and we're gonna miss dinner," he said. He came around beside me and froze when he saw what I'd been drawing.

I fidgeted on my stool. "I'm sorry. I shouldn't have done this without asking you."

His hand settled on my shoulder, but his eyes stayed on my work. "I'm not upset, honey," he said. "Just, well . . ."

"I know you're not comfortable with me drawing you naked. I'm sorry. I'll just put this aside. I won't finish it."

"Like hell you won't!" he said, surprising me into looking up into his eyes.

"You like it?"

"It's beautiful," he said. "Don't tell my brothers I said that, but it really is, Divine. I don't know what to say."

"It's gonna be full color," I said, trying to hide my embarrassment by telling him my plans. "When I started, the sunset was just starting, and the colors were amazing. I took some pictures with the camera so I can get it right later."

He grabbed the camera and looked through the pictures. He blushed, but didn't comment further.

"You're not going to sell this one, are you?" he asked.

"Of course not." I took his hand. "I did this for me." The words were out before I could stop them. I looked at the picture. Even as a rough start, the emotion in it was alarming. It was as plain as day what I was feeling when I looked at him. It wasn't an emotion I was willing to admit to myself yet, but my art wasn't into denial.

"Divine . . . ?" Mason began.

"Dinnertime," I interrupted him, taking off just shy of running toward the door. He stayed to look at the drawing for a moment before following me without another word.

Chapter 13

I LEARNED TOO LATE that controlling Zach was impossible. He had an amazing ability to trick me into saying yes to everything he wanted. He had a reporter interview me and Ray for a public interest piece in the local paper. The headline read, *Aspiring Artist Given Chance of a Lifetime by Long-Lost Father*. Ray and I were horribly embarrassed by it, but I had to agree with Zach that our story would stir up a lot of interest in my work.

I spent a lot of my time out on my bike. I loved drawing people, which meant I had to go where they were. Provincetown became my second home. I spent most afternoons on the docks. I befriended one of the old Portuguese fishermen and took a series of pictures of him on his boat doing repairs, which I could turn into drawings later. There weren't many boats or fishermen left in Provincetown. My new friend grumbled irritably about the complicated political situation that had his boat sitting at the dock. I asked him if he thought any of the other local fishermen would be interested in participating in a series of artwork, to raise awareness about the state of the fishing industry. He gave me some names and numbers and suggested I go down to the Chatham Fish Pier where all the gillnetters were docked.

I loved doing portraits of working-class people at their jobs. My obsession with hands came into play. I loved well-worn, strong hands. They expressed emotions much more clearly than words. I thought about the gentle way Mason's fingers stroked across my cheekbone. I watched as a man knelt down to tie his daughter's shoes. A little boy climbed up onto a large anchor and posed for his laughing parents. I took pictures of it all.

I spent my nights in the studio turning the photographs into art. I arranged to meet with a few of the Chatham fishermen when they offloaded, so I could get some pictures and ideas for my work. I was afraid to mention the idea of the fishermen series to Zach. I knew if he heard about it, he'd take it and run, until it was so big I died under a pile of sketchbooks.

I was lucky I had just finished with the father tying his daughter's shoes when someone came up the stairs to the studio. When I was actively working I never heard anything, something Mason always exploited. He looked disappointed when I looked at him and smiled as he walked into the room.

"No scaring me today," I said.

"It's early yet." He bit my shoulder and leaned over me to look at the picture.

"I like it," he said.

"I'm happy with it."

"Good, 'cause we have plans today."

"We do?"

"I know you've gone up to P-town a few times, but this time you're not going up to work. We're gonna go have some fun."

I laughed at the boyish look on his face. "Aren't you getting tired of me?" I asked. "Your friends must think you died."

He frowned at me. "If I'm smothering you I'll back off."

"I didn't say that. I've just never had anyone find me so entertaining before."

The sound of a truck roaring into the driveway caught my attention. Mason let out a long-suffering sigh as he glanced out the window. I had a feeling I knew who had just arrived. I followed him down the stairs.

Bo emerged from her truck. She slammed the door and looked toward the house, not seeing Mason and me emerging from the studio.

"Mason!" she yelled. "I know you're here, you jackass!"

I stayed behind him as he approached her. There were tracks of tears down her face, and her hair was messily pulled back by a rubber band. That was going to hurt when it came out.

"What did Zach do now?" Mason asked calmly.

Bo whirled on him. "He . . ." she cut off when she saw me. Mortification replaced her anger and she quickly wiped at the tear streaks on her face. "Oh, sorry, Divvy. I didn't see you there. You two are busy. I'll just go."

I knew what I had to do. I ran to catch her as she retreated to her truck and caught her arm.

"I'm fine," she began.

"You're not. But you will be. Go talk it out with Mason. I can't let you go home like this. If I do, you'll just kill Zach, and I need him to make me famous."

She smiled at me with genuine emotion for the first time. "You don't mind? I'm not normally like this. This pregnancy bullshit makes me go crazy if he so much as sneezes."

"I've got some work I can finish up. Mason and I were going to go up to P-town for some fun. You're welcome to come along."

"You two had plans. I don't want to be a third wheel."

"I like third wheels. Being balanced makes me uncomfortable."

I left her with Mason and headed back to the studio.

I felt inspired so I pulled out the large canvas of Mason on the bed. I didn't work on it when he was around because it embarrassed him. I was nearly done with the details, and could start adding the color. I spent a few minutes perfecting the slight smile on his face.

"Hey Divvy, Mase sent me up to . . . oh, wow!"

I jumped off my stool and stood in front of the canvas. Bo was staring at it with her mouth open. I moved over so I was blocking the section with his half-exposed ass.

I had no idea how to explain. I tried, "I'm sorry, Bo. I didn't hear you coming. This is, well, I promised him I wouldn't let anyone see it."

She kept staring at it.

"Bo?"

She shook her head and turned her eyes to me. "Wow," she said again. "That's more of my brother than I was prepared to see." She took a deep breath and smiled at me. "You're really talented. Zach's been talking about you, but I was being petty and pretending he was lying. You can move, Divvy. Now that I'm over the shock, I'd like to see the whole thing."

"Mason is going to kill me," I sighed, but I moved away.

Bo blushed a bit but looked at the portrait with interest. She smiled. "He looks peaceful."

"He was."

She turned to me. "My brother has never been peaceful before."

I took that moment to grab the portrait and move it back to face the wall. Bo's eyes caught the other portrait of Mason I had finished. She grinned at it. "That's so him," she said. "Confident, cocky . . . and obvious!"

I shared a tentative laugh with her.

"He's not very subtle," I said.

"No. Look, Divvy, I owe you an apology."

"No, really," I began.

She shook her head at me. "I do. You make my brother happy. He's a big boy and he knows what's best for him. I hate that we got off on the wrong foot. I'd like to start over."

"I'd like that too," I said. "So why don't you come to Provincetown with us?"

A smile lit her face. "Well, we have to go to a drag show. They love Mason up there, they always pull him up on stage."

I grinned. This day was getting better and better.

Chapter 14

I JUMPED AT THE KNOCK on the studio door. Zach peered around it and smiled at me.

"Sorry to startle you, ma'am."

"Come on in, Zach."

The big man who had taken over my professional career stepped into the room. I had done a second interview for another paper, even more embarrassing than the first. People were starting to talk about the coming show, and it was making me feel sick to my stomach. Surely my work wasn't good enough to earn that kind of attention.

"Why do you always jump like that?" he asked.

"Years of conditioning," I said, stretching.

"What do you mean?"

I hated that lately I'd begun to talk without thinking. The amazing sex with Mason was killing my brain cells. "My mother was a con artist. Numerous times a door was slammed open and we had to climb out a window and head for the hills. So I still jump." I shrugged, wondering why I was telling this to Zach. I still hadn't told Mason anything about Mama.

Zach didn't throw me a pity party, which was a relief. Instead he just got to the point. "Bo sent me to pick you and Ray up. Party is starting. She said she didn't want to come herself, in case you were working on a particular drawing of her brother. Do you know which one she was referring to?"

I blushed and shook my head. "No idea what you're talking about."

He laughed one of his rare, beautiful laughs and held out an arm in an old-fashioned gesture. "May I escort you to the party, Miss Divvy?"

"I just have to give this to Dad before we go," I said, picking up an intricate metal frame. It held six pictures. I had a flash drive with all the pictures I had from my childhood. I'd chosen the best ones to give to Ray for a Father's Day present.

"Interesting frame," Zach mentioned.

"I found it in a gallery in P-town, though to be honest, I only got it as an excuse to talk to the artist. I asked him to model for me." I laughed at the memory. "He blushed bright red and tripped over this giant metal lighthouse."

"What about him drew your attention?" Zach asked.

"He's huge," I said. "His name's Rafael Shore. He's about six-five and a bodybuilder. But being close to him is weirdly relaxing. He has an extremely gentle nature. I wanted to draw that. His girlfriend was all for it, but he refused. Well, he did at first. He called me yesterday and asked if I'd do a portrait of him. Not to sell, but to give to his girl. He's really sweet."

Zach waited in his truck while I went inside the main house to get Ray. I wasn't sure if I should have wrapped the gift or not, but seeing as it was weirdly shaped metal, I was guessing it wouldn't have been worth the effort. I found him at the kitchen table with a tray of cookies he'd baked for the party.

"I got you something," I began. "It's not much. And I didn't get a card or anything. But I thought you'd like it." I set the frame on the table and stepped back.

He picked it up slowly, running his fingers over the metal. I watched him, not sure if I'd done the right thing. I didn't have many pictures from my childhood, but I'd chosen the happy ones. He blinked tears from his eyes. "You were such a beautiful little girl. I really wish I'd been there."

I hugged him. "It wasn't supposed to make you sad."

He smiled and tucked me under his arm. "I'm never sad anymore. Let's head over to the party. It's my first Father's Day, after all."

It was Bo's turn to host the family. I sat on the back deck with Bo, Maxine, and Nancy, while the mass of men played football.

The four of us watched the boys grunting, tackling, and growling in the too-small backyard. Trace was holding his own against his sons and the Cutter brothers. Nancy was watching him, with an open lust that surprised me in a couple who'd been married as long as they had. Ray manned the grill, as an excuse to keep from being trampled.

"That is one sexy man I married," Nancy said.

"I'm lucky Mason takes after him," I agreed.

Bo frowned and rubbed at her belly. "Mason might look like Dad, but he doesn't take after him that much."

"How do you mean?" I asked.

"Mason's always been a hothead," Nancy said. "He was always getting into fights and driving cars too fast, surfing during storms. He slowed down a bit in the past year or so, but he's never really been settled at heart. Well, until recently." Her comment tore my eyes from the shirtless Mason to her.

"I told you," Bo said. "He's calm for the first time with you. Peaceful. He hasn't gone out and picked a bar fight."

"Or shown up at dawn to drag Axel on some damn-fool dangerous adventure," Maxine added.

I tried to reconcile my relaxed Mason with the restless man they described.

"Nancy," Trace yelled from the bottom of a pile of bodies, "you gonna come out here and help me teach these boys how to play ball?"

Nancy flexed the impressive muscles of her arms and smiled. "Excuse me, ladies. I have some testosterone to smother."

I watched this mother-of-four/Wonder Woman as she dove into the game. "Your mother is fantastic," I said.

"That she is," Bo nodded. "I wish I was in there with her. Stupid kid. Be ready already." She rubbed at her belly and rolled her eyes. "The things I do for that man."

We sat in companionable silence for a minute amid the grunts, groans, and playful heckling.

"This is going to sound weird," Bo began, "but has Mason talked at all about his old girlfriends?"

I wasn't sure how to read her tone or expression. "Ah, no. Why?"

She glanced at her brother and frowned. "I just think it's important you know something about his past."

"Why?"

"Because it's not something he can talk about, but I know it's something he wants you to know." She glanced around to make sure everyone was busy and not listening to us. "Back when he was seventeen, Mason was accused of beating and raping his girlfriend."

I stared at her in shock. "Mason? He'd never do that."

"Of course not," Bo and Maxine said at the same time.

Bo explained, "Mason and I went to a party with the girlfriend. While we were there, my ex got in my face, called me a few names. Mason attacked him. I had to pull him off."

"That I can see," I admitted.

"He had too much to drink. We were young and stupid. He calmed down and we stayed at the party. It was at this house someone's older brother was watching for the winter. It was on the water and there was a little boathouse. Everyone called the boathouse the sex-shack, because that's what went on in there. Mason and Chrissy headed out that way. When they came back, she was limping, had blood on her shirt and a cut on her shoulder, and she looked like hell." Bo paused and sighed. "Everyone was doing their best to ignore her condition. I mean, she was smiling and wasn't crying or anything. But her brother, Dan, was there, and he made a huge scene and accused Mason of raping her. Mason got pissed and hit Dan, and the fight got really bad."

"What did Chrissy say about it?" I asked.

"Her brother wouldn't let her get a word in," Bo frowned. "She tried to defend Mason, but when he went after Dan, everyone started to believe she was just afraid of him and was lying."

"People still believe he did it." Maxine shook her head. "I can't understand how anyone who's met him could think him capable of it."

"What did happen?" I asked.

"Apparently, Mason had pinned her against a wall in the boathouse and a picture frame fell on them and the broken glass cut her shoulder," Bo said. (I had no trouble imaging that scenario.) "Then, on their way out of the boathouse, she tripped down the steps and sprained her ankle. I was never a big fan of her. She was too quiet and subdued for him. She was so embarrassed about the sex, she wouldn't tell anyone how she got cut, only that he hadn't hurt her. So no one believed her.

"And then she broke up with him the following day. Everyone assumed it was because he had raped her, no matter how many times she told people it was because of the fight he'd had with Dan. She couldn't handle how aggressive he was. Of course, her saying that didn't help convince anyone he hadn't hurt her."

"So people really believed that Mason had raped her?" I couldn't wrap my mind around it. I had no doubt he'd take the first swing at someone without too much provocation, but never a woman. He was aggressive, but not an abuser.

"Some people still believe he did," she said, "Dan in particular. He makes sure that no one around town ever forgets it, either. He and Mason get into it whenever they run into each other. If Chrissy had just grown a spine and admitted to the rough sex, things might have gone differently. But she was a 'good girl.'" She snorted.

"And I'm not," I said, feeling uncomfortable.

"No. And that's the last we'll say about you, I promise. I don't want to make you uncomfortable. But I had to tell you. He doesn't normally date. He's a one-night-stand kind of guy. And one-night-stands don't allow for enough trust for him to be himself."

"What do you mean?" I asked.

Bo rolled her eyes. "My brother likes rough sex. I would have to be deaf not to be aware of that. My childhood home had thin walls, and his bedroom was beside mine."

I couldn't keep the grin off my face. "Well, I like it rough, so that hasn't been an issue."

She winked at me. "While we're on the topic, I just wanted to say thank you. Because now that he gets regular rough sex, he doesn't start bar fights or go surfing in storms."

I laughed. "Glad I could help, I guess." Then I sobered. "Is it okay that you told me about Chrissy? Would he mind me knowing?"

"It's common knowledge." Maxine shrugged.

"Like I said, he'd want you to know," Bo replied.

"Want her to know what?" Mason asked, coming up behind me.

"Chrissy," Bo said simply.

I saw the emotion in his eyes. It had hurt him deeply to be accused of rape. A man raised by Nancy would find rape abhorrent. That people had believed him capable of it must have been devastating.

But I knew Mason well enough to know he wouldn't want pity or coddling. I jumped up and threw my arms around his neck. "Bo says you need a bad girl," I said. "Lucky you, 'cause I happen to know one."

He laughed and kissed me, and the sadness was gone.

Chapter 15

I WALKED INTO Mason's bedroom tentatively. Aside from two piles of clothes on the floor, the room was surprisingly clean. It was also largely empty. He had a queen-size bed, a dresser whose partially open drawers displayed that they were empty, and a bookshelf covered in magazines. The bed wasn't made and there was no top sheet.

"You bring girls here often?" I teased.

"Only the really drunk ones," he said, kicking a pile of porn magazines farther under the bed.

"It's nicer than I thought it would be," I admitted.

He stripped off his shirt and sat on the bed to take off his shoes. I watched the muscles play in his back and shoulders. My eyes caught on the tattoo of the angel with the name Michael scrawled under it.

"Who was Michael?" I asked. As soon as the words escaped I wanted to take them back. I didn't want those kinds of details from him. It would only bring us closer together, and I had to protect him.

He looked up at me, startled. He glanced over his shoulder at the tattoo. "I forget that's there sometimes," he admitted. I hated the broken tone of his voice.

"I'm sorry. I shouldn't have just blurted it out like that. You don't need to talk about it." Maybe he'd let it drop. I hoped he would.

"No, it's okay." He resumed removing his shoes. To cover my discomfort I started stripping. I didn't want this story. If I got naked fast enough, maybe I could distract him.

"Michael was my best friend. We grew up together. He was an only child and his mom worked a lot, so he spent a lot of time at our house. He was a couple years older than me, but in my grade. He'd got held back a few times. He wasn't that bright, poor guy. Some of the other guys used to pick on him. Actually, he was dumb as a stump." He paused to chuckle and removed his pants.

"He ended up doing night school to finish high school. He did work-study and every shop class he could. Man was great with his hands, just not his head. Anyway, after he graduated he went to work for his uncle on fishing boats. Did that for years. He was gone a lot, but he made good money scalloping. A few years ago he got married. They had a little girl and his wife was pregnant with another."

Mason sat on the bed in his boxers and was silent. I had a really bad feeling about where the story was going, but my being naked hadn't distracted him. I was going to hear it. I sat beside him and took his hand, because it was shaking.

"I still remember the last thing I said to him. He was leaving for a long trip and they had just found out the new baby was gonna be a boy. He asked me to be the godfather. I told him I'd be honored. He joked with me that I needed to borrow someone else's kids, 'cause I was never gonna get a girl to stick with me long enough to have one of my own. He left laughing. I never saw him again."

"I'm sorry." I cuddled against his side, unsure if he was done talking or not.

"There was a storm a few days after they left," he continued. "It came up fast, so they stayed out rather than try and harbor somewhere. Something broke loose on deck and Michael went out with our friend Kol to tie it down. The boat got swamped while they were on deck. Michael went over. Kol caught his arm, but the water was too strong and he dropped him. Kol got knocked up really badly on the metal stairs. Almost died. He was in a coma for a few days. They never found Michael's body."

I wrapped myself more firmly around Mason. "I'm so sorry. His poor wife and little girl. How old was he?"

"He was twenty-eight when he died. Kol blames himself to this day for dropping his hand. But it wasn't his fault. There was nothing he could have done."

I had no idea what to say to make the pain in his eyes lessen. I realized I was now humming Stacey's song. I let the words come, glad that I had a decent singing voice. He listened to me, one hand stroking my short hair.

"That's pretty," he said when I was done.

"My friend Stacey taught it to me. Her mother used to sing it to her when she was a baby."

"Stacey who loved faeries?" he prompted.

"Stacey who is the faerie tattooed on my shoulder." The words came unwelcome to my mouth, and then continued. "Mama always dragged me from place to place. I wasn't allowed to have friends. But when I was fifteen, we moved to Jamestown, in Rhode Island. I enrolled in the high school, despite Mama bitching it was a waste of time. After all, I knew how to con someone out of their money, what good would school do me?" I snorted this, hearing Mama's Irish in my ear, then continued. "I met Stacey in school. She was so unlike anyone Mama had ever let me spend time with. She was from a solid middle-class family—not wealthy enough to be a good mark, so beneath Mama's notice. They were good people. I started spending the night as often as I could. Mama was stripping and hooking, as well as conning a millionaire out of a large sum of money, so she wasn't around much. But the con went south. She showed up at Stacey's door and told me we were leaving."

"How long had you been living there?"

"Six months. It was a real long time for us. But I didn't want to go. I know I haven't talked about Mama, and I really don't want to. Let's just say that I saw a chance to escape, and I took it. Stacey's mom offered to let me stay with her. There was a big scene with me and my mother. It could have been worse though, a lot worse. In the end she gave me five grand and told me the name of a guy who'd give me a car. She said I was a fool to think I could stay. I was a gypsy, just like her, and we didn't belong anywhere. I'd leave eventually.

She told me how to get in touch with her when I came to my senses. Then she was gone."

"How old were you again?"

"Sixteen. Stacey's mom helped me get my driver's license. I was happy there. They treated me like family. But Mama was right. I didn't belong. There was this horrible thought in my head, this pull to move on. I can't explain it. It's like a sickness. All I wanted in the world was to stay, but I couldn't sit still. I lost weight. I couldn't sleep. So one day I got home from school, packed up my car with my clothes and the few things I owned, and drove away. Stacey tried to stop me. We got in a huge fight. She didn't understand why I was going. I told her I had to. I never thought she'd follow me. She jumped in her mom's car and clung to my bumper. I was so angry with her. I started speeding, trying to lose her. It was winter. The roads were icy. Stacey's car hit a patch of ice and she lost control...."

Mason's arms wrapped tighter around me. I could see it all over again in my head: glancing in the rearview mirror to watch the top-heavy Jeep slide off the side of the road and start rolling down the hill; the horrible sounds of shattering glass, bending metal . . . and screaming . . .

"I tried to save her, I really tried. But I couldn't get her out of the car. It had rolled upside down. I climbed in to try and get her out, but I couldn't. She was screaming. There was so much blood." I lost my voice and tucked my head against his neck. He held me while I cried. His hands stroked my bare back, all tenderness and compassion. I had never told anyone about Stacey before. I had no idea why I'd told Mason. I hated it now that I'd told him, that I'd let him see just how vulnerable I could be. I let myself cry until I had no more tears.

"Stacey died three weeks before her seventeenth birthday," I said, hearing the bitterness in my voice. "She died because of me."

"It was an accident, Divine," he said into my hair. "It wasn't your fault."

"She was out there because of me. She was going way too fast, trying to catch up to me. Trying to make me stay. Trying to make me belong. But I don't belong. I never have. I always leave. I try to stay. I try so hard. But I just can't."

I shifted on the bed, pulling my legs up against my chest. "Stacey's mom told me that it should have been me that died. She told me at the funeral, in front of everyone. I ruined them. My mother was right. I tried to be something I'm not, and I broke a wonderful family."

"Divine, it wasn't your fault," he repeated. "It was no more your fault than it was Kol's that he let go of Michael's hand."

"It doesn't matter anyway," I snapped, letting go of my legs to wipe at my tears. "She's dead. I learned my lesson. I've never made the same mistake again."

"What mistake was that?"

"Letting people get too close. People who get close to me get hurt."

"You don't honestly believe that, do you?"

"Stacey died. I slipped up in North Carolina and broke this poor guy's heart when I left him behind. I let my sweet little landlady get too close once. She begged me to stay. Cried like a baby as I drove away. I hurt people, Mason. I'm going to hurt you."

He tried to pull me into his arms, but I slid across the bed away from him. He sat back with a sigh. "You may be right," he said, surprising me. "It's gonna hurt like hell when you go. But that doesn't change anything."

"It makes you a masochist if you don't kick me out of this bed. In fact, I should go."

I didn't get to stand up. Mason sprang across the bed and had me pinned down so fast I didn't have time to scream.

"Let's get this clear, Grace Divine," he said, so close his lips brushed against mine. "You don't get to decide what's best for me. If I want to risk getting hurt, that's my business. If you want nothing to do with me because I'm an aggressive, possessive ass, that I can deal with. But don't you think for a second I'll let you push me away to protect me."

"I don't want to hurt you."

"There is no pleasure without pain, honey." He proceeded to demonstrate his meaning. It was all I could do to hold on. The raw emotion poured out of him in the form of harsh thrusts and rough hands, biting teeth and the scrape of stubble against tender skin. There was pain, but only enough to bring the pleasure to an explosive crescendo. He robbed me of my argument, of my armor. He broke right through my wall and into me, claiming me, owning me. And I loved it. I was terrified.

Chapter 16

I CREPT OUT of Mason's room at dawn, careful not to wake him. I hadn't wanted to put on my dirty clothes from the night before so I wore a pair of Mason's sweatpants. They dragged on the floor and even though I drew the drawstring as tight as it would go, they barely stayed on my hips. The sweats and a borrowed tank top made me look like a small child dressing in her daddy's clothes.

I explored the house as silently as I could. We'd spent most of our time at Ray's because there was so much work to do, so I didn't really know the layout of Mason's place. There were two bedrooms upstairs; Gage was snoring loudly in his. The idea of going into a bathroom that two men were responsible for cleaning scared me, so I ignored it. The downstairs wasn't very interesting, just the kitchen to the side of the house and the large living room. The basement door was open, so I headed down to see what there was to see.

The washer and dryer sat in one corner. Spare clothes were scattered everywhere, amid spilled pools of dried detergent and balls of lint that had missed the small trash can. It was obvious two bachelors lived there. I was so distracted by the chaos it took me a moment to notice the rest of the room.

The floor was covered in gymnasium blue mats. A punching bag hung from the ceiling and there was an assortment of boxing gloves on a table. There was a bench press and a menagerie of free weights.

I should have known he'd have something like this. He didn't go to a gym, and his muscles couldn't be explained by construction work alone.

I stretched and selected a pair of boxing gloves that fit me. I had a feeling they belonged to Bo. I attacked the punching bag to burn off some of my unease about the night before. I didn't want to think about Mason. Unfortunately, I started thinking about Mama, as I often did when I was hitting something.

Mama had taught me to fight as soon as I'd been old enough to walk. She'd never told me anything specific, but I had a theory she'd been badly abused as a small child. She had wanted me to be able to defend myself. I learned a variety of fighting styles as we moved from place to place. The result was a mixed batch that basically boiled down to dirty street fighting with finesse.

"Who are you mad at?" Mason asked, startling me.

"What?"

"You're hitting that bag like it killed your puppy."

I hit it again with a right cross. "I've never had a puppy."

"Are you mad at me?"

I turned to face him. "No. Why would I be?"

He shrugged, but I saw wariness in his eyes. "You snuck out of bed to come and beat on something. Just makes a man wonder, that's all."

I shrugged and held up my gloved hands. "Wanna spar?"

"No." There was an edge behind his tone that caught my attention. It kept me from teasing him. He shifted his feet uncomfortably. "I don't hit women, not even in a friendly sparring match."

I remembered Chrissy and nodded. "It's no problem. You think Gage would spar with me?"

Mason laughed and I relaxed. "Gage is a dancer. He'd never risk you hurting him. And he's not a fighter. You'd kick his ass."

I sighed. I wanted a good workout.

"I can work with you though," Mason said. "I have some pads. You can use me as a target. I'm happy to oblige."

We passed a sweaty half hour of him blocking my kicks and punches with the cushioned pads that strapped to his forearms. He moved amazingly fast for a big man. I never managed to get past his guard. To end it, he surged at me unexpectedly and I dodged into the punching bag and nearly knocked myself out.

He knelt beside me, laughing too hard to offer comfort or even ask if I was all right. The fact that I was muttering swears was a good indicator I wasn't badly hurt.

"You did that on purpose," I accused.

"How was I to know you were gonna dodge that way?"

"Ass."

"Are you okay?"

I cracked my neck and rotated my shoulders. I tasted blood and checked my teeth. They were all still there, but there was a cut on my lip. Mason noticed it and the playfulness left his eyes. "I'm sorry, honey. I didn't think you'd hit it that hard."

"It's no big deal. I just bit my lip a little. It's already stopped bleeding, see?"

He pulled me to my feet. "Let me make you breakfast," he suggested.

I watched him in the kitchen as he cooked bacon and made French toast. The smell of the bacon lured Gage downstairs. He took one look at me and burst out laughing. I remembered I was wearing Mason's clothes and rolled my eyes.

"Bite me, Gage," I said.

"I think Mason would object to that," Gage said.

"Damn right." Mason glanced over his shoulder at us. "She's mine."

"What happened to your lip?" Gage asked.

"I was beating up your brother when he tricked me into cracking my face into the punching bag."

Gage sat beside me and reached for my face. He had slender, long-fingered hands, very different from Mason's. He turned my face into the light. "I think you'll live," he said.

Mason grunted and the brothers exchanged a look I couldn't read. Gage sat back from me casually. "How goes the work on the gallery show?" he asked.

I groaned. "Zach is relentless. I thought it was just gonna be a small thing, a couple people walking around making polite sounds. From what Zach says he's got over a hundred people seriously interested in viewing my work. The man is insane. I do sketches, for fuck's sake!"

"Your work is beautiful," Mason said without turning to look at me. "Zach sees that. So will everyone else. Zach is a businessman; he wouldn't back you unless he knows you're a sure thing."

I laughed. "I'm not a sure thing. I'm a gypsy."

"I like gypsies," Mason said, depositing bacon and French toast on my plate. He kissed my hair. The tenderness was bothering me. I needed him to stay demanding and harsh. I found the idea of intimacy threatening.

"I read that thing in the paper about you," Gage said. "It was full of drama, more drama than the reality of the situation."

"Hey, blame Zach. All that stuff is his doing. He wants to stir up public interest. An estranged daughter given a chance of a lifetime by her rediscovered father is a great story."

Gage sat back in his chair and chewed contemplatively on his bacon. "You take it all in stride," he said after a minute. "I'm not sure I could do it."

"What?"

"You settled into being a daughter so easily. Seeing you and Ray together, you'd think that you'd never been apart."

"I'm a gypsy, we adapt easily," I said. Then I realized I was hearing my mother's words, and nearly choked on my breakfast. I took a drink of orange juice to clear my throat. This time I spoke with my own thoughts. "I got the father I always wanted. I was the unwanted kid for twenty-four years, and then there was Ray."

"You're not mad he wasn't there? That he left you?"

I laughed at the idea. "He didn't leave. He was chased from the house by Mama brandishing a cleaver." I realized both men were staring at me. "What?"

"Did your mother ever hit you?" Gage asked. He blushed red and looked down at the floor the moment the words were out of his mouth. I was surprised the question didn't make me lose my appetite. But I had long ago come to terms with who and what my mother was. Once the truth was accepted, allowing it to hurt you was pointless.

I decided to be honest. "Wanda Therese is a violent, unstable menace to society. But she rarely bothered me. I was a useful tool for her. She took care of her tools. Sometimes she'd lose it, slap me or throw things. I was good at hiding. She went at me a few times, until I was old enough to hit her back. Then I left her when I was sixteen. I haven't seen her since."

Mason sat beside me, but neither man was eating. I shrugged my shoulders and smiled reassuringly at them.

"It's fine. Shit happens. I had a crappy childhood and a psycho con-artist mother. That doesn't matter. I turned out okay. And now I have Ray. So ditch the pity. I don't need it."

Gage nodded but the heavy mood remained. Suddenly, he grinned. "What kind of cons did you do?" he asked.

I laughed. "You mean can I pick pockets and play card tricks?"

"Can you?"

"I lifted a fair share of wallets in my day. Mama would set me up with a lemonade stand sometimes. I'd ask if I could see their wallets and make the change myself. No one suspects a six-year-old."

Gage and Mason laughed and shook their heads. I was surprised I was telling them all this. I normally avoided any talk of my childhood misadventures. But I knew that neither of them would consider me at fault for my crimes. I'd been just a kid. Besides, stealing a wallet was a small price to pay to avoid a beating.

I settled into my breakfast, talking between bites. "Her favorite con was a real estate thing. We'd go to houses for sale, never at open houses or anything, but just randomly showing up. Mama's a great actress. She'd talk the owner into letting us look around. She'd distract the owners while I stuffed small electronics and jewelry into my little pink backpack. If I got caught, we had a whole dramatic scene worked out where she'd scold me and say how I kept picking up everything shiny I saw."

"Interesting childhood you had," Gage said.

"You could say that. Mama kept me out of a lot of her cons. She liked to screw rich men out of their money. Literally. She loved blackmailing married men after she filmed them with her."

Mason and Gage shifted uncomfortably in their chairs. "Your mother sounds like a charmer," Gage said.

"My mother is a monster."

"You haven't seen her in how long?" Mason asked.

"Eight years, two months, seven days, and . . ." I checked my watch. "Two hours." I ate the last bite of bacon and licked my fingers. "She almost caught up to me, twice. Once in Florida, and again in New Orleans."

"She's looking for you?" Mason asked.

"Of course. I belong to her. She lost a useful tool."

"And you run whenever she catches up." Mason said it as a statement.

"I want nothing to do with her."

"When was the last time she got close?"

"Two years ago. I've been careful since then. That's why it was so hard for Ray to find me. Can we talk about something else? I don't like thinking about Mama."

Gage launched into a story about dancing that made us all laugh, but I didn't miss the look that remained in Mason's eyes.

Chapter 17

I SAT ON THE COOLER in the back of Mason's truck, watching the ocean. We were on Nauset Outer Beach, one of the few beaches you could drive out onto, provided you wanted to spend the money on a sticker and had a dependable four-wheel-drive vehicle. Axel followed in his truck with Maxine and Ray in the cab, Bo and Zach in the back. Mason drove with the sounds of Aerosmith beating out of the open cab windows. Gage and James were stuffed into the cab with him. Nancy and Trace had opted to ride with me and Danny in the bed of the truck.

Mason picked a random spot on the beach, well away from everyone else. I jumped down, and was startled when Nancy held Danny out to me. I took the toddler, surprised that he didn't protest as I lowered him to the sand. He took off like a shot, howling as he ran toward the water. Instinct had me running after him.

He put one toe in the water, shrieked, and ran away. He wrapped his chubby arms around my leg and started babbling. I could understand one word in three, but I got the gist that the water was cold. I picked him up and carried him on my hip toward his waiting parents.

"He's fast," I said as Danny climbed down and latched onto Axel's leg.

"He knows he can't go in the water alone," Maxine said. "Thanks for going with him, though. Those waves can come up high sometimes."

I looked down to the water, needing to feel it engulf me. I loved the ocean and most of my traveling had kept me close to it. I noticed Mason untying the surfboards from Axel's truck and grinned. I hadn't been surfing in months. Mason noticed me watching and called me over.

"I was gonna offer a lesson but something tells me you don't need one," he said.

"I learned to surf in California when I was eight."

"Show-off."

I gave him a quick kiss and stripped off my shirt. He growled in approval as he took in my small black bikini.

"Race you to the water," I said. I kicked off my shorts and took off running. I heard Mason coming after me. We reached the water at the same time and I splashed right into the frigid waves. He plunged in beside me and we dove into the wave as it crashed over our heads.

His arms wrapped around me as I came up for air. We were both gasping from the shock of the cold and laughing. His body felt extremely warm and I wrapped my legs around him. He grunted a little and glanced toward the beach.

"You realize my parents are watching, right?" he asked.

I glanced up at Nancy, who gave me a thumbs-up. "Your parents love me," I said, realizing what I had said immediately. Love was not a word I tossed around. I saw something in his eyes and was afraid he'd ruin everything, but he only smiled and kept the thoughts in his head. We floated for a while in the freezing water, enjoying each other.

James stood at the edge of the water. Mason and I laughed as he slowly made his way in, one agonizing step at a time. He bitched and complained about the cold the entire time. I finally lost my patience and dove. I caught his ankles and hauled him under.

Zach was watching from the safety of the high-tide line when I returned to the surface. He was laughing. Bo waddled her very pregnant body down the beach and right into the water without flinching. She floated like a top and grinned at me.

"Zach won't come in," she said. She looked at her husband. "Chicken shit!"

"That's my delicate wife, respectful and gracious as always," Zach called to us.

"I love New England ocean water," I admitted, climbing onto Mason's back.

"Good. The last couple of women Mason brought to the beach just sat in chairs and texted the entire time. They wouldn't go near the water. I have to ask, how is that scrap of bathing suit staying on?"

I glanced down to double-check it was still in the right place. "Magic. I'm a gypsy, remember?"

"I bet I could get it off," Mason rumbled, stroking my thigh under the water.

"Not in front of me," Bo complained. "I'm pregnant and horny and I look like a whale."

"You look beautiful," I said. "The real reason this suit stays on is that it doesn't have much to cover. I'm not curvy."

"I beg to differ," Mason said.

"I'm athletic, not curvy."

Bo snorted. "Having big boobs is more trouble than they're worth. Mine keep getting bigger, it seems. Zach is thrilled."

"I really don't want to talk about my sister's boobs."

Axel and James carried the surfboards down to the water. Axel lent me his, because he was busy digging a giant hole with Danny. I watched the father and son for a moment, wishing Danny could understand just how lucky he was to have such a loving family. Mason tugged on my arm and we went back into the water to see if we could catch any waves.

Cape Cod isn't California. The waves are small and hard to ride. It took me a few tries to find my balance on Axel's board. Mason and I caught the same wave. I didn't notice how close he was until he reached out and pushed me sideways. I coughed up some water as I surfaced. Mason stood close to me, offering his hand. I took it, but only to haul him into the water with me.

Mason and I stayed out surfing long after everyone else had returned to the beach to warm up and relax. Axel and Danny had dug a gigantic hole and were defending it from the encroaching high tide with Zach's help. I couldn't stop myself from watching the happy little boy. Being around kids always made me a little sad, since I'd never gotten the chance to be one.

Ray had grilled up some burgers on the portable propane grill, and the promise of food drew us out of the water. We settled on towels and beach chairs. The trucks' windows were down and both radios were tuned to the local rock station. I hummed along to Poison while enjoying my meal.

"I could get used to this," I said, then wanted to slap myself. I needed to stop talking like that. I was going to start itching to move on soon, and I knew I would leave. Talking like I was going to stay was not a good idea.

Mason didn't notice my unease. He sat beside me, pressing his leg against mine and settling one arm behind me so I was leaned on his shoulder. Every time I tried to stay distant he pulled me close. I gave up trying and rested my head on his collarbone.

"So, Divvy, think you're gonna be ready for the show next month?" Zach asked.

"I'll never be ready," I said. "But I should have enough work done so people can get a good laugh."

"Cut that out," Nancy said. "I've seen your work. It's wonderful."

"When did you see it?" I asked.

"I stopped in to give Mason his paycheck, but you guys were in P-town. I let myself into the studio. I hope that was okay?"

"It's fine," I said, trying to remember where the naked Mason picture was leaning.

"You have a fascination with hands," Nancy mentioned.

"Yes. I love drawing them."

"And fishermen, I noticed."

I glanced at Zach. "I've been talking to some of the local guys. I'm thinking of working on a series to raise awareness, and some money to support the local fisheries."

I watched Zach's eyes as his brain started working. I knew I was done for.

"It would have to be a separate show," he began. I listened to him talk as the simple idea became a grand scheme. I knew now I would stay to do it. Zach would hound me into working on the series, organize the charity, and then have some other greater idea before we were done.

Mason nuzzled my hair. "This is a great idea," he said. "I can talk to Kol and Michael's uncle. And Kol's friend Tony. They'd all love to get involved. Kol wouldn't admit it, but he'd be a great poster boy for the cause."

"Why do you say that?" I asked.

"Because Kol is a Viking god," Bo said. Zach rolled his eyes. Bo continued, "Kol is six-foot-four, white blond hair, extremely blue eyes, with a body that reminds me of trashy romance novel covers. He's also completely oblivious to how good he looks, and is the most down-to-earth, decent guy."

"I like him already."

"He's a good guy," Mason said. He hadn't bristled or gotten possessive over me. I took that to mean that either he trusted Kol implicitly, or Kol was gay.

"I have to finish enough stuff for this show first, though," I said. "So I have some time before I have to figure any of that out."

"You don't have to do anything," Bo said. "Zach's got it in his head now. He'll do it all."

Zach was busy muttering to himself, but he kissed his wife's hair absently.

Mason pulled me aside after the food was gone. We started walking down the beach at the tide line so the end of the crashing waves slapped against our ankles.

"I wanted to ask you if you'd be interested in meeting some of my friends," Mason said.

I hesitated.

"It's okay to say no," he continued. "I'm babysitting Michael's kids tomorrow while their mom does some shopping. Then I was going to go out with some friends."

I walked beside him without speaking for too long. I did want to meet them. I wanted to become a solid part of Mason's life. It was a dangerous wanting. I knew I was going to leave. But this time I had Ray. I'd come back to see my dad time and again. Mason would be here. Maybe we could settle this into a friendly while-I'm-here relationship. I knew it wasn't going to work, but I wanted it to.

"Sure, I'll hang with the kids and your friends tomorrow. I don't change diapers, though," I warned.

He put an arm around my shoulders. "My godson is two. His sister is five. I'll handle the diapers, don't worry. And you can talk to Kol tomorrow about the fishing series."

"You'll introduce me to the Viking god without pawing at me and grunting *mine*?"

Mason laughed. "I don't need to. You'll understand when you meet him."

Chapter 18

I FROWNED AS I heard Ray go back upstairs for the fifth time. Something was wrong with him. He'd changed his clothes three times that morning and bothered to shave on a weekend. He practically vibrated with nervous energy and I had no idea why.

"What's with Ray?" I asked Mason.

"What do you mean?" Men were so oblivious. I shrugged as the doorbell gave its horrible choked gurgle. That was on the list to be replaced. The list seemed to only grow as time went on.

Mason opened the door and was pounced on by two squealing children. He picked one up in each arm. Their mother followed them inside more sedately. I looked at Michael's widow. She was a lovely woman in her mid-thirties, with long black hair and happy-even-if-tired brown eyes. Her children both had her hair, but their eyes were green.

"How are you hellions doing?" Mason asked the kids in his arms.

"I have a loose tooth," the girl announced. The two-year-old babbled something. I needed a translator so I could understand toddlers. Mason nodded like it was perfectly clear and set the girl down.

"Hope, I want you to meet my friend Divvy. Divvy, this is Hope . . . and Mikey, and their mother, Laura."

I shook the little girl's trusting hand. I looked at the boy and imagined that he was the image of his father. I met Laura's eyes while I shook her hand. There was strength in her that touched me. I couldn't imagine how hard her life had been since losing her husband.

Ray walked into the entryway, trying for casual but failing. The moment he looked at Laura, I knew why he was acting so strangely. Mason seemed unaware of my father's interest in his friend's widow.

"Laura," Ray said, offering his hand awkwardly. "It's always nice to see you."

Laura smiled warmly and hugged him. I wasn't sure if she was aware of Ray's interest, or she was just the hugging type of person. He wasn't normally so awkward. His attention turned to the kids, who hugged him easily. He'd obviously spent time with the family. How had no one else noticed his attraction to Laura?

"Are you in a hurry to be off?" he asked her. "There's coffee and some muffins if you're hungry."

"And donuts for the monsters," Mason added.

Hope ran for the kitchen and Mikey struggled to get down and follow her. Laura smiled after them but didn't move farther into the house.

"My mother is waiting in the car. She's got the whole day planned out for me. She says I need some adult time. Thanks for taking the kids, Mason."

"Anytime. You're gonna come get them around six, right?"

"That's the plan."

"Want me to feed them?"

"If you want to. If not, I can get them pizza on the way home. My mother has decreed I am not to do any work today."

"You deserve a day off," Ray said.

"Thanks again. I'll see you later." Laura went out and I watched him watch her go. There was a crash from the kitchen and he headed in that direction. I grabbed Mason's arm to keep him in the entryway with me.

"You are aware that my dad has the hots for Laura, right?"

Mason stared at me blankly. "What?" he finally managed.

"My dad has a thing for Laura. It's so obvious."

"Seriously?" Mason looked out the window as Laura drove away. "I never noticed. Laura is still Michael's wife in my eyes. He's been gone almost three years, now. She went on a few casual dates with some guys her mother set her up with, but she wasn't really interested. She's busy raising the kids alone and running the flower store."

"What would you think of Ray dating Laura? Would it bother you?"

Mason seemed unable to grasp the idea at all. "Ray? Laura?"

"Ray is only forty-two years old. He's clean and sober now, with a good, steady job and an increasingly nice house."

"I've just never thought about it," Mason admitted.

"Well, think now. Would it bother you?"

He shrugged. "Well, no. Laura loved Michael, but he's gone. He wouldn't want her to be alone, and I don't either. I just never thought of Ray like that. He's always been alone. He's never dated anyone, not in the seven years I've known him."

"Well, I'm gonna make it my goal to fix that," I said.

He raised an eyebrow. "I wouldn't have figured you for a meddler."

"Normally I'm not. But I know Ray. He'll never ask her out. I'll just have to give him a shove in the right direction."

We found him, juggling donuts in the kitchen, to the giggling delight of the children. I threw on some rose-colored glasses and allowed myself to see the possibility. Ray had lost his chance at a family with me and Mama. Maybe he had a second chance here.

We spent the day ripping apart the kitchen. The kids got bored with the destruction after a while, so I set them up on the kitchen table with art supplies. Mikey ended up wearing most of the paint but they had fun, which was the point. Mason barely had to watch the kids at all, since Ray rarely left them.

We ordered a pizza and sat on the rotted back porch eating it. The kids started an impromptu game of tag with Mason, and Ray and I sat in the cheap, creaking beach chairs and watched.

"So," I said. "What am I going to have to do to convince you to take Laura out on a date?"

Ray jumped like I had hit him and the chair nearly gave way. "What?" he gasped.

"You heard me."

"I couldn't."

"Why not?"

He didn't answer me, just watched the kids running around.

"Is it about you thinking you're not good enough, or is it about Michael?"

He considered my words for a minute. "I knew Michael. He was a good man, a good father. I was always attracted to Laura, but she was his wife. I ignored it. Then he died." He paused and the silence was filled with the laughter of the kids. "Laura was amazing. She is such a strong woman. I wanted to give her time to grieve for Michael."

"It's been three years," I mentioned. "She's been on a few dates. So why don't you ask her out? Her kids adore you already, so that's not a worry."

"I was a drunk for a long time. A loser. She deserves better than that."

"You're sober now. Gainfully employed, owner of a nice home. Not too shabby."

"I have no idea what to do on a date."

I laughed but ended the conversation as Hope climbed onto his lap.

"Protect me from Mase!" she begged.

"You little creep," Mason said, walking up with Mikey hanging from his neck. He was as natural with the kids as Ray was. I imagined that he'd been a stand-in for Michael on many occasions. It was a Tavish trait to extend the love of family to outsiders in need. It made me think of my mother, who'd scoffed at love of any kind and only used it to hurt and steal. What could I know about love and family?

Chapter 19

KOL DID INDEED make me think of a Viking conqueror upon first glance. But within five minutes, I understood why he didn't trigger Mason's possessive hands-off-my-woman routine. Kol Amundson looked at me without a shadow of sexual interest. He greeted everyone with the same level tone and friendliness. He was genuinely unaware of how attractive he was, and the result was the most mellow, easygoing man I had ever come across. But also I recognized something in his eyes, in the way he moved.

The other friend of Mason's who accompanied us to the bar was Paul. He was a police officer in Eastham and made me nervous. I'd been groomed to despise cops as a child, and hadn't ever really succeeded in overcoming the conditioning. Mason, Paul, and Kol had been on the football team together in high school, and had stayed close. We next greeted James, who showed up claiming to have narrowly escaped a beating from his sister-in-law.

The bartender was an attractive short blonde named Quinn. Mason introduced me to her and she shook my hand. "A brunette." She raised an eyebrow.

"I'm trying something new," Mason said.

"Does this one know how to use big-girl words?"

I laughed and Quinn grinned at me. "Mason has terrible taste, on principle," she explained. "But James came in, and he told me about you. I can see you're the exception to the rule."

"Thank you."

"When are you going to take me up on that offer for a date, Quinn?" James took her hand in a dramatic gesture.

She slapped him off. "If I was going to date a washashore it sure as shit wouldn't be you."

"Would you ever date anyone?" He asked, his tone teasing. "What about Kol?"

Both Kol and Quinn laughed. "Kol is as much my brother as Ben is, despite being born to different parents."

I realized that was what it was about Kol. He exuded a sibling vibe rather than a single-attractive-man one. He wasn't gay, just entirely platonic. What a waste!

Kol shrugged. "Your dad was more of a father to me than Nils. The best thing Nils ever did for me was die." He said it casually, without the force of emotion I would have suspected.

"I sympathize," I said, realizing I'd spoken aloud when everyone else had stopped talking. I took a long drink of my margarita. "I haven't seen my mama in almost nine years. If I see her in another decade, it'll be too soon."

"Sorry to hear that," Quinn said.

"Don't be. I've got Ray now." I was hoping to turn the conversation.

Quinn narrowed her eyes at me. "Ray?"

"Ray Tivens. This is his daughter," Mason said.

Quinn smiled at me. "The long-lost daughter. Ray is my brother's sponsor."

I had no idea what she was talking about. She leaned closer to me so random bar patrons couldn't overhear. "His AA sponsor. Ray helps my brother stay on the wagon. You do look just like your dad. Same cool-colored eyes." She said the last part more loudly to everyone as she leaned back.

"I like them," I admitted.

"You have that faint Irish accent, though. You must get that from your mother. I know Ray's never been overseas."

"Mama's an Irish-born gypsy. May she keep moving on far away from me." I raised my glass. Mason and the others clicked theirs with me. Kol looked at me a moment. We exchanged a look that held the understanding of what it was like to have been an unwanted child.

"So you should all come to the gallery opening next month to see Divvy's work," Mason said. I kicked him, but it only made him laugh.

"Keep it up and I'll put the portraits of you in the show," I muttered. That got all the guys harassing Mason, until he mumbled something and went to the bathroom.

A man approached the bar in the spot Mason vacated and asked Quinn for a beer. It took a lot of self-control, especially considering I was already on my second margarita, to resist the urge to ask if I could draw him without even bothering with a hello. He was incredibly handsome, but aside from that, he was wearing a black eye-patch. He ignored my existence entirely, despite being only an inch away. He took his beer and retreated to the pool table.

Quinn raised an eyebrow at me and I snorted. "What? I'm with Mason, I'm not blind. What's with the eye-patch? Is that just a look or something?"

"He was in a bad car accident when he was a teenager," Quinn said quietly. "Ended up wedged in the wreck with his dead mother for hours. He's what I like to call a hot mess, and you're better off without that kind of crazy in your life."

I took one more glance at the guy, thinking that I could actually use that kind of mess in my life. Not in a romantic sense, but I always gravitated to other damaged souls. My eyes drifted to Kol. There were scars on his arms, and a distinctive one starting on his forehead and going into his hairline. I remembered Mason telling me he had been in a coma after he and Michael were hit by the wave. I watched his large fishermen's hands on his glass of beer.

"Something interesting?" he asked, startling me.

"Oh, I'm sorry. I love drawing hands. Yours are very distinctive. I'd love to draw them."

He smiled at me calmly. I wondered if it was possible to fluster him. "Sure. As long as you don't mind some calluses and scars."

"Scars add character."

"Especially the ones that don't show." He glanced at the TV above the bar. There was a report on the news about some singer engaged to a football star. She was stumbling drunk and supposedly hooked on diet pills. I'd heard her sing before. She had a beautiful voice. It was a shame she was killing herself with her lifestyle. I glanced at Kol, wondering why he'd take interest. And I saw in his eyes the kind of broken loss only true love could bring. Quinn snatched up the remote and changed the channel.

"I'll be right back," he said, and escaped out of the bar. I glanced at Quinn, who looked almost as upset as Kol had.

"What was that about?" I asked, against my better judgment.

Quinn glared at the TV, although she'd changed the channel. "That singer is my cousin. She left Kol behind to be famous." She sighed and looked out to where the big blond fisherman had gone. "He's never loved anyone else."

Some might have considered it tragically romantic. I just thought it was sad. What kind of woman gave up the love and devotion of a good man to become cannon fodder for *paparazzi* and then get hooked on diet pills?

Mason returned from the bathroom and put an arm around me. What kind of a woman was I then? I was going to run from a good man. I finished my margarita and asked for another.

Chapter 20

I SPENT MOST of June and July in my studio, or out doing sketches among the masses of tourists. There were so many people, I never lacked for material and inspiration. When I wasn't in the studio I was in the house with Ray. Mason dragged me to the beach on weekends and for sunsets, and into a bed as often as was possible. All told, it was a nice way to live.

The gallery show was scheduled for August 20 and that date approached so quickly I wanted to scream. I had a few pieces I was very proud of, but most of them I was considering throwing into the trash. Mason and Ray talked me down from hysterics, but they were unable to convince me I wasn't just a no-talent charlatan.

I also worried about how close I was getting to everyone. I was breaking all my rules, but I couldn't seem to stop myself. I hadn't felt the desire to pack a bag and go, but I had started running every morning. I was up to three miles. That worried me, because the need to run had always precluded the driving impulse to leave.

I returned from my morning run one late July afternoon to find Ray home early from work. I found him in the kitchen. It smelled suspiciously of baking.

"What's going on?" I asked.

"Nothing. It's hot as hell today," Ray said. "Trace let us go early."

"I smell cake."

"Do I look like the kind of man who knows how to bake a cake?" he asked.

I rolled my eyes and went upstairs to shower. I had a bad feeling that Ray had remembered my birthday. I had been extremely careful not to do anything to trigger his memory. I should have known better. I showered and dressed in cutoff denim shorts and a blue halter top that showed off my navel. I spent a little time on my hair and makeup, because by that time I was positive that Ray had planned a surprise party.

I jumped when my cell phone rang. I glanced at it and smiled at Isabella's picture. I hadn't seen Izzy in person in over a year, so the picture was probably outdated. I doubted she'd changed much, though.

"Hey, Izzy," I answered.

She burst into a loud rendition of "Happy Birthday" in Spanish. She knew I could only understand the few words of Spanish that she'd managed to teach me during the nine months we lived together, but my ignorance had never stopped her from expressing herself in her mother's native language. I loved hearing her Cuban accent. It almost made me cry to realize how much I'd been missing her.

"How are you doing, girl?"

I sat on my bed. "I'm avoiding going downstairs because Dad remembered my birthday and is throwing me a surprise party."

She snorted. "I told you he'd remember. I can't wait to meet him. I'm going to be moving on from here soon and I'm heading right for Massachusetts."

"I might not still be here," I muttered.

"Then I'll find you wherever you are. I need to see you. It's been way too long."

We talked for a little while. I'd met her when I was seventeen, shortly after Stacey died. I'd just cheated a scary-looking female Harley rider out of her bike at a game of poker, despite not actually knowing how to drive a motorcycle. I'd managed to run it out of gas and been stranded on the side of the road. Izzy pulled over to help me, and I'd ended up going home with her. Eight years later, she was the only friend I'd ever kept.

I said good-bye eventually, knowing I couldn't hide forever. I took a moment to admire the new woodwork on the stairs, delaying the inevitable for one more second. I still jumped with an undignified squeak when the kitchen erupted with a chorus of "Surprise!" I had been prepared for my dad with a lopsided cake, and Mason, maybe Gage. I hadn't expected the entire Tavish family, the Cutters, Kol, Paul, Laura and her kids, and a few others Mason had introduced me to but I had forgotten.

I was passed around from hug to hug until I nearly had a panic attack. I wasn't used to so many people. Mason sensed my unease and managed to pull me aside and out the back door.

"You okay?" he asked, kissing my forehead. The tenderness in the gesture threw me off even more.

"I'm not used to being the center of attention," I said lamely.

"Ray was worried it would be too much," Mason frowned. I loved when he got that look on his face. It was comical enough that I relaxed.

"I'm okay, Bear," I said, leaning into him.

"Bear?"

I hadn't realized I'd called him that until he repeated it. I had been thinking of him that way since the night he'd first burst into the house and pinned me to the wall. I grinned up at him.

"Don't tell me I'm the first to call you that," I said.

"The one and only."

I didn't like the way he said it. He was saying a lot of things that made me twitchy lately. He kissed my hair again. "Want me to kick them all out?" he asked.

"No. I just needed a moment. Thanks for offering, though."

We went back inside. I guzzled down a margarita and felt much calmer. There was pizza and after two more margaritas and two slices I settled into a festive mood. As long as I pretended we weren't celebrating me I was okay.

Ray had baked me a cake, but he credited the frosting and decorating to Bo. Small fingerprints had found their way into the decorative edges of the frosting, but none of us said anything about it. Danny buzzed around the party with a little girl I was informed was Quinn's niece, River. Laura's two kids added to the herd, and I was fascinated to watch them. They required little adult supervision and raced around the yard amusing themselves. I had never had other children to play with.

Mason noticed me watching the kids. "What's going on in that beautiful head of yours?" he asked.

"Just wishing I'd had a childhood," I said. I hated that Mason made me want to speak the foolish words I normally kept locked inside my head. He took my hand and kissed my knuckles gently.

"You need to stop doing that," I muttered.

"What?"

"Being so nice to me."

"What would you prefer?"

"Aggressive and demanding."

I watched a brief battle of emotion in his eyes before he lowered his head and nipped my neck under the pretense of whispering in my ear. "I have a present for you later," he said in a tone that made my body sing.

I pulled away from him so I could better resist the impulse to drag him upstairs, party be damned. I found Ray sitting on one of the rotting beach chairs on the back porch. I sat beside him, listening to the talk and music flowing out of the house.

"Are you mad at me?" he asked.

"Not at all." To further reassure him I got up to kiss his cheek. "This was wonderful. I normally don't celebrate my birthday. Mama referred to it as *the day my life went to shit*." I deepened my accent to imitate her brogue.

Ray shook his head and closed his eyes. "You were the most beautiful little baby. So perfect. I couldn't stop staring at you. The day you were born was the best day of my life. Well, until the day I found you again. And every day since then."

I blinked the tears out of my eyes shamelessly. I jumped onto him, wrapping my arms around his neck. The chair collapsed and we hit the deck with a thud that brought everyone running. Both

Ray and I were helped to our feet, laughing like idiots. Everyone thought the tears were from the laughing, and we were content to let them think that.

We sat on the lawn and Mason fed me cake, to my immense pleasure and embarrassment. The kids passed by our romantic display and broke out in a mix of *yucks*. We abandoned the cake to chase the kids around the yard. Mop loped along with us, proving to be a big help as he accidentally tackled Danny.

The party wound down and people drifted home. By eleven the only ones left were Mason and Gage. Gage was stumbling drunk and speaking in a language no one could understand. Mason and I helped him to the couch. I sat with him while Mason went to get a pillow and blanket.

"You 'mell great," Gage said. His nose was pressed into the freshly Febrezed couch. I ran a hand through his short brown hair.

"If you have sex with that couch you're bringing it home with you," I warned him.

"Coush?" He started to snore and Mason arrived with a pillow and a blanket. We rolled him onto his side and threw the blanket over him. He snored louder, punctuating the noise with, "Won' wear th' pink one."

Mason and I exchanged a look. "He's going to explain that comment in the morning," Mason said. Then his eyes went darker and he grinned at me. "Time for your present. Have you been a good girl?"

Chapter 21

I WASN'T SURPRISED when Mason threw me over his shoulder and carried me upstairs. I was surprised when he set me down on the bed gently. He pulled a small box from the pocket of his jeans. At my look of horror he shook his head.

"Take a breath, honey. It's not a damn ring, although it is something shiny."

I forced air into my lungs. I took the small jewelry case from him, embarrassed that my hands were shaking. I let out a sigh of relief as I opened the box. The sigh caught in my throat as I saw what was really inside.

It was a belly-button ring. Not only that, a silver grizzly bear. I looked closer and noticed the rose in the bear's teeth. For a long time I stared at it. "Why a bear?" I finally managed to ask.

"To make you think of me."

I looked up into his too-blue eyes. "But I never called you Bear until today."

He traced my chin with his fingers. "Honey, you talk in your sleep."

I stared at him in shock.

He shifted his weight. "Do you like it?"

I blinked in surprise. "What?"

"Give me something, Divine. Are you staring at me 'cause it's all wrong, or because you like it?"

"It's wonderful," I heard myself say. I looked down at the faerie ring currently on display on my navel. Without another word I switched her for the bear. Mason lowered his head and kissed my belly. He grasped my hips and pushed me farther up the bed. It wasn't a rough shove. His hands didn't dig into my hips. His lips were gentle and caressing on my belly as he kissed circles around the bear.

I waited for the harsh demand, the rough shove that would end the tenderness. I waited while he gently stripped off my shirt and bra with slow, deliberate movements. It was making me want to scream. What was he doing? Where was my Mason? I needed to be taken. If he was this gentle, I would have to give. I couldn't do that.

"Mason." His lips were cutting a slow trail down my body, but he paused with a hum at the bear.

"Mason, enough foreplay already!"

He lifted his head to look into my eyes. I choked on the rest of my words. It was too late. He wasn't going to take me. He wasn't going to possess me. He was going to love me. If his hips hadn't been pinning my legs against the bed, I would have run. He lowered his head but kept his eyes on mine. He kissed me just above the button of my shorts.

"Don't do this," I whimpered. His hands unbuttoned my shorts and slowly slid them down.

"Don't do what?" he asked.

I had no words for him. He rubbed his cheek against the outside of my thigh, his hands ghosting over my skin, so lightly it made me shiver. He pulled off his shirt and stepped out of his jeans. I pushed myself up the bed, hoping the fast retreat would trigger him to pounce. He watched me, standing at the end of the bed.

"You're so beautiful," he said. His tone was soft, almost reverent. I glanced at the door. He followed my look and shook his head.

"What are you afraid of?" he asked.

"Nothing. Get over here already."

He slid his big body down onto the bed beside me, but didn't touch. He propped his head on one arm and ran the other arm lazily over my breasts and down my body.

"Cut it out," I muttered.

He ignored me, his attention fully on the hand that was stroking down my thigh and back up. I couldn't take it anymore. I slid sideways and off the bed, and nearly screamed in frustration when he didn't stop me. He lay back, relaxed and patient as a crocodile with a toothy grin.

"Where to?" he asked, his tone soft and unworried.

"What the hell is wrong with you?" I demanded.

He shrugged, drawing my attention to his body. I pried my eyes away from the various edible muscles and back to his face. Looking in his eyes was the mistake. There was so much vulnerability in the blue depths that I nearly cried out. I needed to run from him. I needed to protect him. He was going to break himself on me. But I couldn't move.

"Divine," he whispered. I took a step toward him. A boyish grin lit up his face. "That's my girl. Come on, honey."

I looked at him.

"Please," he winked at me. "This Bear needs some lovin'."

I felt the smile on my face. I wanted to cry, but he made me too happy. He was too perfect. He said all the right things. I walked to the bed and framed his face with my hands. I wanted to tell him to run away. I needed to tell him that falling in love with a broken thing was going to hurt more than it was worth. But all I said was his name. He kissed me, pulling me on top of him. His hands were still gentle as he pulled me down onto him. I could have made it rough. He gave me the control. But I didn't. I rocked on him, gentle as a lily pad on a pond. He held me, stroking me, saying my name. He loved me. And I loved him. But it changed nothing.

I lay in his arms afterward, listening to the steady thunder of his heart. He kissed my neck, my hair, my closed eyes. His fingers danced over the bear on my navel, warm from the heat of our bodies. He didn't say the words, but I heard them just the same. I owned his heart, and I couldn't give it back. The last kiss on my lips wasn't a harsh claiming, but an admission of surrender.

Chapter 22

MASON'S ARMS TRAPPED me as I tried to slip out of bed. His teeth nipped the back of my neck.

"Where do you think you're going?" he asked.

I had been planning on running screaming. I'd slept deeply but had awakened with the knowledge that something truly dangerous had happened last night. I now needed distance between us. Mason only tightened his hold.

"We need to get up and help Ray clean up from the party."

He nipped my neck again. "Later. I want to play first."

"Maybe I don't feel like playing."

He rolled on top of me, pinning me down with the power and force I was used to. The gentle giant from the night before was gone. His teeth closed on my throat and I nearly came from the sensation. He then proceeded to show me what he considered playful morning behavior.

I limped to the shower and soothed my pleasantly sore muscles with the hot water. Mason joined me, washing my back and my hair. This back-and-forth between tender and rough was going to give me a complex.

We dressed and headed downstairs. Gage was still snoring loudly on the couch. I could hear Ray whistling outside while he cleaned up the party debris. Mason and I cleaned up the empty booze and beer bottles to save him some discomfort. I was wondering how so few people had managed to make such a mess when I heard cars in the driveway.

I glanced out the window and blinked. The Tavish and Cutter clan were all stuffed into Trace and Axel's trucks. There were coolers and surfboards and towels. Nancy was the first to the door. "We came to help clean up," she said, "and then drag you to the beach for a continued birthday celebration."

"We come bearing gifts," Bo added, holding out an industrial-sized box of coffee. I was feeling the four or five margaritas from the night before, so I didn't argue. Within fifteen minutes the house was cleaner than it had been since I'd moved in. I hadn't been allowed to help.

"Okay," Nancy announced, "ziss house is clear." She said it in an eerily accurate *Poltergeist* voice, then grinned. "Let's go to the beach."

I went upstairs to change into my bathing suit while the rest of them trooped outside. I thought about changing out the bear ring for the faerie, but knew I couldn't do it. It might as well have been a brand.

I skipped down the stairs, determined to be chipper and enjoy my day. As I opened the front door, however, a fire-engine-red convertible skidded into the driveway. The driver's door swung open and all glorious five feet of an enraged Wanda Therese sprang into view. Mama's waist-length sable hair was in a single thick braid. She wore skintight jeans and an intricately tied red scarf for a shirt. Her exotically dark eyes burned with madness and hatred as she looked at Ray, who froze like a deer in headlights.

Wanda Therese shrieked like a banshee, pulled the knife from her hair, and rushed at Ray. I dove off the front steps and tackled her before she could gut my dad. I knocked the knife from her hand as we hit the ground. She screamed and went for my eyes with her fingernails. I grabbed her wrist and twisted her arm behind her back. I forced her smaller body down onto her knees and kept going, until she needed her free hand to hold herself out of the dirt.

The entire process took seconds. No one else had moved. I looked up to see everyone staring at me. Mama let out a shriek.

"Give it a rest," I snapped, giving her trapped arm a sharp twist.

"Let go of me, you fucking little whore," she yelled.

I closed my eyes and counted to ten. Mama struggled and I shoved her harder into the ground, forcing the air from her in a grunt.

"Stop, or I'll dislocate your shoulder," I ordered, my voice steady and calm.

"You little traitor. Stupid bitch. How dare you?"

"Save the speech."

Wanda Therese finally stopped struggling. I could feel the sanity and control returning to her violent little frame. I couldn't make myself look at anyone. I knew they were all there, staring at us. I couldn't deal with it, so I went into my private world of calm. Everything but Mama disappeared.

I shifted my grip on her, releasing the pressure. She didn't lunge at Ray. I took that to mean she was over her mindless rage. Talking to her might have some impact now.

"If I let you go, will you attack Ray?" I asked.

"That piece of shit isn't worth my time," she said.

"I'm going to let you go. And you're going to get back in your car and slowly drive away. I'll meet you tomorrow at Campground Beach at 7:00 p.m. We can talk there."

"Agreed."

I waited another count of ten before releasing her. I stepped back from her, ready to pin her again if she went for Ray. She rose to her feet with impressive dignity, dusting off the knees of her jeans. She lunged at me so fast I almost didn't block in time. I twisted aside as her fist grazed my cheek. I caught her shoulder and used her momentum to throw her onto the ground.

"I told you when I was fifteen you'd hit me for the last time," I muttered.

She lunged to her feet and smiled at me, making me think of a snake about to strike. "I should have strangled you with the umbilical cord."

I shrugged. "Lost your chance. Now get in the fucking car and go. I'll meet you tomorrow."

"Fine."

I watched her walk slowly to the car. She opened the door and paused, looking back at me.

I watched her coldly. "Go," I growled.

I didn't know what she'd thrown at me until the rock had glanced off my upraised arm and hit my temple. I fell to my knees as I felt hot blood trickle down my face. I felt people around me and steadied myself with my hands.

My vision swam a little, so I closed my eyes, focusing on my hearing. I heard the comforting rumble of the convertible's engine. I didn't relax until I heard it going away from me. I wouldn't have put it past her to try and run me over, or Ray.

Mama was gone at last. It was time to come out of my quiet place. I didn't want to. There were people all around me. Hands were touching me, voices were comforting and gentle. I shoved at them, because I was still in the quiet place. There was blood on my face. I could feel it on my arm as well. I started being able to hear the individual voices. I heard Mason and Ray first.

"Please don't touch me," I said, my voice sounding far away and painfully close to tears. I would not cry. I would not let Mama make me cry. I felt pain on my hand and realized I was digging my fingernails into the hard ground.

I opened my eyes, leaving the quiet place. There were too many people around me. I held out the arm that wasn't throbbing and waved everyone away. "I'm fine. Just back off," I said.

Everyone but Mason did what I said. When Mason didn't back away, Ray stepped back toward me too.

"I mean it, Mason," I said, trying to keep my voice steady. My eyes were blurry with unshed tears. He said my name and laid a hand on my shoulder. I shoved at it. "I said fucking leave me alone!"

His touch had pushed me over. The demand came out in a sob as the tears overwhelmed me. I would have crumpled to the ground but Mason's arms wrapped around me. Without a word he picked me up, cradling me against his chest. I gave up on being strong and let my mother win. I cried harder and buried my face against his shoulder. My body shook with the gasping breaths I could manage.

I held on to him as he brought me into the house. I heard Ray following, telling everyone else to stay outside. I was grateful to have fewer witnesses to my breakdown. Mason sat in a chair with me on his lap. He hummed deep in his throat and stroked my hair. I felt Ray take my arm that was throbbing. Something cold that stung was pressed against it. I was already crying and the slight external pain had nothing on the emotional damage so freshly bleeding.

"We need to look at the cut on your head, honey," Mason said. I let him shift my face so Ray could clean the small gash on my temple. I kept my eyes closed, so I wouldn't have to look at them. I felt Mason's arms relax when he saw how small the cut on my head was. I knew from experience that head wounds bleed a frightening and misleading amount. It was already stopping. The gash on my arm from the initial hit was worse.

I kept crying but the sobbing had stopped. I opened my eyes and watched Ray clean the gash on my forearm and cover it with a large square Band-Aid. He tilted my head to the side and pressed a warm washcloth to the cut on my head.

I sniffed back the last of my tears. "You'll ruin the towel."

He looked at me for a long moment. He didn't say anything, just lowered his head and kissed me gently beside the cut. It nearly made me cry again. He cleaned the wound and put another Band-Aid over it. Then he pulled me up and into his arms.

"I'm so sorry," he said. "I should have stopped her. I should have done something."

I shook my head against his shoulder, but the tears were coming back. "I know how to handle her," I said.

"I should have protected you," Ray said. "That's the way it's supposed to go. Why did you jump between us?"

"Because she would have killed you if she could. She might throw a punch or a rock at me, but she'd never really hurt me." I heard the lie in my words. She had hurt me much more deeply, but not physically.

I heard Mason grunt and looked at him. I realized he was vibrating with anger and barely holding it in check. I looked into his eyes and he looked away. It made me hate my mother even more. Mason also thought he had failed to protect me. There was nothing he could have done to stop Mama. He couldn't make himself hurt a woman, even to protect me. I hadn't wanted him to, but that didn't change anything.

"I'm sorry to intrude," Nancy said, drawing my attention from her son. She stood in the kitchen doorway, her hands clasped tightly in front of her in an anxious gesture. She glanced at Mason and frowned.

"I know you probably don't want us around, but I had to come in and check on you. I know I'm not your mother . . ." she faltered a moment then smiled bravely at me. "But I am *a* mother. Are you okay?"

I looked at Nancy Tavish, wishing with all my heart that she *was* my mother. Nancy would never have hurt her child. She would never have thrown rocks or broken bones. She would never have wished, even silently, that her children hadn't been born. I tried to tell her that I was fine, but the sound I made instead wasn't open to interpretation. Nancy crossed the room and took me into her arms. I sank into the warmth and comfort, experiencing for the first time what being held by a mother should have been.

"Poor baby," Nancy said, stroking my hair. "It's okay. You cry it out now, that's a good girl." I couldn't stop myself. I cried and held her like I was sinking. I heard her say, "Mason, go outside and break something. Take that anger somewhere else. Ray, go with him please. We need a moment."

I had no idea how long I stayed in Nancy's arms. I soaked up the feminine comfort, a strange new experience. I thought about Mama. Even during a con when she was pretending to be a doting mother, her hugs had never felt like Nancy's. Mama had never hugged me. She had never brushed away my tears.

After my tears were gone I sat down at the table, and Nancy took my hand.

"Thank you," I said.

"I'm glad I could help." Her fingers were calloused and strong. Mason had her eyes. I thought of Mason and sighed.

"Poor Mason," I said.

Nancy shook her head at me. "Only you would think of him at a time like this."

I shrugged. "I knew who and what my mama was. I knew what would happen if she found me. I wasn't surprised. As far as this goes," I indicated the Band-Aid on my temple, "she's done a lot worse. I was expecting it. But Mason doesn't understand what Mama is. He can't protect me from her. She'd hurt him and he wouldn't fight back. He can't. I don't want him to ever get in her way."

"How dangerous is she?" Nancy asked. I saw the flash of protective instinct in her eyes, and wished my mother had even a trickle of it. But Mama had never protected anyone but herself.

"She goes into rages where you can't reason with her. She calms down pretty quick, then she's just mean, not really violent. That's why I held her down. If she's trapped, she calms down, and starts thinking." I sighed and rubbed at my eyes. "Hopefully I can get her to go away."

Nancy watched me a moment. "You're not gonna run?"

The question hit me hard. I blinked in surprise, as I realized I wasn't running already. The last two times I'd seen Mama I'd taken off running before she could even speak to me. I'd gone right to my apartment, thrown my stuff in my bags, and left without another thought.

It hadn't occurred to me to run from her this time. I didn't want to leave. I wasn't going to let her chase me away from Ray. And Mason. And Nancy and the rest of the family. I had friends and family here. For the second time in my life, I had something to fight for.

"No," I said, still surprised at myself. "I am not going to run. She stole me away from Ray once. I won't let her scare me off now." The fact that when I pictured Ray I saw Mason standing beside him unnerved me. I wasn't ready to admit that I needed Mason, especially not to his mother. I might not let my mother chase me off, but that didn't mean I would change my nature and stay permanently.

Nancy stood up and offered me a hand. "I say we go to the beach and celebrate your birthday some more. That's the best way I can think of to stick it to your bitch mother."

I laughed and took it. "Sounds great."

Chapter 23

MY HEADACHE WAS GONE by the time we settled on the beach with our chairs, towels, coolers, and beer. Mason fired up the portable grill on the bed of the truck and started cooking. The Tavish family was always eating and drinking, it seemed. It was a wonder they weren't all horribly fat.

Kol arrived in his beaten old truck with River, Quinn's niece. I wasn't entirely sure of the relationships within that group, but River treated Kol like he was her father. I had met her father, Ben, at my birthday party. Ray was his AA sponsor. No one ever mentioned River's mother, and I was going to let it go at that.

Kol sent River down to the water with Danny and Axel. I was sitting in a chair, watching the waves and trying not to cry. Kol sat beside me in the sand, hugging his knees to his chest. His eyes were the same blue as the water. He looked at the Band-Aids on my temple and arm; I saw the storm in his eyes.

"Rough morning?" he asked. His tone was casual, which surprised me.

"My mother found me."

He nodded. "My mother never looked for me. Even when I was right in front of her."

We watched the waves in shared sadness for a while. Everyone else gave us a wide berth. I wondered if Mason had called Kol and asked him to talk to me. Coincidence or a setup, it didn't matter. Having his quiet, wordless understanding helped a lot more than the beer.

I glanced at the scar on his arm. He caught me looking. He hesitated a moment, looking up and down the beach. No other cars were parked particularly close. We had a good stretch of beach to ourselves. Slowly, with a deliberateness that made it clear he was doing it for my benefit, he removed his shirt. I almost started crying when I saw his back. I knew what it felt like to be hit by a belt, but Mama had never hit me bad enough to scar. Kol's back was a ruin of belt scars. I could even see the buckle on some of them.

His steady blue eyes met mine and he shrugged. "The worst scars are the ones that don't show. The ones on the inside. None of them understand." He looked at the happy family around us. "Mason called me because he doesn't know what to do to help. I don't really know either, but I figure a shared understanding would have to do."

"It helps. For what it's worth, I'm sorry." I indicated his back.

He shrugged again. "Those are beside the point. I hide them because they disturb people. I hate those pitying looks. The real damage Nils did was to my soul." He closed his eyes and took a deep breath of the salty air. "They can't understand what it's like to be given so much hatred. To feel the anger burning inside, building and building, and being terrified that you really are the monster they've tried to make you."

I understood him. I knew exactly what he meant. "I can't be like my mother," I said.

"I can't be like my father," he nodded. "I slammed his head into a truck window the day he told me he was dying of cancer. I have to live with that, with knowing that he put so much violence in me. I fight it every day."

"I run," I admitted. "I avoid making friends. I hurt people because she trained me to. She's a con artist. She trained me to lie, to cheat, to break people and then take what they had while they were down. I'm so afraid I am what she tried to make me."

"You're not," he said, giving me a smile.

"Mason is more than half in love with me, and I'm going to leave him high and dry, just like Mama said I always would."

Kol settled back on his elbows and watched River and Danny. "You're not conning Mason," he said dismissively. "You may have some strange compulsion to move on, but it has nothing to do with him. Besides, why haven't you run already?"

"What?"

"Your mother found you. You said you run. Well? What are you doing here?"

"I don't want to run from her. She stole me from my dad. I won't let her run me off now."

Kol nodded. "You're lucky to have one parent who loves you. I envy you that." He sighed and shook his head. "It's not about me. I've found my peace. Besides, both my parents are dead, so I have nothing to fight anymore. I have to live with the anger, though. What do you do when the people who are supposed to protect you are the ones who hurt you?"

I blinked away my tears. "I don't know."

He sat up and took my hand. "I'll tell you then. You find new people, good people. People to stand by you. You can only run so far, and you can't win a fight with your mother. Hurting her will only make you hate yourself."

"So what do I do?"

"You take the help that's offered. You let us stand with you. You may not be able to fight her, but the rest of us can protect you."

"Why would you do that for me? You in particular? You've only met me twice."

He smiled and touched my temple with a long calloused finger. "Because Mason is my friend. Because you are good people. And because I had someone to stand beside me all those years ago when I told Nils he'd hit me for the last time. Because I have people who pull me back on the ledge when my anger pushes me off. And I have this desire to protect a fellow battered child. If my father were still alive and threatening me . . ."

"I'd kick his sorry ass," I muttered, wiping away my tears.

"Exactly." He looked at the Tavish and Cutter family. "They may not understand it like I do. They're lucky for that. But that doesn't mean they can't stand with you. Let them."

"It's hard to let people in," I said.

"I thought about killing myself not so long ago." He said it casually. "I had it planned out, too. My father was dead, my mother had killed herself, and Raina." His voice now caught in his throat and he shook his head. "I lost Mike. I can still feel his fingers slipping through mine. I remember the terrified look on his face. I still dream of it." He closed his eyes. "I was done. I'd taken all the abuse and loss I could."

"What stopped you?" I asked.

He smiled and looked down at River.

"My family stopped me. And I don't mean my blood relations. I have none. I chose my family. They chose me. That little girl is more important to me than breathing. She may not be mine by blood, but she damn well is my daughter." He smiled again. "Ben grudgingly shares her with me. It was Quinn who found me that night, sitting with an empty bottle of whiskey. I told her I was going to end it, and she hit me. Yelled at me. That's what stopped me. Because I have people that love me. And now, for the first time in your life, so do you."

I bit my lip and looked at Mason.

"Scary shit, huh?" Kol said.

"Terrifying."

"Let it sink in. I speak from experience. From one unwanted child to another." He stood and offered me a hand up. "Letting people love you is hard to do. Let's go play in the ocean with the kids. Saltwater heals all wounds."

"Even the ones that don't show?"

"Especially those."

The fire burned warm in the metal fire pit Axel had pulled out of his truck. Trace had two fishing poles sticking out of the sand. Whenever the beach patrol drove past, he'd trot down and pretend to be fishing so we weren't asked to leave. It was getting close to ten o'clock and they would kick us off eventually anyway.

I'd spent the day letting the ocean, children's laughter, and the sun wash away my troubles. I was calm and centered, and prepared to deal with my mother. This was my home now, and even if I wasn't going to stay permanently, I would come back to it. I was going to fight for this place, for these people.

The fire danced in Mason's eyes as he sat beside me in the sand with his arm wrapped comfortably around me. I leaned into him, for once content with his tenderness. I was too bruised and raw to want the aggressive bear now. I needed a teddy bear to cuddle and Mason was happy to comply.

The country station was pumping out of both of the open doors of the trucks that provided shelter from the wind. The song changed and Mason stood up, offering me his hand. "Dance with me," he said softly.

I let him pull me to my feet. His arms wrapped around me as the lyrics of the song sank through me. *Crazy girl, don't you know that I love you? I wouldn't dream of going nowhere. Silly woman, come here let me hold you. Have I told you lately I love you like crazy, girl?*

He'd found a way to tell me how he felt without actually saying a word. It was the only way it would have worked. If he'd told me in so many words that he loved me, I would have run. He knew me too well. He danced with me, holding me close as our toes sank into the sand. He pulled me closer until I was pressed against his chest and we were doing little more than swaying. He kissed my hair. I curled into him and let the rest of the world go away.

Chapter 24

IT HAD TAKEN some work to convince the family I didn't need an entourage to go see my mother. The most persistent were Nancy and Ray. I explained that seeing another woman there, especially one who radiated protective-mother-bear energy, would just send Mama into one of her rages. Nancy relented, but told me to call her afterward so she knew everything had gone all right. Ray took my word that Mama would likely try and kill him on sight, and opted to stay home.

Mason ended the possibility of argument by simply stating, "Either you take me with you, or I follow you. Nothing short of rendering me unconscious will keep me away."

I could have tried to knock him out. I seriously considered it. But I understood his nature so I didn't put up a fight. He wanted to protect me. The need to do so was bone deep, and it would hurt him more if I rejected his help. I wouldn't hurt him on my mother's behalf. Mama did tend to play to any audience she had, but any extra antics would be worth the protection of a two-hundred-thirty-pound bear.

Mama was sitting on the hood of her red convertible in the parking lot of the beach. She wore a short brown dress with a golden ribbon tied around her waist and in her hair. Her eyes were dramatically decorated and her lips were as red as the car.

I got out of Mason's truck before it had entirely stopped moving, to keep myself from chickening out and begging him to just floor it and take me away. I wore my leather pants and corset, because I knew my mother hated that outfit. She hopped down from the hood of her car to perch on her stylish three-inch heels. Even in the shoes she was six inches shorter than me. I was still terrified of her.

"Mama," I said, years of her conditioning lending my voice a bored, formal quality that hid my fear.

"Grace," she said, smiling at me like I was a pet that had finally learned a new trick. Her eyes flicked to Mason as he stepped up beside me. "Who's the guard dog?"

"Mason, may I introduce Wanda Therese."

He didn't offer his hand, which only made her smile wider.

"And exactly what are you to my daughter?"

I held my breath while his dark blue eyes studied her. He appeared calm outwardly, but I knew him well enough to see the violence barely held back. What was he going to say? We had never really talked about what we were to each other. He glanced down at me and put a hand protectively on my shoulder. "Like you said, I'm her guard dog," he said.

Mama let out a sharp bark of a laugh. "You've got some balls. But Grace doesn't need a guard dog. They are just as likely to bite the hand that holds the leash."

"You came to talk to me, not harass Mason," I reminded her.

"You can go now, Fido." Mama shooed him away with painted fingernails.

Mason crossed his arms and looked down at her. She looked ridiculous glaring up at him. She weighed about ninety pounds, soaking wet. He was a foot and a half taller and his thigh was as thick as her waist, but I knew which was the dangerous one.

I whistled sharply to get Mama's attention. "Talk to me or I leave."

She laughed, the sound light and eerily girlish. "I was just having a bit of fun with your boy, that's all. Really though, Rover, you can go wait in the car."

"His name is Mason, and he stays."

Mama's eyes widened at my tone. "Really, Grace, I'm not going to do anything. I'd never hurt you."

I elbowed Mason to keep the furious outburst inside his mouth. She was goading him, hoping he'd lose his temper. I needed him to stay calm.

"Rocks don't count?" he muttered.

I sighed.

"That was her fault," she said, shrugging. "I taught you to always be on your guard. It's not my fault you dropped it."

Thankfully, Mason seemed to realize that rationalizing with Wanda Therese was a waste of time. He remained blissfully silent, and I could have kissed him.

"Why have you come here?" I asked.

She blinked at me, looking genuinely surprised. I didn't buy it. Mama could smile innocently into the faces of people while she was stealing their baby. "Why, I'm here to protect you, of course," she finally said.

Mason made a sound I couldn't really identify but said nothing.

"How did you find me, anyway?" I asked.

She glanced at the water. "I came to the Cape a week ago. You know tourists, darling. I do adore them. Anyway, I had to come down here to collect some money from this lowlife banker who wants to keep his wife from seeing this colorful video I have of him." She smiled sweetly and pushed her hair behind her ear. "That man is as twisted as they come. You wouldn't believe what he had me do to him."

I rolled my eyes, because I knew it irritated her. "Drop the theatrics, Mama. Mason knows what you do."

"You're such a spoilsport. Fine. So anyway, while I was at the banker's house I ended up reading the newspaper . . . after beating him with it."

I forced my face to be calm and relaxed. If she knew she was getting to me she'd just give me more details. When I didn't react, she continued with a less enthusiastic tone.

"So I read this disgusting drivel about some long-lost daughter and her father handing her her dreams on a golden fucking platter.

And what do you know, it was you, and that waste-of-flesh old fuckup! Well, I just had to find you. So I asked around. I found out you were hanging with Fido here from a waitress at a bar. The bartender was this nasty little blonde who threw me out, but I'd already got the address from the waitress."

I'd have to remember to give Quinn a big hug later.

"So you found out where Mason lived and drove there?" I asked.

"I went by Ray's first," she said. "I was hoping to find him there. It woulda been simpler that way."

"What are you even doing here?"

"I have to protect you," she said, as if it were obvious.

"Protect me from what?"

"From Ray."

"From Ray?" I hadn't managed to hide my surprise this time, and that was a big mistake. I watched the wild gleam enter Mama's eyes, and I braced for the storm.

"I can't believe I raised such a stupid little cunt." She threw her hands in the air in theatrical extravagance. "I took you away from him. I saved you from him. I didn't do that so you could run back to him."

"What exactly do you think Ray will do to me?" I asked carefully.

She looked at me like I was an idiot. "He's a daddy. Daddies hurt their little girls. Everyone says that they don't, but they all do. Everyone is just full of shit. They just pretend it's not happening. But I know the truth. I know what daddies are really like." Her voice had gone high now, and she strung her words together in growing panic.

"Daddies like to touch. Daddies call you pretty." She curled her lip, mimicking some voice from her past. "'Come sit on Daddy's lap, baby. . . .' Dirty . . . filthy . . . twisted . . . I saved you from that, girl. I saved you!" She was pacing now, and I knew she was lost in her own sordid nightmares.

I glanced up at Mason. There was pity in his eyes now, as he watched my mother frantically pacing and muttering to herself. Mama had never told me any details, but it didn't take a genius to see that she had been badly abused. When she went into the fits it was best to stay quiet and still until she calmed.

"I took care of you," Mama ranted. "I did. Me. I didn't let him hurt you. No, I saved you. And now you've run back to him. It was all for nothing. I have to stop it. I can't let him do it. Daddies are bad. You don't need one. No one does. I'll get rid of him. I'll just..."

I stepped into her pacing, forcing her to stop. Very calmly, I touched her shoulder. "Are you seeing me, Mama?" I asked.

Her dark eyes met mine and she blinked a few times. "Who are you?" she asked. Then she shook her head and smiled. "Oh, Grace. I really hate your hair like that."

"I like my hair short."

"A woman's hair is a weapon. It provides mystery and a shield. You cut it all off, and you have nothing left to hide behind."

"I don't like hiding." I took a deep breath and risked it. "Ray isn't going to hurt me, Mama."

She snorted. "Of course he is."

"Even if he was," I said, relieved she hadn't just started raging again, "you taught me how to defend myself. I'm not a baby anymore. I'm safe. I'm okay."

She narrowed her eyes. "I did teach you well. Not that you use your talents."

I shrugged. "I'll go pick a pocket tomorrow if it will make you happy." The scary thing was that I meant it. No matter how horrible she was, I would always somehow need to try and please her.

She played with the ribbon in her hair. "Child's play. You were such a useful tool. Oh, the cons I pulled off with you. I've missed it."

I noticed that she hadn't said *us*, and that she meant she missed the cons and not me. "I'm an artist, not a con artist, Mama."

"Those stupid scribbles?" She waved a hand dismissively. "Why would anyone pay for that?"

Mason opened his mouth, but shut it when I shook my head.

"I have a show in a few weeks. I have a very knowledgeable businessman backing me."

"Who?"

"His name is Zach Cutter. He's Mason's brother-in-law. And he's not connable, Mama, so forget it. He'd see right through you."

"I hate the smart ones." She shrugged. "I've always preferred men who think with their dicks." She glanced at Mason. "Which are you?"

"I pick the right organ for the situation," he said.

Mama laughed, and it was her real laugh for once. She smiled at him. "You're not so bad, after all. Still not good enough for my daughter, but not a total waste of air."

"Thanks."

"So, Mama," I said, not entirely relieved that she liked Mason. "How long are you staying on the Cape? And can you be trusted not to kill Ray while you're here?"

She frowned like a put-out five-year-old. "It would be so easy to do away with him. I have a few fishermen friends. They have the best ways to dispose of bodies."

"I want your word you'll not harm, maim, or kill Ray. And you won't harm, maim, or kill him, even using a proxy." Mama did have one redeeming quirk. If she gave her word, she wouldn't break it. You had to be very careful with the wording of the promise, because she could twist words around in ways mere mortals couldn't imagine.

She watched me warily.

"Your word," I repeated.

"Fine."

"Say it."

"I give you my word of honor as a gypsy that I will not harm, maim, or kill, either personally or by proxy, the piece of shit known as Ray Tivens."

I sighed in relief. "Thank you. So, how long are you staying here?"

"Well . . ." She played with one of the ribbons in her hair. "My daughter is having an art show in a few weeks. I should be there, don't you think?"

Fear stayed wrapped around my gut. She could do a lot of damage in that amount of time.

Chapter 25

MASON WATCHED ME as I sat beside him in his truck. We were parked in my driveway. We had been for about ten minutes. I was too afraid to try and get up, because I was still shaking from seeing my mother.

"Can I talk yet?" he asked.

"No."

"Are you okay?"

"What part of not talking didn't you understand?"

He sat back in his seat with a grunt. I looked over at him. He was angry, and not just at my mother.

"Why the fuck are you having dinner with her tomorrow?" he asked.

"I said no talking."

"I don't take orders."

"Fine!" I threw the door open and jumped out. I walked to my bike and picked up my helmet. I needed to be alone. Mason grabbed the helmet out of my hands and threw it across the yard.

"What the hell!" I yelled in his face.

"You want to avoid me, want to hide, that's fine. But you are not getting on your bike right now. You're fucking shaking, Divine. It's not safe. Take my truck if you want to get away." He held the keys out to me.

I realized he was right. I was out of my mind. I was acting like my mother. I shoved the keys away and ran without thinking. I ended up in my studio. I slammed the door and leaned against it. I heard Mason coming after me. "Open the door, Divine," he said.

"Go away."

"No."

"I don't want you near me right now. Please, just go away."

"No."

I started to cry. Why wouldn't he leave? I crawled across the room onto the mattress and hid under the sheets.

He knocked again. "Divine, open the damned door!"

"It doesn't even have a lock, you ass!"

"I still want to be invited."

"Well, I want a pony."

The door opened. "You're going to have to settle for a bear." He walked to the bed and knelt beside me.

"Why won't you just go away?" I whined.

"Because you are so used to being alone that you don't realize when you need someone. I'm not going to let you fall back on old habits. You're not alone anymore. You have people to hold you when you cry. Not just me, I'm just the one here right now. I'll go get Ray if you want, but I am not leaving you alone."

I wanted to hate him. I wanted to be angry at him for being so controlling, but I couldn't. I could never hate him. I was pushing him away because for the first time in my life I'd allowed someone to stand beside me. Mama had taught me never to do that. She'd taught me to push everyone away. But I was not my mother, and I was not the daughter she'd tried to create. I reached out from under the sheet and grasped his hand.

He lay beside me and held me. I accepted the comfort while I tried to let go of the fear. I was terrified of my mother. I was terrified of what she might do while she was here. Not that she'd hurt Ray, but that didn't mean she wouldn't go for everyone else. I didn't want her to target Mason's family. And I could imagine the spectacle she'd put on at my show.

Mason stroked his hand through my hair and told me everything was going to be fine. No one had ever done that for me before. I liked it. I let him say it for a long time, long enough so that I started to believe it.

"I'm better now," I said. "I'm sorry I freaked like that. Thank you for not letting me get away with it."

"You're okay?"

"Better. I know it must look crazy, agreeing to have dinner with her. But if I see her, at least then I can keep tabs on her. If I avoid her, she'll just seek me out. I want to keep her away from your family. I don't want her to hurt anyone. When she's calm, she's not always bad—never nice or anything, but not dangerous. Maybe I can keep her calm the whole time she's here."

He kissed my nose. "She's not what I expected," he admitted. "I really hated her at first. But after the things she said, well, I still hate her, but I feel sorry for her too."

"I don't know what happened to her exactly," I said. "I know she was molested. She never talks about her family. She says the past is dead. I always wished she'd get the help she needed. If she was on medication and talked to a therapist, maybe there is a real person hiding in there. I always wanted that for her. For myself, really. No matter what, she is my mama."

"I understand."

I sighed. "I have to call your mom and tell her it went all right. I don't want her to worry."

He smiled and stroked my cheek. "Divine, I lo . . ." he cut himself off with a flinch, but it was too late. I'd heard the unspoken part. Panic roared into life in my head and I scrambled out of his arms.

"Come on, Divine, please." He followed me, catching my wrist. "I didn't say that. I wasn't going to say that. I was just gonna say, ah, that I love that you don't want my mother to worry."

I stared at him.

"Yeah," he sighed. "That sounded more believable in my head."

There were now a thousand voices in my mind, all demanding that I run. Mason gently held my wrist. I could have easily pulled away to flee. I looked into his eyes. He looked miserable and apologetic. I hated that I was making him feel he needed to apologize for loving me. What the hell was wrong with me? I didn't have to say it back. What the hell was so scary about *I love you*?

"I'm hungry," I said.

He blinked. "Oh." There was a long pause. "So we're gonna go with the whole *that didn't just happen* idea?"

"Let's order pizza," I said, and walked calmly out of the room.

Chapter 26

I COULDN'T SLEEP. Mason's arms, which normally made me feel safe, made me feel confined instead. I stared at the darkness, my mind filling it in with childhood memories: Mama in one of her rages; Mama smiling and pretending to love me; Mama standing on a tenth-floor balcony, her arms spread wide; Mama crying.

I slid out of Mason's arms, surprised when it woke him.

"What's wrong?" he asked, his voice beautifully slurred by sleep.

"Nothing. Just go back to sleep."

"No," he frowned and sat up, blinking and shaking his head. "Is there anything I can do?"

"No, I just need to work right now. Go back to sleep."

He frowned. "Work?"

"I have to draw something. I'll come back to bed when I'm done."

"Oh." He grunted. "I'll come sleep in your studio to keep you company."

"You don't have to," I began.

"I want to."

I put on cotton shorts and a little shirt before heading as quietly down the stairs as I could. I didn't want to wake Ray. Mason followed me, looking adorable as he stumbled along in his boxers, his eyes half-closed. He kissed my nose once we were in the studio, then crawled onto the mattress on the floor. He was asleep in seconds.

I loved that he was there. His steady breathing was calming. I put on some music, relieved when it didn't wake him. Once Mason was asleep, he usually stayed that way. I sat on my stool and began to work.

I closed my eyes and let the images of my mother play across the canvas of my mind. I let them take shape, merge, and become a new reality. I drew that reality. Her face emerged on the paper—half of it hers, the other half a demon. The demon side was no less beautiful, but her beauty was terrifying and lethal. She had fangs to accent her seductive smile. I used colored pencils to change her skin from pale Irish white to demon red, in a slow progression across her face.

I put it aside and started another. The dualities of my mother emerged from my hands, released at last from my mind. I had never drawn her before, never dared risk what I would see. I drew my fear of her. I drew my confusion, my desire to please, my love.

The sun had risen long before Mason woke. My eyes were blurring and my hands were cramping. I had a half dozen pieces in front of me. All were beautiful, and they told the world what it was like to be Wanda Therese's daughter.

Mason put his hands on my shoulders and kissed the top of my head. I leaned back against his bare chest and closed my eyes.

"These are amazing," he said.

I looked down at the most recent one. I'd drawn my mother's hands holding mine. Our fingers were interlocked. One of her hands was normal, but the other had claws that sank deep into my skin. Blood trickled from the wounds, and I'd drawn my face leaning down, kissing the back of my mother's clawed hand.

"I'm not sure there's a word for these," I said. "I'm going to put them in the show."

"I think you should."

I could picture it. I'd set them all together under the title, *My Mother's Love*. Mama was surely going to make a spectacle at my show anyway. Might as well beat her at her own game and put her on display as I saw her.

Mason put his arms around me. "Are you tired now?" he asked.

"No," I said, surprised. "In fact, I'm kinda wired." I glanced at the clock. "Oh, shit. Aren't you late for work?"

"I told Dad I was taking the day off," he said.

"When?"

"Yesterday, before we went to see your mother."

"Why?"

"Because I have better things to do than work today."

I smiled. "Like what?"

He gently took the pencil out of my hand. "Are you done working?"

"Yes. For now. These aren't done. I need to finish them, but it can wait."

He picked me up and turned me around so I was facing him. I wrapped my legs around his waist and he grinned at me.

"I love when you get like this," he said, walking backward until he was against the bed. He lowered us both down so that he was on his back and I was straddling him.

"Get like what?" I asked, ducking my head to nip at his throat.

"When you make something that you love, when you are really happy with your work, you go all playful. It's like you become pure joy."

I laughed. I liked the way he said it. I felt suddenly free and alive. My body was alive with energy, almost like electricity was running through my veins. It was an amazing natural high. Mason was capable of producing a different kind of high. I decided that combining the two was just what this gypsy needed.

Chapter 27

I SAT ACROSS from Mama, my wooden chair scraping noisily on the floor as I forced myself to move closer to her. She grinned at me, but the grin vanished when Mason put his hand over mine where it lay on the table. While I'd fought with him for an hour about it, I was glad now that he'd come with me to dinner.

"Tell me again why you brought Rover?" Mama asked.

"His name is Mason, Mama."

"Who cares?"

"I do."

"Whatever." I didn't like the way she looked at him. She knew she couldn't con him. She wasn't looking at him like she wanted to hurt him. She was looking at him like he was lunch.

"Nice to see you again, Wanda."

She laughed. "The boy has manners. How quaint."

"I aim to please."

"I bet you do," she said, with enough sexual innuendo that I squirmed. "So, tell me, Rover, what is it that you do?"

"I work construction."

"Oh," she cooed. "I love a man who's good with his hands."

He stared at her, then glanced at me. "Is she serious?"

Mama laughed and sat back in her seat. "Of course. What good is a man who doesn't know what he's doing? Hell, even the ones who are semi-competent are only good for a few uses before discarding."

I had a feeling Mason was beginning to regret wanting to come with me. She was going to attack him for trying to protect me. If I'd been alone with her, she'd be displaying better behavior.

The waiter arrived with a smile. He was my age, and I watched as he got lost in Mama's cleavage and big, sultry brown eyes and pouting lips. "How are you all doing tonight?" he asked.

"Much better now, sweetie," she said, in her fullest Irish accent. "Aren't you just the cutest thing? I could eat you up."

I rolled my eyes while the waiter blushed. What he didn't realize was that she meant it. She could have destroyed him in a day, probably less. I was going to have to make sure she left the restaurant without him. She'd strip him of everything he owned, then ride his dignity and self-worth all the way to the bank.

"Why don't you tell us the specials?" I suggested when the waiter couldn't find his voice.

Mama played with the pendant of the necklace that hung between her breasts. The waiter forgot what he was saying twice. I ordered tequila, since that was the kind of night it was going to be.

Once the waiter was gone, I leaned across the table. "Mama, leave that poor kid alone."

She laughed. "Don't get your panties in a bunch. He's not my type."

"The next time he comes to the table, put that money back in his apron."

She grinned at me and tossed me a wad of bills with a rubber band around it. "You give it back to him. Spoilsport."

Mason remained quiet, but he seemed very relieved when the waiter arrived with his beer. I slipped the money back into the apron, glad he hadn't noticed it was gone. I hated playing Mama's games, but it was easier to play than to get run over by them.

"So," Mama said, sipping at her wine. "What exactly are you planning on doing?"

"Doing?" I asked.

"Well, I know you don't intend to stay here." She drummed her manicured fingers against her glass. "This art thing you're doing, or whatever it is, might actually make you some money. It could get you introduced to some influential people."

I took a long sip of my drink. I was going to need a second one soon. "I am not a con artist, Mama."

"Don't be a little cunt." She waved her hand at me. "Of course you are. You just need to get back into the game. I've got some great ideas. Have you ever considered doing forgeries?"

I closed my eyes and counted to ten. "I will not work cons with you."

"I got you to return the money to the waiter."

"That wasn't a con."

She grinned, and I hated her.

"Oh, come on, sweetheart," she pouted at me. "We had so much fun together. I've missed you so much. Can't you just give it a chance? Just a little con?"

"No."

"Oh, come on. I'll consider leaving town a little sooner if you pick someone's pocket tonight."

"Really?" I asked.

"My word as a gypsy."

I reached into my purse and pulled out Mason's wallet. He stared at me.

"That was in my back pocket when we sat down," he said.

I patted his arm. I'd taken it when we left the house. I took it a lot, actually. It was a miracle he'd never realized it. I guess I had a tendency to touch his ass, so he didn't notice anything amiss when my fingers got sticky.

"That's my girl," Mama said.

I shrugged. "So, when are you leaving town?" I asked.

She smiled as our food arrived. To my relief, she ignored the waiter and didn't steal from him again.

"I am going to stay until your show," she said. "Depending on how I feel after that, I might even head out the next day."

"You have any plans while you're here?" I asked.

"I've got some fun lined up," she said, finishing her wine. "Aside from the guy on the Vineyard, I've got another one in Chatham. You should see the house I'm staying in. Right on the water. This guy is so afraid his wife is going to find out, he gave me the house for the month. Even threw in the weekly maid service."

"Sounds lovely," I said.

"I'm gonna tell his wife, anyway," Mama added, her eyes watching Mason for his reaction. "As soon as I'm done with the place."

He just drank his beer and said nothing.

"Where to after here?" I asked.

"Wherever the wind takes me. Are you sure you won't consider coming with me? I've got this great idea we could do in Florida. I've had it planned for years."

"No thanks. But you have fun."

Mama shrugged. "I always do. But anyway, back to you. Where are you going next?"

"I don't know. I like it here."

"Of course. It's lovely here. And you get to fuck that every night." She pointed at Mason. "I'd stick around for a few weeks myself for that kind of action. But you know you'll go. We don't stick, dear. Gypsies don't have homes."

"I do."

Mama laughed. "That shack your loser daddy calls a house? Be worth more if you burned it to the ground. You were meant for so much more than that, baby. You and I, we're meant for mansions on the water, for champagne and servants."

For barred windows and padded walls, I thought, but said out loud, "I like the house. My studio is there."

"Oh, yes, your scribbles." She waved a hand.

"Excuse me," Mason said, standing. "I'll be right back." He headed toward the bathroom, and I wondered if he was coming back. There wasn't an exit back that way, though, and his shoulders were too wide to fit through a bathroom window.

Mama flagged the waiter for another glass of wine. She smiled at me; it made my skin crawl. "Are you into sharing?" she asked.

"Leave Mason alone!"

"He's a big boy." She licked her lips. "I'm sure he can take care of himself."

"He can."

"Good. If you insist on keeping a man for any length of time, at least it's not some pathetic, clingy one. Now if you'll excuse me, I'll be right back."

I wanted to scream as she stood up. She was going to ambush Mason. There was nothing I could do. If I got up to follow her, she'd make a scene. I knew she would. Mama loved an audience. So I stayed in my seat and prayed I was right, and that Mason could take care of himself.

Mama's wine arrived. I drank it in two gulps and ordered another drink for myself. The waiter looked concerned until I told him I wasn't driving. "Oh, and by the way, my mother is a psychotic con artist. If she fucks you over now, it's your fault, not mine."

On that note, I decided she'd been gone long enough. I headed toward the hallway leading to the bathrooms. I heard her voice before I turned the corner and saw them. I couldn't hear what she said; the noise from the kitchen drowned it out. Mason stood, his back against the wall, arms crossed. Mama wasn't touching him, but she was standing close.

He didn't see me. He kept his eyes on Mama. I knew him well enough to see the hurt and fear in his eyes, but I could tell Mama wouldn't see it. She wasn't trying to con him, she knew she couldn't. But that didn't mean she couldn't hurt him. She reached out and touched his arm in a soothing gesture, and he flinched.

I'd seen enough. I walked up behind her. "Playtime is over," I said.

She smiled at me. "We were just having a nice little talk, weren't we?" Her innocent-looking eyes were on Mason.

"Yeah," he said. "It's fine."

I followed him back to the table, even though by that point I desperately had to pee. There was no way I was going to leave him alone with her again. If she ordered dessert, I was going to dump my leftover salad over her head.

"What did she say to you?" I asked for the third time. Mason climbed into bed and pulled the covers over his head.

"Nothing worth repeating."

"I'm sorry, whatever it was."

"Don't apologize for her." He was angry, but too tired to be animated about it. I slid into bed beside him, but he didn't try and hold me. He stayed on his back with the covers over his face.

"I shouldn't have let you come tonight," I sighed.

"I make my own decisions."

"Not when it comes to my mother."

"Dammit, Divine." He shoved the blanket away so he could glare at me. I flinched at the sharp movement, but he didn't seem to notice. "It's late. I'm tired. So either shut up and go to sleep or I'm going home." He rolled over onto his stomach with a grunt.

I blinked back tears and stayed quiet. I didn't know what my mother had said, but what scared me was, it was likely true. She wouldn't have bothered lying to him. I was fairly certain she'd said something along the lines of *"She's using you, she's going to leave, and she doesn't really care about you at all."* And Mason had no reason not to react to that truth. Not that it was entirely true. I wasn't using him. And I did care for him. But I wasn't his, and he knew it. She'd reminded him that I was going to leave him, sooner or later. I couldn't be mad at him for being hurt and unhappy.

I lay awake, wondering if I needed to go to the studio to work more. But no image came to mind. Mama wasn't the bad guy this time, I was. And I was too afraid to draw myself.

Chapter 28

I WOKE TO MASON'S cell phone alarm. He didn't touch me when he got out of bed. He disappeared into the bathroom, returning without glancing at me. He got dressed without a word.

"Are you all right?" I asked.

"Fine," he said, looking at me for the first time. "Just running late for work." He headed for the door.

"Are you coming by after work?" I asked.

"I'm not sure. I'll text you later."

He was gone before I could think of a reply. I sat in bed, stunned. Mason had never left without kissing me. What the hell had my mother said to him? I jumped out of bed, glad that Ray would already be gone with Mason, so I wouldn't have to deal with him. I didn't stop to get breakfast, heading right to the studio.

I worked on the series of my mother, but now it didn't feel right. I set them aside, afraid I would ruin them if I tried to force it. I grabbed a random sketchbook and let my mind go. I was so engrossed in my work, I didn't notice someone coming up the stairs until Nancy called my name. I actually screamed and fell off my stool.

"I'm sorry, Divvy," she said, helping me up. "Didn't mean to frighten you."

"It happens a lot." I shrugged. "Mason scares the hell out of me as often as he can."

"My son has a sick sense of humor," she admitted. "I'd blame his father, but we all know the truth."

I smiled. "What can I do for you?"

She bit her lip, something I'd noticed Bodel doing when she was nervous. "Well, I came by to check on you. You've seen your mother twice and, well, Trace called me and said Mason is in rare form this morning and I'd better come see what's going on. So I took a long lunch to see how you are."

I sighed and sat on the table amid the portraits of my mother. Nancy sat on my abandoned stool. Her hands were streaked with grease and grime. My mother would never have let herself get dirty like that. She'd have scoffed at Nancy, and it made me angry just to think about it.

I took a breath and began. "It wasn't easy seeing her," I admitted. "But it wasn't terrible either. Well, it wasn't as bad as it could have been. I tried to get her to leave, but she's going to stick around until after my show."

Her eyes had traveled to the portraits. "Are those going in the show?" she asked.

"A last-minute addition."

"They are wonderful. Aren't you worried your mother will make a scene?"

"She was going to make one anyway. This way I get to tell my side of the story."

She laughed and continued looking at my work. "So tell me, how was it talking to her again?"

"It felt the same as it always has, like the floor is about to drop out at any moment, but I still have this need to do or say the right thing to make her happy."

"What does make her happy?"

"Me leaving with her to run cons." I snorted at the idea. "She knows I won't. She just keeps asking to piss me off."

"What about Mason?" she asked. "How does your mother treat him?"

I wasn't sure how to answer that question. She was trying to hide it, but her mama-bear claws were showing. Mason had learned his protectiveness from her. Hoping she wouldn't be too angry, I said, "Well, she alternates between flirting with him and calling him Rover."

She blinked. "Excuse me?"

"The first time she met him, she called him my guard dog. She thinks it's clever to call him Fido and Rover, and she knows I hate it, so she's continued." I could tell Nancy had a thing or two to say about Mama calling her son Rover, but she kept her thoughts to herself.

"Are you and Mason okay?"

I looked down at my bare feet, unable to meet her eyes. "I don't think we've ever really been . . . okay."

"What?"

I was feeling guilty, which meant I was going to get defensive. I jumped down off the table and began to pace. "Look, I was honest with him from the start. I told him I was going to leave. That I wasn't the long-haul girl. I told him I couldn't be with him at all, because I knew I wasn't what he was looking for."

"So how did you end up with him?" she asked, crossing her arms.

"He stormed into my house, pinned me against a wall, and said 'Take me or tell me to leave.' It was kind of an impossible offer to refuse."

To my surprise, Nancy laughed. "That's my son, as subtle as a heart attack. You don't have to defend yourself, Divvy. I know my boy, and I know you pretty well too. I'm positive you told him exactly what you intended to do, and he ignored all your warnings and insisted on being with you, anyway."

"Pretty much." I sighed, and sat back down on the table. "I never wanted to hurt him. My mother said something to him last night that set him off. I don't know what it was. She managed to get him alone without me. I shouldn't have let it happen."

"What did she say?"

"I don't know, and he won't tell me. But I have a feeling it was along the lines of *She's using you, she doesn't care about you, she's going to leave* . . . that kinda thing."

"You are *not* using him," Nancy snapped.

I studied my toes. "No. I'm not. And I do care about him. I really do. But I am going to leave. I never planned on staying here forever. I told him that. I tried to protect him from me."

"Have you considered asking him to travel with you?" she asked.

I snorted. "I'd never ask him to do that. Mason's a homebody. He loves working for his father. He loves his family and his happy, simple life here. Moving around like I do would make him miserable. I'd never let him come with me."

She sat down beside me. "I'd hoped you'd noticed by now that my son does what he pleases. No one *lets* him do anything. He makes up his own mind."

"Not when it comes to following after me," I said, as I felt the cold shoot up my spine. Images of Stacey filled my head, and I shut my eyes. "I will never let anyone try and follow me again."

Nancy took my hand. "What are you talking about?"

I was surprised to realize that I trusted and cared for her enough to tell her about my past. The words began to pour out, almost on their own. "I tried to become part of a family once. When I was sixteen. I made a friend, Stacey, and her mother invited me to live with them. It was a chance to get away from Mama, so I stayed.

"But no matter how happy I was there, I didn't fit. I didn't belong. I couldn't explain it, and Stacey didn't understand. She was so angry that I was leaving. She said she was my sister, and I couldn't abandon her. But I packed up my car and left. She followed me. It was a bad night. The roads were icy. I was trying to lose her, get far enough ahead that she'd give up and go home. But she lost control of the Jeep and rolled off the side of the road."

I felt an arm around my shoulders. "I'm so sorry."

"Stacey died before the ambulance arrived. I stayed with her, but it was too late. I stayed for the funeral, but that was a mistake too. Stacey's mom told me I was the one who should have died. I agreed with her, but it didn't seem to make her feel better."

"It was an accident, Divvy!" Nancy was stroking my hair. "It wasn't your fault."

"It was an accident," I agreed, "but it was my fault. She was chasing after me. Trying to make me stay. Trying to force me to belong. And I won't let anyone else get hurt like that."

Nancy leaned away from me so she could look in my eyes. "I'm sorry that happened. But Mason is not a teenage girl."

"That doesn't mean he won't get hurt. I know rationally that he's not literally going to chase after me. He'd follow me doggedly, but he wouldn't get hurt physically doing it. But being dragged from place to place would kill him in a different way. He belongs here, with his family. I won't let him lose that."

"Well, then why exactly can't you just settle here?"

I decided I could be honest with her. I hadn't even dared say these thoughts to Mason, but I felt safe with Nancy. "I've been thinking that maybe, someday, I can."

"Someday?" she asked.

"I have been on the move for twenty-five years. Never had a home, or a family, or friends. I was raised to use people, to hurt them. I was told from Day One that love is a disease. I've tried not to become what Mama tried to make me, but some lessons have run too deep. I am not going to recover from a lifetime of conditioning because I've had a month or two of good sex with a man who loves me."

Nancy cocked her head. "You make a good point. At least the sex is good."

I smiled. "Look, Nancy, your son is very important to me. I know how he feels about me, even though he's tried really hard not to show it. But I don't know how to love him back. I want to. I want to say 'Fuck it, I'll just settle here and stay.' But I don't know how. I need to keep moving. I don't know how to belong somewhere."

"Honestly, I can't understand that," she admitted. "But I've always had a home."

"I don't know how to have one. But I do want one. I want this place to be my home. I know I'll come back here. Not just for Ray. I've made friends here. I plan on leaving shortly after my show. But I don't think I'll be gone long. Maybe only a month. I'll be back. And each time I come back, I'll try and stay a little longer. And maybe one day I'll learn to stop leaving."

"Have you told Mason any of this?"

"No."

"Why not?"

"Because it's not fair to ask him to wait, to ask him to leave his heart on the line while I rip it out and put it back, over and over, with no guarantee I'll ever really be his."

"There are no guarantees in love." She shook her head. "I think you should tell Mason what you just told me. Let him make up his own mind."

I didn't want to tell Mason. I knew he'd wait for me. And I couldn't give him hope, when I wasn't sure there was any to be had. He was twenty-eight years old. He wanted a family, I knew that much. He wanted kids, and pretty soon. How long was he going to wait for me? What if I couldn't stop moving? What if ten years from now I still hadn't stopped leaving? He'd have missed his life waiting for it to start. I couldn't let him do that.

"I'll think about it."

After Nancy left, I looked at the sketchbook I'd been working on. I'd drawn two shadowy figures, a man and a woman. The man stood with his arms outstretched as the woman walked away, casually tossing the heart she'd ripped from his chest, over her shoulder and onto the ground.

Hunger pains made me stop working. I looked at the clock and realized that it was seven thirty. I hadn't eaten anything since those few bites of dinner from the night before. I'd spent the day drawing the reality of me: a sequence of departures and broken hearts. I'd drawn myself as the wind sliding through a man's fingers. It felt good to be honest but depressing at the same time. I wanted to be substantial. I wanted to be more than just a passing breeze.

For now, I'd have to settle on eating something for substance. I left the studio and noticed that Ray's truck wasn't there. He hadn't come home from work yet. It was Friday, so maybe Trace had taken the crew out for dinner. He did that from time to time. I was on my way inside to check my cell phone when Ray pulled up to the house in his truck. He didn't look happy as he got out.

"What's up?" I asked. "Where's Mason?"

Mason's truck was in our driveway from the day before. He'd hitched a ride to work from Ray. I'd assumed he would come back for his truck, if not to see me.

"I wanted to bring him here, but he insisted I drop him at home. He got in a fight and he's banged up, but he told me not to tell you."

"He got in a fight?" I gasped.

"Yeah. I knew it was a bad idea for him to go anywhere near Wanda. I warned him. He was in a pisser of a mood all day. Trace took us out for drinks and dinner at the Stowaway to try and calm him down. But he ran into a guy he knows and they went at it in the parking lot."

I was stunned. I'd been told that Mason had been prone to bar fights and other acts of aggressive stupidity before he'd met me, but I'd never really been able to picture it. I had no problem imagining him defending someone, but attacking was another matter.

"Look, sweetheart." Ray put a hand on my shoulder. "Mason's a good man, but he has his flaws. He doesn't handle strong emotions well. He starts fights when he's frustrated or angry. I've seen it happen many times. I think you should stay away from him for a bit, and let him calm down."

"Like hell I will," I muttered, heading inside to get the keys to my bike. I could have walked to Mason's house, but I wanted to make an entrance.

Chapter 29

I ROARED INTO his driveway, probably looking like a crazy woman without my helmet. My hair was windblown into crazy spikes, but I didn't care. My hair matched my mood as I stalked to his front door. Gage's car was there, which meant Mason and I were going to have an audience for our fight.

I didn't pause to knock, just barged in. Mason was in the kitchen drinking a beer. Blood from his split lip tracked down his face and stained his T-shirt. One of his eyes was swelling and going to be black and blue. He was leaning against the counter, glaring at me.

"What are you doing here?" he asked.

"Don't ask stupid questions. You're bleeding."

"Yeah. So?" He drank more beer. I went to take the can from him, but he didn't let go.

"I think you've had enough to drink."

"I don't give a shit what you think." He shoved my hand away and finished the beer, tossing the can in the sink. He wiped the trail of blood off his face with the back of his hand and went to get another beer out of the fridge. I stood in his way.

"Get out of my way, Divine."

I leaned my back against the fridge. His hands slapped against the fridge around me as he caged me in. I wasn't afraid of him at all.

He lowered his head to look into my eyes. "You are not my keeper. You've made it perfectly clear that you aren't my anything. So get the fuck out of my way."

I rolled my eyes in the face of his aggression and kissed him. I felt the shock go through his body. His hands dropped from the fridge to settle on my waist. He tasted like blood and beer but I didn't care. I pulled back from the kiss and wiped his blood off my lip. He backed slowly into a kitchen chair and sat down, pulling me against him. His arms wrapped around me and he buried his face against my stomach. I stroked my fingers through his hair as he held me.

"I'm sorry," he said, not raising his head.

"For what?" I asked.

"For talking to you like that."

"I know how to handle my Bear," I said, realizing I shouldn't have called him that. He flinched and pulled away from me. I caught his face in my hands. His eye was swelling shut but the split lip wasn't bleeding as badly anymore. I grabbed a washcloth from the sink and wiped the blood off his face and neck. He didn't stop me or say anything. I found a package of frozen peas in the freezer, wrapped them in a piece of paper towel, and pressed it over his eye.

"You should see the other guy," he muttered.

"Did you throw the first punch?"

"Maybe."

I took his hand, noticing the bruised knuckles. "You know you're an idiot, right?"

"Yeah."

"As long as that's clear. Are you hurt anywhere else?"

"Not badly. He got a few lucky punches to my ribs but nothing is broken."

"You know what broken ribs feel like?"

"Yes. I've got some bruises but I'll be fine."

I grabbed the bottom of his bloodstained T-shirt and pulled it up. He grunted a little as he raised one arm, but helped me remove the shirt. I gave him the bag of peas to hold against his eye and wiped at his lip again. Bruises were forming on the right side of his chest. I went over his body gently with my fingers, searching for more serious injuries.

"Why are you here?" he asked.

"You know why."

"No, Divine. I don't. And that's the problem."

"I'm here because I care about you," I said. "Because you matter to me. I'm sorry I don't have the words you want to hear. I just, well, you have as much of me as I've ever given anyone. I hope that counts for something."

He cupped my face in his hand. "It counts for a lot. I'm sorry I didn't talk to you about this. I just needed to hear that you cared. At least a little."

I kissed his nose. "Of course I care, Bear." I took his free hand. "You didn't need to get beat up just so I'd say it."

"I didn't get beat up," he muttered.

"Who did you hit anyway?" I asked.

He rotated his shoulders. "Does it matter?"

"Yes."

"Guy's name is Dan. He's Chrissy's brother. We've hated each other since high school."

"Do you always hit him first?"

"Not always." He sulked, which was kind of cute but annoying. "He's the one that said I raped Chrissy. He told the entire school. You don't know what that was like."

"That was ten years ago," I mentioned. "You were teenagers."

"He's kept the rumors going," he said. "He's gone out of his way to tell any girl I'm seen with that I'm a rapist."

I considered that a moment. "Okay, so I understand hitting him first. How come he hasn't come around me?"

"'Cause I'm pretty much always with you. He doesn't have the balls to lie with me right there." He sighed and pressed the peas against his eye. "I still shouldn't have hit him, though."

"No, you shouldn't. You should introduce me to him, so I can hit him."

He smiled, causing his split lip to start bleeding again. I pressed the washcloth against his mouth.

"Stop smiling," I scolded.

"Can't help it when I'm around you."

"I know the feeling. I'm supposed to be mad at you."

"I'm too pathetic and cute to be mad at."

I scanned my eyes down his bare chest. "Cute isn't the word I'd use to describe you."

"You know, sex is a great painkiller," he said, discarding the peas in the sink.

"Don't you think we should talk some more about this?" I asked.

"About what, exactly?"

"Us."

He looked at me for a few heartbeats before shaking his head. "I don't want to talk any more. I know I won't like what I'll hear. I'll take what I've already got and leave it at that for now."

"Mason," I began, but he pulled me to him and kissed me.

"No more talking, honey," he said. "I know you care about me. That's enough for now."

"But . . ."

He tossed me over his shoulder, proving he wasn't badly hurt at all. He carried me upstairs and kept me from talking for a long time.

Chapter 30

I SLIPPED OUT of bed without waking Mason. I figured some extra sleep would help him feel better. His eye was black, but the bruise on his ribs wasn't that colorful. Mason told me that Ray and Trace had broken up the fight after the first few punches. It scared me to think what happened when Mason picked a fight without supervision.

I tiptoed downstairs to find Gage sitting at the kitchen table, eating cereal. He looked up at me and smiled, but I could tell he had something on his mind. Gage wasn't really a deep-thought kind of guy. He was mostly unfocused, and generally happy to float along in whatever way he happened to be going. It wasn't like him to mull over problems or worry. The fact that his forehead was now creased with worry lines was notable.

"Morning," I said.

"Morning."

I got a bowl of cereal for myself, not liking the silence. Gage was never quiet. He was always tapping on things and in constant motion.

"What's up?" I asked.

"Thank you for what you did last night," he said, not looking at me.

"What I did?"

"For Mason." Gage gave up the pretense of eating and sat back. "Look, I love my brother, but he scares me sometimes. When he gets like that, it's like he's this whole other person. I hate it. I don't know what to do. I just stay out of his way."

"That's probably the best idea."

"Then why did you get in his face? You weren't afraid of him at all."

Something occurred to me. "Did you see us last night?" I asked.

He ran a hand through his hair and rubbed at the back of his neck. "I heard you come in, and went to try and help. I saw the whole thing from the doorway."

"Oh." I wasn't sure what to say.

"Why weren't you afraid of him?" Gage asked. "I mean, I didn't think he'd actually hurt you. But when he pinned you against the fridge, that scared the shit out of me. I'd have pissed myself. But you weren't scared at all. You kissed him, and then he was back to being my brother again. How did you know to do that?"

I shrugged. "I didn't know. I just followed my instincts."

"But how did you do it? No one else has ever managed to calm him down like that. Not my mom, not Bo. None of his stupid girlfriends ever tried. They'd just take off and I'd never see them again."

I shrugged. "Mason would never hurt me."

"But how do you know that?" Gage asked. "He was yelling in your face, slamming things."

"I've been hurt many times in my life," I said. "I grew up with Mama and her rages. I know what real violence looks like. Mason could never look at me like that. He might lose his temper and yell and throw things, but he'd never even think of hitting me. He's not a fluffy little kitten. He's a big, aggressive guy. He'll start a fight, yeah, but he's not going to seriously hurt the other guy. Real malice isn't in him."

"I hate it when he gets like that," Gage said. "I'm afraid he's going to lose it when you go."

We sat in silence. I'd been thinking the same thing all night. Being reminded that I was leaving had caused him to go pick a fight. What would he do when I left, when I wouldn't be there to calm him down?

"He'll be okay," I said, because I had to believe that. "It's not like I'm going to disappear off the face of the earth. He can call me anytime. And I won't be gone forever."

"You're coming back?" he asked, sounding completely surprised.

"Of course I am. My dad is here. You guys are here. I'll probably only be gone a month or two."

"Then why leave at all?" he demanded, some of the anger he'd been hiding now coming to the surface.

"It's complicated."

"No it's not." He stood up and dumped his cereal in the trash. "You're just a chicken shit. Hell, why did you even get involved with him in the first place?"

"I don't think this is any of your business..."

"He's my brother," Gage snapped. "That makes it my business."

"Well I'm sorry, but I don't know all the rules of being a family." I threw up my hands. "I've never had one. I've been alone my entire life."

"You have one now."

"Right." I stood up to be at his level. "And three months of having a dad and a boyfriend are going to make me a new person? I don't know how to share my life with people. I'm trying, okay?" I was embarrassed to realize I was starting to cry. "I'm giving as much as I have to give. There just isn't that much there. I don't know how to belong. I don't know how to stop leaving."

Gage caught my frantically gesturing hands and pulled me to him in a hug. He stroked my back and made comforting sounds. I rested my head on his shoulder and wished he was my brother. I'd give anything to have grown up with someone who was always there.

"I'm sorry, Divvy," he said.

"For what?"

"Making you cry. That's not what I wanted. I didn't want to hurt you. I just don't understand why you have to go. You know that we all love you, right? You know we want you to stay?"

"I know," I said, stepping out of his arms. "And I want to stay. But I don't know how. I just hope you can be patient while I learn."

"What do you mean?"

"I plan on trying to make this my permanent home," I admitted. "I think I could make a life here—no, I know I can. My plan is to stay as long as I can each time I come back. And maybe someday, I'll stop leaving. That's the best I can hope for right now. I know it doesn't make sense, but it's the way it is."

"Mason thinks you're leaving and not coming back. Why haven't you told him you are going to try and stay?"

"Because I don't want him waiting around forever for me. I might never be able to settle, and I won't let him put his life on hold."

"Nobody *lets* Mason do anything," Gage said, reminding me of his mother. "Divvy, it's his choice if he wants to wait for you. If you are what he wants, then you can't make him change his mind."

I was tired of being told that. Mason had said it repeatedly, Nancy said it, and now Gage too? It was my life. I was going to live it the way I wanted to. And if part of that was tricking a man to fall out of love with me, then so be it. I would not let him suffer because of me. That was my decision to make, not his. I'd lie to him if I had to. If I couldn't settle, I'd tell him I didn't love him. I'd tell him I didn't want him. He'd hate me, but he'd move on and live his life.

"Divvy?" Gage touched my shoulder, bringing me back to the moment.

"I'll do my best not to hurt him," I said, as honestly as I could.

Chapter 31

I LOOKED AROUND the gallery and sighed. I was regretting insisting on cleaning it myself. I should have let Zach hire the cleaning company like he wanted. It was only one large, open room with some old furniture stacked in piles for storage. How dirty could it be? I had spent an entire day dragging furniture around, dusting, scrubbing, and de-spidering. I'd found homes for the good furniture in the house and broken the rest into little pieces with a sledgehammer while picturing my mother's face on each one.

Now that the furniture was cleared and the floor and walls were as clean as they were going to get, it was time for a fresh coat of paint. I bought a pair of overalls to paint in, because I was in a mood and had never owned any before. I wasn't sure what you were supposed to wear under them. I figured Mason was coming by after work, so I settled on a red thong and a black sports bra. I could have worn a shirt, but I'd probably just have gotten paint on it. I looked cute, which was a new thing for me. I wondered what he would think.

I'd tried to talk to him about us, but he wasn't willing to listen. He said he was living in the moment, and wasn't interested in anything else. I worried about him, but he made it clear that there wasn't anything I could do about it. He made up his own mind, and as he said, it was his heart and he was responsible for what happened to it.

A car pulled up while I was still cutting in. I looked out the window to see Laura. She didn't have her kids with her. I wondered why she was there. I wrapped the paintbrush in a plastic bag and greeted her at the door.

"Hey, Laura," I said.

She looked me up and down. "No leather today? Trying a new look?"

"Hey, I don't always wear leather," I said, motioning her inside.

"Oh, don't get me wrong, if I had your body I'd show it off too," she said. "But this body had two kids, so I think I'll stay on the conservative side."

I rolled my eyes. "You look fabulous. I'd never guess you had two kids."

She laughed. "You're sweet. My hips just aren't the same, but it's worth it."

"So, what can I do for you?" I asked.

"Well, I had to do a flower delivery in the area and decided to give myself a long lunch break. I am the boss, so might as well enjoy it. I've never seen your work, and I wanted to come look. I'd come during the show, but honestly, crowds aren't my thing. And I'd have to find someone to watch the kids. Can I have a little pre-show?"

"Of course," I said, starting up the stairs. "I've got everything organized and ready for next week. Zach is driving me crazy. But I think I'm driving him equally crazy, so it's fair."

I watched her as she looked over my art. I wasn't sure how to bring up Ray, and after a few minutes, decided on my usual style of bluntness. "So," I said. "What do you think of Ray?"

She cocked her head at me. "Ray? Well, he's a very nice man. He's wonderful with my kids. I don't know him as well as I'd like to. He seems really shy. Why do you ask?"

"Are you attracted to him?" I prompted.

She blinked. "Oh. Well, sure. He's a good-looking guy. I like that he's letting his hair go gray. It looks good on him."

"Would you date him?"

She raised an eyebrow. "Are you trying to hook me up with your dad?"

"Yes."

"Oh."

She looked confused, so I steamrolled on. "He's interested."

"How do you know?" she asked. "He's just nice to me because he feels bad that I'm alone with the kids. That's all."

"I know because he told me. That and he changes his clothes multiple times when he knows you're coming by the house. And he watches you the entire time you're around. You just don't notice."

She sat on a stool. "Oh. I . . . uh . . . I guess I didn't notice. I guess I should have. It's just that after I lost Michael, it took me a long time to really see men again. And Ray's been my friend for years. So I just never thought of him that way. But now that I am thinking it . . ." she trailed off, tapping her lip with her painted fingernail. "Well, he's a sweetheart. He is wonderful to my children. They're already comfortable with him. But seriously, why would he want to get involved with me?" she asked. "He might like the kids, but that's a far stretch from getting really involved. I'm a package deal. Three for the price of one."

"Ray's an orphan who grew up in foster care," I told her. "He's always wanted family. I know he'd welcome a chance to be closer to you and the kids."

She frowned. "Then why hasn't he asked me out?"

"He thinks he's not good enough for you, because he was a drunk for all those years."

She snorted. "He's been sober for as long as I've known him. I don't know what he was like before, but I really don't care. If I wanted to live in the past, I'd stay alone the rest of my life. I loved my husband, but he died. He had a dangerous job. We knew the risks. He told me what he wanted for me if something happened."

"What did he want?" I asked.

She smiled. "For me to be happy. He didn't want me to be alone. So I'm not going to be. I'm going to ask Ray on a date."

I suppressed a whoop and settled for a smile. "Mason and I can watch the kids."

She jumped up from the stool. "I want to surprise him," she said. "I mean, I know he'll say yes, so no pressure. I've always wanted to do something really bold, you know?" She laughed and shook her head. "Of course you know. You do bold things all the time. I want to be more like that."

"Do not use me as a role model!" I shuddered at the idea. "Boldness is often cowardice in disguise."

"What do you mean?"

What I meant was that moving place to place without a plan wasn't actually bold, but more of a continued flight from something inescapable. I wasn't even sure what I was running from. But I didn't say that aloud. "I have an idea. I'll tell Ray that Mason and I are gonna watch the kids while you go out on a date. Then when you come to drop them off, you can grab Ray and tell him the date's with him."

She clapped her hands. "You think that'd be okay? He wouldn't be upset that I had a date with someone else?"

"He'll be jealous, which will make it even better when he finds out he's the lucky guy."

She wrung her hands. "I don't know. Maybe I should just be formal and ask him normally."

I shook my head. "You wanted bold, Laura. I gave you bold."

I knew Ray never had plans, and Mason's only plans were whatever I was doing. So Laura and I schemed for Friday night, and she left with a giant grin on her face. It had taken three months, but I'd finally managed to get my dad and Laura on a date. Delighted with myself, I returned downstairs to paint.

Chapter 32

I SHRIEKED as Mason's hands slipped under my overalls from behind. He laughed against my neck and kissed me.

"I like this new look," he said. I could barely hear him over the music I'd been blasting while I painted the gallery walls. I wriggled free of his groping hands and turned the music down. He was dressed as he always was for work: old jeans and a loose T-shirt with his father's company logo across the back. He hadn't bothered to shave that morning. He looked amazing, scruffy and sweaty.

"So what do you think of the color?" I asked.

"Honey, it's white," he laughed. "And I can't really take my eyes off of you to notice."

"Since when are overalls sexy?" I asked.

"Since you started wearing them. With nothing underneath them."

"I'm wearing underwear."

He hooked his fingers into my overalls and pulled them out so he could see my panties. "So you are. That's a shame." He pushed me backward toward the wall.

"Mason, I think the paint is still wet," I said.

He shrugged and shoved me against the wall anyway. Luckily, it was the first wall I had rolled and the paint was dry enough that I didn't splat against it. Mason grabbed my hips and lifted me, bracing his knee against the wall and settling me on his thigh. It reminded me of our first night together.

"I missed you today," he said, unsnapping one of the straps of my overalls.

I grabbed the bottom of his shirt and pulled it over his head. He smelled like sawdust and sweat, which was becoming an intoxicating combination. I licked his neck, enjoying the scrape of his beard stubble and the tang of salt on his skin. He unsnapped the remaining strap of my overalls. He kissed my neck and I tilted my head to give him better access.

I opened my eyes . . . to see my mother standing in the open doorway of the gallery!

She grinned at me. "Don't stop on my account."

Mason dropped me without ceremony. I snapped the straps back into place, while he struggled to untangle his shirt.

"Oh, please don't put that back on," she said, licking her lips. "I'm enjoying the view."

He pulled his shirt on, inside out and backward. I stepped between them for good measure. "What brings you here, Mama?" I asked, adding, "Without calling or being invited?"

She continued to stare at Mason like he was an entrée. "Oh, I was in the neighborhood. Glad I could catch the show."

Mason cleared his throat. "Ah, nice to see you again, Wanda."

She put a theatrical hand to her heart. "The manners again, just adorable. Take your shirt off again, stud. I'd appreciate that a lot more."

"Mason, Ray needs you for something," I said without taking my eyes off my mother.

He leaned down and whispered in my ear, "She's between me and the door."

"Come and give me a hug, Mama," I said.

She laughed. "He's afraid of me. It's cute."

"It's smart," he said.

The playfulness left Mama's eyes, and the real woman looked out at us. "Yes, it is. Run along now, Rover."

He squeezed my hand and gave her a wide berth as he escaped out the door. I was glad he hadn't argued with me about leaving. Apparently, he'd learned his lesson when it came to Wanda Therese.

"I get it now," she said, watching him walk to the main house. "He's not rich or particularly bright, but that body..." She closed her eyes. "Yes, I have a few ways I could use that body."

"You know he'd never..." I began.

She laughed, waving my anger away. "Of course not. Because you warned him. But if I'd met him first? Well, let's just say that a man like that is worth a few uses before discarding."

"That's all you ever do is use people." I shook my head in disgust. "So why the hell are you here? What use do you have for *me* today?"

She flinched. I stared at her in shock. Nothing I said had ever seemed to bother her before. I hadn't said anything particularly damning this time. So why was she looking at me like I'd hurt her?

"I... ah..." she stumbled on her words.

My mouth was hanging open. "Who are you, and what have you done with my mother?"

And just like that, she was back. "You've always been an ungrateful little cunt, you know that?"

"Yes. What do you want?"

"Maybe I just wanted to see you," she sniffed.

"What's the agenda?" I asked, hands on my hips. "There's always a scheme. Always some underhanded bullshit going on. I'm not stupid, Mama. You raised me to be smart. I don't let people play me. Especially not you."

Anger replaced the sadness I had seen in her eyes, making me wonder if it had been real. "From the look of it, you've let Rover play you."

"He's not playing me."

She snorted. "No, but you're playing him."

The statement felt true, and I hated it. So I did what I always did. "Get the hell out, Mama."

"Oh." She moved closer to me. "Didn't like me saying that, huh? I was just guessing, but thanks for confirming it."

"Just shut up."

"Oh, Grace." Mama rolled her eyes. "That boy is in love with you. The stupid, slobbering kind of love. And you know it. And you knew from the start you couldn't love him, but you let him get close anyway."

"I said, get out!" I snapped, pointing to the door.

She shrugged. "Don't get mad at me. I didn't do anything to hurt Rover. You did that yourself."

"His name is Mason, Mama," I yelled, "and he and I are none of your business."

"You are my daughter."

"Only when it's convenient for you!" I yelled, getting into her face. To my surprise, she backed up. "I've never been your daughter, just a tool to use in your cons, a hostage you could use to manipulate the world. Everything you ever taught me is twisted and wrong. You fucked me up so badly, I can barely stand myself."

"I taught you how to survive."

"Survive?" I snorted. "You taught me how to cheat and steal and hurt people. You taught me how to end up miserable and alone. I don't want that, Mama. I don't want to be this twisted thing you turned me into. I want a normal life. I just want to be normal."

She frowned. "You'll never be normal, Grace. You're extraordinary."

I blinked. Was that actually a compliment? I couldn't remember Mama ever having a single nice word to say about me. Nothing I did was good enough. I was stupid and ugly and a subpar liar. Extraordinary? Did Mama even know what that meant? Did I?

"What are you doing here?" I asked, instinctively going on the defensive.

"I told you," she said. "I was in the area and I wanted to stop in and say hi. I'm your mother. I'm allowed to do that."

"I won't run cons with you again," I snapped.

"It would be a waste of time anyway." She shrugged. "You've gone all soft. You couldn't pull a half-decent con out of your perky little ass." She frowned. "Speaking of which, what in the hell are you wearing? Overalls? Rover must have the sex drive of a prize stallion to get off on that. The farm-girl thing is so tired."

I sighed. "I'm tired . . . of this conversation. Please leave, Mama."

"Fine. I'll leave you to your rodeo." She blew me a kiss and left me alone.

Chapter 33

I FOUND MASON and Ray sitting in the living room of the main house. They'd been watching through the window as Mama left. Mason looked like he could use a drink. Ray looked like he could too, which worried me.

"She's gone," I reassured them.

"What did she want?" Ray asked.

I sat down on the window seat, needing some distance from Mason until Mama's words had gone out of my mind. "I'm not really sure," I admitted.

"She's usually pretty direct." Ray shrugged. "Crazy, but direct."

"She said she just wanted to stop in and see me." Ray looked as unconvinced as I was. The three of us sat there puzzling over the craziness of Wanda Therese for a while.

"Maybe it's true," Mason said. When we stared at him, he continued, "I mean, she's crazy. No doubt. But like you've both said, she has her lucid moments. She is your mother, Divine. Maybe there's a good part of her in there that knows that, and is trying."

"So I should just overlook years of abuse and welcome her?" I snapped.

"No, but . . ." he began.

"There is no but," I cried, jumping up. "I don't want there to be any good in her. There's not enough to make it matter. She's always going to hurt me. She's always going to be crazy. I'd rather her be truly awful. Five minutes of actual kindness from her hurts a lot more than all the years of abuse."

"Why?" Ray asked.

"'Cause if I know she's capable of loving me, then why didn't she?"

Neither of them said anything. There wasn't really anything to say.

"I'm done talking about this." I threw up my hands. "I'm going for a ride."

"Want company?" Mason asked.

"No, I want to be alone for a while."

"Call me if you need me."

I went upstairs and changed into jeans. I owned a pair of black leather chaps and strapped them on too. I laced up a black corset with red laces and grabbed my leather jacket and boots. I always dressed suggestively when I was angry, probably because my style was so different from Mama's, and it was comforting. I kissed both men lightly on the cheek before I left. I didn't want them to worry and think I was angry at them. They were such fragile creatures. I knew I was going to break them both.

I was halfway through my second margarita when a man sat down beside me at the bar. I was in Provincetown, so the odds of the man being gay were high, but the way he was looking at me confirmed he wasn't. *Great! All I want is to be left alone and I find the one straight man in town!*

"Can I buy you a drink?" he asked.

"Have one." I took another sip from my glass.

"Can I buy you another?"

"No."

"Oh, come on. Don't make me use a lame pickup line."

I glanced over at him. He was a little older than me, I guessed Mason's age. He was attractive enough, but there was a meanness in his eyes that ruined it. He wasn't wearing a wedding ring, but he had a nice watch. If he became too annoying, I'd steal it. Maybe his wallet too. Not that I'd keep them. I'd turn them in to the bartender before I left, claiming I'd found them on the floor or something.

"I'm driving home soon," I said. "So this is my last drink."

"I could give you a ride home," he said, winking at me.

I rolled my eyes. "You can buy me a drink, but I'll be calling my boyfriend for a ride home."

"If you've got a boyfriend, why are you here alone?"

"I'm not alone. I'm being pestered by an asshole."

"Dan," the bartender said to my companion. "Leave the lady alone."

The name was familiar for some reason. I glanced at him again. I hadn't originally noticed in the dim light of the bar, but he had the remnant of a recently blackened eye and a faded bruise on his cheek.

"You've got to be kidding me," I muttered into my drink. I finished it, deciding I had to get away from Dan before he realized who I was.

"What?" he asked.

I pulled out my card to pay for my drinks. He must have read my name off it.

"Wait, are you Mason's girlfriend?"

"You don't want to go there with me."

"'Cause there are some things you should know about him," he said, putting his hand on my shoulder. I flinched under his touch, but he didn't let go.

"You have three seconds to remove your hand," I warned him.

"Mason's a rapist," Dan began.

"One second left," I said.

"What?"

I grabbed his fingers and ducked under his arm, twisting it behind his back. I didn't actually hurt him, unless you included his pride. His chest was pressed against the bar and I was standing behind him, keeping just enough pressure on his trapped arm to keep him from moving.

"Look, Dan," I said, ignoring all the people around us who'd jumped away. "I did not invite you to touch me. I asked you nicely not to. I'm going to let you go now and walk away. If you say another word to me, I'll make what Mason did to you seem like a massage. Got it?"

"You two deserve each other."

I released him and tossed an extra twenty on the bar. "Sorry for the scene," I said to the bartender. "You make an awesome margarita." I grabbed my jacket off the chair and walked out.

Mason was asleep on my bed when I got home. He was still dressed, and looked to have fallen asleep waiting for me to return. I gently shook his shoulder to wake him. His eyes opened slowly, as they always did.

"You're home," he said. "I . . . I must have fallen asleep. I'm sorry. I should have gone home. I was just worried about you."

I pushed him back down when he moved to sit up. "I'm glad you're here," I said. "Being alone didn't work out for me."

He rolled his eyes. "If you wanted to be alone, you shouldn't have gone out dressed like that."

"I went to P-town. The men there are gay."

"You are hot enough to turn them."

I laughed. "No, I'm not. But I did manage to attract Dan."

Mason sat up. "Seriously?" he asked. "What are the odds of that?"

"Fairly good, seeing as he hit on me."

Mason grunted. "I'm breaking something the next time I see him."

I shoved his shoulder. "You are not. Besides, I think it'll take him awhile to recover his ego after tonight."

"What did you do?" he asked.

I told him while I removed my chaps and corset. He laughed and undressed with me. We crawled under the covers and he held me.

"Oh," I said, remembering earlier in the day. "I also ran into Laura today. I set her up on a date with Ray for tomorrow."

"What?" he asked. "Ray doesn't know about it. He would have said something."

"It's a surprise. I'm gonna tell him you and I are going to watch the kids while Laura goes on a date. She's gonna show up to drop off the kids and take Ray out."

"Whose idea was this?"

"She said she wanted to do something bold." I shrugged.

"Your alternative childhood is showing."

"Hey, it's not a con if it's to benefit the person."

"And that shiny gold watch you put on the bedside table?" He indicated Dan's watch.

I shrugged again. "I never claimed to be a good girl."

He kissed my neck. "Good thing I like bad girls."

CHAPTER 34

I SMILED TO MYSELF while Ray went through his usual Laura-encounter routine. It served my purposes, since he always wore nicer clothes when he'd see her, so he wouldn't have to change for their date. She had called twice for encouragement, nearly backing out. I was glad she had embraced her bold side as I heard her pulling into the driveway. The back windows of her little car were plastered with stickers and fingerprints. It made me sad because Mama had never let me do anything like that.

I was about to go out and help her unload the kids and their bag of toys, when Mason walked into the yard. He'd gone home to shower after work and get clean clothes. He saw me in the window seat and blew me a kiss. I settled back on the pillows and listened to Ray, scrambling around like a rat on acid.

Hope burst into the room and ran right to me. "Can we draw?" she asked with no preamble.

I smiled and pulled her up onto my lap for a hug. "Of course. What else would we do?" I'd already set up the kitchen table with crayons, paints, and colored pencils. I'd also bought fun-shaped cookie cutters, and found a recipe for sugar cookies. I loved playing with the kids. It was a way I could relive the childhood I'd never had.

Mason entered the room with Mikey hanging around his neck, as usual. Laura followed more sedately. She was a beautiful woman, but she never drew attention to the fact. She rarely wore makeup, and her clothes had been chosen based on function rather than fashion. She had little kids wiping their snot on her jeans and shirts; she wasn't going to waste money on fancy things. But tonight she wore a simple cotton dress, black with red roses. A light dusting of rose eye shadow and lipstick brought her looks even more sharply into focus.

"You look great," Mason said.

"You think?" she asked. "I'm terrible at this. I don't know how to do the whole makeup thing."

"You don't need it," I said. "Natural is your look."

"Do you think Ray will like it?" she asked.

As if on cue, Ray jogged down the stairs. Laura's back was to him, so she missed the show of his mouth dropping open. I smiled innocently at him. "Hey Dad, what do you think of Laura's dress?"

Laura turned to face him. He wasn't drooling, but he didn't really need to answer the question for us to know what he thought. He took a moment to collect himself and said, "You look absolutely beautiful. Whoever you're going out with is a very lucky man."

I was afraid she would chicken out, but she smiled and said, "That would be you."

He didn't respond. It was like he was a machine and someone had unplugged him. He stared at her blankly, in complete shock.

"Dad," I said, loudly. "Say 'Thank you, Laura, I'd be honored to take you to dinner.'"

He blinked, unable to take his eyes off her. "You have a date, right?"

"Yes. With you."

Ray still wasn't getting it. I walked up to him and slapped him on the back to try and clear his mind. "Well, you two should get going. And don't worry about the kids. Take your time, don't rush home."

"I'm going?" Ray asked. Laura just laughed and threaded her arm through his, gently leading him toward the door. "Come on, Ray."

I watched them walk out together, shaking my head at my father. I wondered how long it would take for him to realize that he was actually on a date.

Mason and I amused the kids with art for a while, but Mikey got bored, so Mason took him into the living room to watch his favorite movie. He wasn't old enough to actually sit through a whole movie, but he would sit for part of *Frozen* before wandering off. Hope and I continued painting in the kitchen.

"Mommy is on a date with Mr. Ray," Hope said, with no preamble.

I set my paintbrush down. "Yes. What do you think of that?"

She kept her eyes on her paper, adding sweeps of color with a carelessness that didn't match her tone. "I like Mr. Ray."

"That's good."

"Mr. Ray is your daddy, right?"

"Yes."

"So your daddy is on a date with my mommy?"

I hadn't really thought too much about it. If things worked for Ray and Laura, this little girl could be my stepsister. The idea was too foreign to really settle in my mind, but I was strangely comfortable with it.

I wasn't sure what the right thing was to say to a six-year-old, so I tried, "My dad really likes your mom."

"I know," Hope said. "It's sooo obvious." She rolled her eyes.

"Are you happy they are on a date?" I asked.

She shrugged. "Mommy talked to us about it before we came here. I told her it was okay." She frowned down at her painting. "He's not going to be my new daddy, is he?"

I was not qualified to have this conversation. My exposure to children was very limited, and I had no idea what the right words were. But I had to say something. "No, Hope. Mr. Ray isn't going to be your new daddy."

She nodded with a very serious look on her face. "'Cause I have a daddy. He's in heaven now, so I don't get to see him anymore. But he's always watching me." She considered her artwork for a minute. "But it would be nice to have someone to take me to the park. Mommy needs help with the dishes, and when things break at the house. Mr. Ray could do all those things, and that would be okay. He could do all those things, but not be my daddy, right?"

"Yes," I said. "Your daddy loves you, and he's watching you from heaven. I'm sure he'd be really happy that you have someone to take you places, and help out your mom."

She nodded. "Good. Okay. I wasn't sure. But Mr. Ray is your daddy, and you are happy he is on a date with my mommy. So if you're happy, then I guess I should be too."

"Happy is good," I said. "Are you done with your painting?"

"Yes. All done." She smiled brightly at me.

"Why don't you go into the living room and watch *Frozen* with the guys while I clean up? Then you can help me make cookies."

Her eyes went wide. "We're making cookies?"

"Yep."

She hugged my leg. "You are the best babysitter, ever."

I laughed as she ran into the other room. My mind tried to embrace the situation while I cleaned up the art supplies. I let myself wander into the world of possibilities. What if Ray and Laura fell in love and got married? Ray would get a second chance, a second family. He adored Laura's children, and I knew he would be respectful of Michael's memory. Laura would then be my stepmother. That idea was a bit too weird. I put it aside to mull over later. But the idea of having Hope and Mikey as my step-siblings was appealing. They were great kids, and I could be the fun big sister.

But you aren't staying here, I reminded myself. Was it really fair to let the kids get attached to me if I was going to be leaving? Stability was important for children, and I wasn't good with stability. Even though I was planning on leaving, I was going to come back, and often. I hoped with time I could spend most of the year on the Cape. So befriending the children wouldn't be a bad thing. At least I hoped so.

Mason walked into the kitchen and kissed me. For a long time I'd been worried about what my leaving would do to him, but now I was equally worried about myself. Could I leave him? Why the hell did I even want to? It wasn't about wanting, though; it was a need, a deep subconscious need to move on. I didn't think I was strong enough to overcome it. But leaving Mason was going to hurt me too, possibly more than I could bear.

"What's wrong, honey?" he asked, running his thumb along my cheek.

"Nothing," I lied. "Let's make cookies."

Chapter 35

I THANKED VICTORIA for the fifth time, shaking her hand vigorously as she headed out of the studio toward her fancy sports car. I'd originally objected when Zach had said he was going to hire her to set up the gallery. I'd been convinced I could do it myself. After all, it was just hanging things on walls, how hard could it be? But now that I'd seen Victoria work I knew that, as usual, Zach was right. I was good at making art, but I should leave displaying it to the professionals.

She had found the best ways to group my work in an attractive way. She'd organized the prints and told me how many I should have. I was lucky the old owner of the gallery had left so many frames behind, or I'd owe Zach even more money. It worried me how much he was doing for me. What if I didn't sell anything? I could never pay him back.

"The caterer will be by tomorrow at eight to set everything up," Zach said, making me jump.

"I told you that a caterer is overkill."

"And you're wrong, again." Zach patted my head. "It's not extravagant. Some wine, cheese, and crackers. Trust me."

I ran my hands through my hair and produced a frustrated grunt.

"You should try not to do that tomorrow," Zach said. "When your hair stands on end like that, you look a little scary."

I stuck my tongue out at him and had a sudden desire to dye my hair purple.

"While I'm thinking of it, what are you planning on wearing tomorrow?" he asked.

I stared at him in complete shock. I looked down at the strappy little shirt that exposed my stomach, and my cutoff shorts. No one would take me seriously if I dressed in my normal clothes. I didn't have much of anything nicer, though. Unless leather was acceptable art show attire. I grabbed onto my hair and let out a shriek.

Zach flinched beside me. "Please never do that again."

Mason came running from outside. "What's wrong?" he asked.

"I have nothing to wear!" I yelled.

He took a step back. "Oh. I thought there was, like, a giant mutant rat or something."

I snorted. "I've dealt with giant rats before. This is so much worse."

"We'll go up to the mall and you can get something," Mason said. "It's no big deal."

Zach shook his head at Mason. "You have a lot to learn."

"No big deal?" I shrieked. "What should I wear? Should I get a dress? Should I wear a pantsuit? Or a skirt with a nice top? Should I buy a wig, so I look like I have normal-girl hair?"

Mason held his hands up. "Relax, honey. Your hair is fine. Lots of famous people have their hair cut short like yours now."

"But they have professional people style it. It always looks great. I look like I stuck my head in front of a fan."

"That's only 'cause you keep pulling at it," Mason said.

I growled, and he took another step away from me.

"Stop talking," Zach suggested to Mason. He smiled at me and put a hand on my shoulder. "Why don't you ask Laura to go shopping with you?" he suggested. "She's done the flowers for a lot of fancy events. She knows a lot more about women's fashion than I do. She'd make sure you look professional, but not stuffy or boring. You're a young artist, you don't want to downplay your wild side."

I did my best to calm down. Zach was right. Laura would help me find something that was appropriate but made me feel comfortable.

I hoped she wasn't busy. I watched Mason walk around the gallery while I called her. She calmed me down and assured me she'd be over as soon as she could leave the store. Mason could watch the kids while we shopped. We would find something perfect at the mall and get dinner, and probably a lot of drinks.

I hung up with Laura and went over to where Mason was standing. He was looking at a series of six I had done using a man I'd met when I took my bike in for an oil change. He was the mechanic and I'd embarrassed him horribly by asking him to model for me. He was a beautiful man with an amazing body. His skin tone was Anglo-Colombian, and his mixed race gave his features an exotic quality. He had posed for me in a series of seemingly impossible yoga positions.

"Who the hell is that?" Mason asked, crossing his arms.

I laughed, unsurprised by his possessiveness. "That is Shadow."

"Seriously?"

"Yeah. That's his name, as far as I know."

"You had this guy here, I'm guessing multiple times, alone with you, and you don't know his real name?"

I rolled my eyes. "His boss calls him Shadow too, so I wasn't suspicious. He's a mechanic at Randal's Garage."

He relaxed a little. "Oh." He looked at the pictures again. "Why didn't I ever meet him?"

I decided on being honest. "I kept you away from him, actually."

He frowned. "Why?"

"He has serious PTSD," I explained. "He's really jumpy and afraid of, well, big, aggressive guys like you." I put a hand on Mason's arm. "You're possessive of me. And you'd get the way you get and you'd freak him out. So I only invited him by when you were busy."

Mason's shoulders relaxed. "I get it. I would have overreacted. Why would he be afraid of me?"

I looked at the images I'd drawn of him. "I didn't draw his scars because he asked me not to, but he has a lot of them. He wouldn't talk about what happened, well, he can't actually talk."

"He can't talk?" Mason asked.

"He's a selective mute," I said.

"A what?"

"It's a psychological disorder. He's incapable of speaking. Hasn't been able to say a word in years, I guess. Since he lived through something someone didn't want him to live through."

"Poor guy," Mason said. "Wait, if he can't talk, then how do you communicate?"

"He signs." I shrugged.

"Signs? As in sign language?"

"Yeah."

"You know sign language?"

I laughed and signed as I spoke. "Mama taught me when I was little. It was a way we could talk to each other during a con without anyone understanding."

Mason stared at me.

I shrugged. "Hey, I'm glad she taught me. You should have seen the smile on Shadow's face when he realized I could understand him. He's a real lonely guy."

"Is he coming tomorrow?" Mason asked.

"He said he'd try, but crowds tend to trigger panic attacks."

"I'd like to meet him," Mason said. "I promise I won't be an asshole. I just, well, a guy like that could probably use a friend or two."

I smiled. "You promise not to growl at him? He is pretty hot."

"Don't push me, little girl," Mason growled in my ear.

Chapter 36

"YOU'RE KIDDING, RIGHT?" I asked.

"Nope," the woman said for the second time. "I've been doing Laura's hair for years. She said you were worried about looking professional today, so I volunteered to come help you out."

"You really don't need to," I said, but found myself sitting in a chair.

"It's my pleasure," she said. "Short hair like yours is fun. And I can do your makeup if you like."

I gave up. "I'd really appreciate that. I end up looking slutty, which is normally fine with me, but not good for this occasion."

"Well, you have beautiful skin. A little color around your eyes and some lipstick is all we'll need. Just relax and let me take care of it."

So I did. She washed and trimmed my hair, and styled it to look as beautiful as the women on TV. I was relieved when she was done with my makeup. I still looked like me, just with pinker lips and a slight shimmer of silver on my eyelids.

I put on the black pencil skirt I'd purchased the day before. The blue silk blouse I paired it with was sexy in a sophisticated way. It draped attractively and showed a little cleavage but nothing to raise an eyebrow at.

I adjusted the strap on my black slingback three-inch heels and looked up to see Mason in the doorway of my bedroom. I stood up straight and struck a hopeful pose. "What do you think?" I asked.

"I'd say that if you didn't need to be downstairs in five minutes, I'd have you naked in that bed screaming my name."

I smiled. "Well, we do have five minutes."

He laughed. "I'm not even gonna risk kissing you. That lipstick is going to haunt my dreams."

I rolled my eyes. "Seriously, though. Do I look professional? Will they take me seriously?"

He walked up to me and kissed my nose. "Yes, honey. You look beautiful and sexy and professional. I got you something, actually. I hope it goes with the outfit." He held out a box. It wasn't a ring box so I didn't have to panic, but the idea still occurred to me. I opened the box. They were silver earrings in the shape of pencils, with little diamonds at the points.

"Are those real?" I asked.

"Yeah." At my look he continued defensively, "Look how small those are. You're gonna get mad at me 'cause I got you earrings with two tiny little diamonds?"

"You shouldn't have spent so much money," I said, though I was already putting them on.

"It's my money to spend." He shrugged. "They look nice on you. Are you gonna hit me if I give you the necklace too?"

I put my hands on my hips. "Maybe."

He handed me another box. "I wanted to get you something nice to celebrate the show. Bite me."

I looked at the pendant. It was a larger version of the earrings, including a much larger diamond. "Did you really just say bite me after giving me beautiful jewelry?"

"Yes. But you deserved it. If you could see the way you looked at me, you'd have said it too."

I gave up. "It's beautiful. Thank you, Mason."

"You're welcome, Divine."

"Divvy," Zach yelled up the stairs. "Show's starting. Time to make an appearance, my dear."

I froze. I'd been too afraid to look out a window to see if there were any cars arriving. Zach had assured me a lot of people were going to show up, but I wasn't sure if I wanted them to. What if they hated my work? What if they laughed at it? I was nobody, just a self-taught ex–con artist who got lucky with connections. No one would buy anything. I'd been living off Ray for months, but with the intention of paying him back with profits from the show. Not that he'd let me, but I was going to insist. But what if there were no profits? What if I was a complete failure?

"Divine?" Mason touched my cheek. "Are you all right?"

"Not at all. I can't go down there."

"Yes, you can."

"Nope."

"Chicken?"

"Yep."

He took my hand. "Come on, honey. Just put one foot in front of the other."

I took a step back.

"That's not quite what I meant." He slapped my ass, making me squeak and jump forward. "That's more like it."

"Stop that," I snapped as he slapped me again. He continued to slap me, until I ran downstairs to escape him. Zach caught me and towed me out of the house before I could protest. At least he didn't slap my ass.

Next thing I knew, I was in the gallery, parked by the tables set up in the middle of the room. There was a glass of champagne in my hand. I resisted the urge to down it in one gulp. Zach stood beside me, repeating reassuring words in his soothing Southern drawl. Cars were parking outside. People were starting to come in.

The first person to enter made a beeline for me. I took a large sip of champagne and plastered a smile on my face. The woman was in her fifties, and she oozed class and money. She held out her hand.

"You must be Grace Divine," she said. "I'm Martha Ruttledge. Zach has told me so much about you. I've been looking forward to this all summer."

"Nice to meet you," I said.

She smiled wider. "An Irish girl. Why didn't you tell me she was Irish, Zach?"

Zach kissed the back of her hand. "I could have sworn I mentioned it, Martha."

"I'd have remembered." She returned her attention to me. "I have a weakness for Irish accents. My second and third husbands were Irish."

I was tempted to ask how many husbands she had, but decided that was unwise.

"My mama is Irish, that's where I got the accent. I've never been there, though."

"Oh, you need to." She grasped my hand. "It's beautiful. Speaking of beautiful, I really can't wait to see your work. I'll come chat again in a minute."

I took a deep breath as soon as she was gone.

"See," Zach said. "It's easy. Just smile and let them do the talking."

Chapter 37

I LET THE WORLD go out of focus as the show progressed. Zach was wonderful about pointing me in the right direction, and answering questions when I drew a blank. He used his charm to distract people when my anxiety became too apparent. He also kept me from drinking wine like it was water, which would have ended badly.

I hadn't expected so many people to come, and from such diverse groups. Zach was old-money wealthy, and even though he'd been Southern-born, his friends up North were affluent as well. I had only been around his kind of people during cons, and they'd always made me feel uncomfortable. It wasn't that they'd be purposefully rude, there was just a cultural gap that was hard to overcome.

While Zach definitely had some wealthy friends, though, he'd also attracted middle- and working-class people. He'd married a waitress from a blue-collar family, something that had upset some of his relatives, but had earned him affection from the less fortunate. He treated everyone the same, which was a rare quality.

I was surprised to see many of the fishermen I'd met at the docks. They looked uncomfortable without their rubber boots, probably dressed in clothes they usually reserved for weddings or funerals. I loved that they were there. Part of the gallery was a section devoted to the portraits I'd done of them. I spoke to each of them, feeling much more at ease than when I had to talk to the more affluent people. Zach was already making plans for a second show, to be a benefit for a fisheries charity. Even though I was planning to leave the Cape soon, I'd come back. I could work on that next show whenever I visited Ray. Even as I rationalized this in my head, though, it still didn't sound right.

I wasn't sure if it was the wine, but I started to feel more comfortable. I left Zach's side to speak to people I knew. I started to notice how many "sold" stickers were appearing on the walls. Everyone was praising me and complimenting my work. I was selling. I couldn't entirely believe it. I noticed many people lingering by the section titled "My Mother's Love." I wasn't selling any of the originals, and hadn't really wanted to have prints made. These weren't the kind of thing people would want for their homes. Still, they were fascinating to look at, even for me.

Two women were standing by them. I realized with a shock of horror that one of them was Mama. I hadn't seen her come in, likely because she was dressed in a gray pantsuit. Her hair was in a single braid down her back. I could see the ornate handle of the knife she always kept in that braid. She was looking at the portraits I'd drawn of her. She hadn't seen me watching her, or at least was pretending she hadn't. It was impossible to tell with Mama.

The woman standing next to her was obviously shocked by the images. She looked to be from the upper-middle class, well dressed but not lavish. She had a wedding ring, and I imagined a few happy college-aged children. What was she thinking as she looked at the images of my mother? Just as I had the thought, the woman turned her head toward Mama. She flinched, looked back at the portraits, then back at Mama, her mouth falling open.

Mama turned to her with a pleasant smile. "My daughter is quite talented, don't you think?" When the other woman only stared at her in shock, Mama's eyes went back to the wall. "And honest. Don't know where she got that. Must be her daddy. He always wore his heart in his eyes. She would have done the same, but I beat that out of her. I forced her to hide it. But she found a way." She smiled at my work. "She outsmarted me. I'd never tell her to her face, of course, but I'm very proud of her."

The poor woman my mother was talking at was mouthing words, but not actually saying anything. I was just as speechless. My mother? Proud of me? Thought I was talented? Why had she dressed so simply and slipped into the show unnoticed? Mama always wanted an audience. I'd been prepared for her to try and ruin everything. But this quiet woman standing in front of me wasn't there to start trouble. I was stunned to realize that Mama wasn't going to make a scene. She was just there to see my work. Did she intend to talk to me at all? Was she just going to slip out again and be gone forever? Was that what I wanted?

The woman Mama was talking to mumbled something unintelligible and scurried off. Mama still hadn't turned around and seen me. She kept looking at the portraits of herself. I was at an angle to her, so I could see she was smiling at her half-demon reflections. She sighed, and started for the door. That was it. She was just going to leave.

I almost ran after her, then barely remembered I didn't want to make a public spectacle. I had to settle on a graceful trot as I followed her. I caught Zach's eye and waved to him that everything was fine as I stepped outside. She was already halfway across the driveway.

"Mama, wait!" I called to her.

She stopped with her hand on the door of her red convertible. She didn't turn to face me as I approached. "This isn't the way it goes," she said, her voice low and dangerous. "Walk away."

"No."

She turned to me, her eyes dark and angry. "Do as you are told."

"Weren't you going to at least say hello to me?" I asked.

"A viper can't give kisses, and a constrictor can't give hugs."

I stared at her, trying to figure out what she meant.

"You are ruining the only good thing I've ever managed to do for you," Mama said. "Go back inside."

"What are you doing?" I asked.

"I'm leaving," she said as a tear escaped her beautiful eyes. "I'm doing what I should have done twenty-five years ago. I'm getting in my car and leaving. I won't come back. I won't come near you again."

I felt something break inside my heart. I'd always insisted that I hated my mother and I never wanted to see her again. But that wasn't the case. It never had been. Since I'd been a little girl I'd just wanted her to love me. I'd wanted her to be my mother.

"But I don't want you to go," I blurted.

She smiled at me. "I know. And that's why I'm leaving."

"I don't understand."

"I can't love you, Grace Divine," she admitted sadly. "I wanted to. I'll always want to. But I can't. I am a monster. A demon. There is nothing good about me. I consume and hurt and steal and cheat. That's just the way it is." She smiled at me, the expression full of sorrow. She put her hand on my cheek. "Lovely girl. I wish I could say I did my best for you. I'm a liar, but I can't lie about that. I failed you. I will always fail you. I couldn't see that, not until now. I've always thought I needed to protect you. But the only thing you needed protection from is me. So for the first time in your life, I am acting like a mother." She removed her hand and stepped back. "I'm leaving. It's the one good thing I have ever done in my life. I'll stay away, too. I'll keep track of you, though." She wiped at her tears. "You're going to be a famous artist now. I can watch you from a distance, and know you are safe that way."

I wanted to tell her not to go, but I didn't. I knew she was right. I knew that she was giving me a gift. But she was still my mama, and I just wanted her to hold me. I didn't want her to leave me, even if I knew it was for the best.

"Oh, don't cry." Mama brushed away my tear. "You've got to look nice for those rich saps in there."

I managed to smile at her. "Where will you go?" I asked.

"I'm the wind, darling," she smiled. "I'll be everywhere, and nowhere. But I'll always be gone." She kissed my cheek and moved to get into the car. I grabbed her in a hug, needing to hold her just once. She felt strange in my arms, small and fragile. She pulled away quickly and opened the car door. She slammed it shut and rammed the keys in the ignition. She put on her sunglasses and glanced over at me.

"You remember that address I gave you when you left me?" she asked.

"Yes." It was burned into my memory, though I'd never tried to use it to contact her.

"I want you to do something for me," she said. "Every once in a while, write a letter and mail it to that address. Write it to the mother you always wished you had. That way we can both pretend I'm that person." She smiled again in that heartbreaking, defeated way. "When you get married and have babies someday, don't tell them about the real me. Paint them a pretty picture instead. You're good at that."

I knew it was over. She was leaving. It was the right thing. It was a good thing. And it was the only way she could show me that she cared. "I love you," I said.

She shook her head and put the car in gear. "You never were very smart."

Chapter 38

I DON'T KNOW how long I stood in the driveway. It could have been hours, but more likely, it was only a few seconds. I now realized Mason was standing beside me. I tried to smile for him, but I don't think I pulled it off.

"You don't have to put on a face for me, honey," he said, running his knuckles along my cheek. "Are you all right?"

I took a deep breath. "Actually, yes. I am. I am all right now."

"Where is she going?" he asked.

"Away. She said that vipers can't give kisses and constrictors can't give hugs."

Mason nodded, following my gaze to the empty spot where Mama had driven off from. "Are you happy she's gone?" he asked.

"She told me I was stupid for loving her." I smiled. "Such a Mama thing to say. It's weird. I haven't really seen her in years. I've only talked to her four times since I was fifteen. But I'm sad that she's gone. Does that make any sense?"

Mason shrugged. "It doesn't need to. Feel how you feel."

"Are you glad she's gone?" I asked.

"Yes," he said with no hesitation. "It's fitting that she describes herself as a snake. That woman scares the hell out of me. But I respect her for making the right choice."

I turned to him. "What choice was that?"

"Letting you go," he said.

I looked up into his eyes. Would he be able to let me go when the time came? Would I want him to?

"Everything okay, Divvy?" Zach called from the door of the gallery.

"Fine," I yelled. "Be right there."

"Sure you don't need a minute?" Mason asked.

I needed a lifetime to process what just happened. I didn't think an extra minute would do any good.

I returned to the show and a fresh glass of wine. It was starting to wind down, which was a blessing. My face was starting to hurt from smiling, and I had a headache that was making it hard to stand up straight. The whole thing with Mama was too big for me to think about, so I concentrated on answering questions and modestly accepting praise.

I realized that despite the show being officially over, people weren't leaving. The strangers had gone, true, but the Tavish family wasn't going anywhere. Neither were the various friends I'd accumulated throughout the summer. They were all gathering to celebrate my success. I didn't want to celebrate. I wanted to go upstairs and cry because I'd lost my mother. I waited for the right moment, when everyone was distracted, and hurried upstairs to my studio. I hoped no one would come looking for me, at least for a while.

I curled up on the mattress and let myself cry. I wasn't even sure why I was crying. I couldn't miss something I'd never had. But now I knew I'd never have it, and maybe that was worse.

I don't know how long I was crying before I realized I wasn't alone. Mason was holding me. My ear was pressed against his steady, comforting heartbeat. His calloused fingers caught on my short hair as they stroked through it. I loved him so much, but it didn't matter. I was going to leave him. And the worst part of it was that I didn't even know why.

For the first part of my life, Mama and I were running together. Then I ran away from her, and tried to belong somewhere, to someone. But I had never stopped wanting Mama. I still belonged to her.

She hadn't given me up, I'd escaped. I had never been able to admit before how guilty I felt for abandoning her. I'd never been able to voice the thought aloud, that abandoning her was what I had done. Maybe that was why I'd left Stacey's. I'd felt so guilty. I had what Mama could never have. And I didn't want it. I just wanted her. So I'd left, doing what came naturally to me. I'd keep telling myself I didn't want her to find me, but I could now admit that it hadn't been true. Moving from place to place was my link to her. It was the only safe way I could have her in my life. I had to be like her.

Mason held me as I imagined my skin covered in scales.

I slept for a time, but I couldn't hide forever. I plastered a smile on my face and went downstairs to join the celebration. I was a good actress; I'd learned from the best. No one realized I wasn't really in the room. I smiled and laughed, telling jokes and accepting toasts and hugs. But it was just an act. I was really still curled up on that bed, alone. The only one who wasn't fooled was Mason.

The party moved to the house and I went where I was directed. I drank more wine and ate some dinner, but I tasted nothing. Nancy had baked me a cake and I knew it was delicious, but it was lost on me. It was like I was trapped in a bubble inside my head. I knew now with horrible finality that I was going to leave soon. The show was over, and had been a huge success. I had money now. I had to go. There was somewhere I had to go. I didn't know where, or why, only that the time had come.

I watched all these people who cared about me. I watched them laugh and smile and love each other. I envied them that. I wanted to be like them so badly, but I wasn't. There was a broken piece inside of me that didn't belong. I had this weird feeling that leaving was the only way to fix that broken piece. But that didn't make any sense, either. Leaving was what had made me broken in the first place.

I was so detached that I didn't even react when Bo started having contractions. I stared at her blankly as the entire family started freaking out. She cursed and told everyone to calm down, that they were just Braxton Hicks contractions and she'd been having them for a few days. In my haze the only thing I noticed was how calm Zach was. Wasn't he supposed to be freaking out the most?

As everyone settled down, I couldn't take my eyes off Bo. She was massively pregnant by this point, due any day. Something my mother had said echoed into my head. "When you get married and have babies," she'd said. I looked at Bo. Me, pregnant? Married? Babies? Gypsies didn't do that. They didn't settle or belong. We were the wind, though I felt like a tornado. On second thought, I was more like a hurricane: I moved more slowly, lasted longer, and left a much larger path of destruction.

"Divine?" Mason prompted, touching my arm. I realized at that moment that he was the only person who had ever called me Divine. No one else called me that. My mother called me Grace. Everyone else called me Divvy. Mason had referred to me as Divine since the day he met me, and I'd never corrected him. Why hadn't I realized that? Why didn't it bother me?

"Divine?" he repeated.

"What?" I asked, remembering what part I was playing.

"Are you feeling okay?" he asked.

"Fine. Tired. I think I've had too much to drink." That sounded like a reasonable thing to say. It seemed to placate him, because he kissed my temple and helped me up.

"I'm bringing you to bed," he said.

"But the party is still going on," I said, not wanting to be alone with him.

"You're all the party I want," he said, nipping my ear.

I followed him upstairs into my room. I let him strip off my clothes. I let him make love to me. I didn't have the heart to tell him that this was good-bye.

Chapter 39

I WANTED TO ESCAPE before Mason woke up, but I couldn't leave without saying good-bye to Ray. Unfortunately, Mason woke up first and insisted on making a big breakfast. I smiled and tried to act like myself. It was a beautiful summer Sunday. I had everything I could want, and I was about to throw it all away.

I choked down my food, amazed that neither Mason nor Ray seemed to realize what was happening. *I must be a better actress than I thought.* Too good, really. I couldn't expect either of them to rescue me if they didn't know I needed rescuing. Not that I'd have let them, anyway.

I wasn't surprised when the Tavish family arrived to bring us to the beach. Zach and Bo weren't coming, seeing as Bo was so close to delivering. I put my bathing suit on, relieved I hadn't put it on backward in my haze, and jumped into the truck as I was directed to.

I carried on conversations, laughed and smiled like I was supposed to. I even managed to have a complicated conversation with Zach about the profits from the show. He assured me that the majority of the money would be in my account by Tuesday or Wednesday. I had no cash at the moment, though. I couldn't wait till Wednesday. I'd have to steal some money from Ray or Mason, just enough to put myself up at some crappy motel for a night until my money went through. I'd pay them back, so it wasn't really stealing. I felt unclean when Mason kissed me. I should never have gotten involved with him. He had been a mistake.

The day passed slowly, as bad days tend to. Pretending to have a good time was exhausting. I was relieved to collapse into bed that night. I was less relieved that Mason was with me. He'd asked a few times throughout the day if I was all right, and he asked one final time that night. When I started to cry, he kissed me. He held me and told me everything was going to be fine. I couldn't stand to listen to him, knowing it wasn't true. I made love to him again, knowing it was wrong, knowing that I had to tell him I was leaving. But I couldn't. I was going to disappear out of his life like the coward I had always been.

In the morning, he got up to go to work. I watched him dress in his swimming shorts and T-shirt from the day before. He leaned down to kiss me. "I've gotta head home to get some work clothes, and I've got some errands to run after work. Will you tell Ray that I'll meet him at the job?"

"Sure," I said.

He kissed me, and I let him go. That was it. That was how I was going to end it? "Sure." Not "I'm sorry," or how I was really feeling: "I love you." I wanted to call him back, but I didn't. What would I tell him? *I'm leaving you for no reason, and while I plan on coming back, I'm not coming back to you, and I have no idea why.* There wasn't a good way to say that. It was better if I just left. I'd have to stay away awhile to give him time to get over me. Maybe I'd see if Ray could come visit me, wherever I ended up for a week or so. How long would it take for Mason to forget me? How long would it take for me to forget him?

I got out of bed. I dressed in jeans and my leather corset and chaps. They didn't travel well in my bags. It took me less than ten minutes to pack everything I needed into a backpack and two plastic bags. The items in the plastic bags would go into the saddlebags on my bike. The only addition I took with me was a framed picture of me and Ray. The earrings and necklace Mason had given me I left on the bedside table. I made the bed. The sheets smelled like him.

I heard Ray wake up and start his morning routine. I briefly considered hiding until he left for work, but I couldn't do that. He was my dad, and I would be returning to him. I would always belong to him. I didn't belong to Mason, though, and I never could.

I left my bags in my room and entered the kitchen with a fake smile plastered on my face. Ray was cooking at the stove, his back to me. His wallet was sitting dead center on the kitchen table. Without glancing back at me he said, "I figured I'd save you the trouble of picking my pocket. There's a hundred in cash in there. And I want you to take my credit card for emergencies."

My mouth fell open. He glanced over his shoulder at me with a sad smile. "Thought you had me fooled, didn't you?"

I collapsed into a kitchen chair. "I'm sorry, Dad."

He scooped the scrambled eggs onto a plate and turned off the stove. "I knew you were leaving, sweetheart. But I also know you'll be back. And you have a cell phone. I plan on calling you every few days."

"You're not mad?" I asked.

"Why would I be?" He sat down beside me. "You have always been honest with me. You aren't settled here. I think you want to be, but there's something undone out there that you need to go do. It might take years to figure out what that is. That's okay with me. I know that even if you're not here, you're still with me."

I threw my arms around him, crying freely for the first time in days.

"Where are you going to go?" he asked once I'd released him.

"I don't know," I admitted. "South, probably. Along the coast."

"Take pictures along the way and text them to me," he said, tapping the new smartphone I'd recently taught him how to use.

"I will."

"How long do you think you'll be gone?" he asked.

"I'm not sure. Originally, I was only going to go a few weeks, but now I think I should stay away longer."

He frowned. "Why?" At the look on my face his frown deepened. "Divvy, you did tell Mason you were leaving, didn't you?"

I couldn't answer him. I was too ashamed.

Ray set his fork down, food uneaten. "You mean to tell me that you kissed the boy good-bye this morning, and intend to just disappear while he's at work?"

I knew I had no right to get defensive, but I felt my hackles rising anyway. "What am I going to say to him? Sorry, I warned you! Have a nice life?"

"What's that supposed to mean? You're coming back. It's not like you're never going to see him again." At my stony silence he sat back and folded his arms. "Why?" he demanded.

"Why what?" I asked.

"Why are you ending it with Mason, when you intend to come back here?"

"It's for his own good."

"Bullshit."

"I'm not good for him," I insisted. "I'm going to keep leaving. Gypsies don't settle down, get married, and have babies."

"And who the fuck says you have to be a gypsy?" he demanded, standing up. He threw his eggs in the trash and dropped his plate in the sink so hard it broke. He whirled to face me. "I thought better of you than this."

"What are you talking about?" I asked.

"How dare you leave him like this," he shouted. "Slinking away without any explanation. Your mother did that to me. I never thought you would sink that low."

His words felt like a blow. I stood up. "I don't know what to say to him," I shouted, as tears tracked down my face. "He won't understand. I warned him. I told him I was leaving. I was so careful to never let him think I loved him."

He scoffed. "You say that like love is something horrible."

"*My* love is," I said, covering my face with my hands. I felt my father's arms around me. I cried into his neck, relived that he was holding me. I was doing everything wrong, but he still loved me.

"Divvy, sweetheart," he soothed. "I'm sorry I lost my temper and yelled. I know you think that leaving like this is the best way, but you're wrong. Mason deserves better than this. He deserves to know why."

"But I don't know why," I admitted.

"Then maybe you shouldn't end it. Maybe you should just take this time to see what it's like without him, and see if that's really what you want. You know he'll wait for you."

"He shouldn't have to."

"And I shouldn't have had to wait twenty-five years to have a daughter, but I did." He kissed my temple. "Life isn't fair, baby. It's not perfect. It doesn't make sense. You just go for the ride and do what you think is best."

I wiped away the last of my tears. "I'm doing what I think is best. If I leave like this, maybe it'll make him hate me, make it easier for him to get over me."

Ray shook his head. "Mason could never hate you. Leaving him like this is wrong. I won't interfere, it's your decision, but it's wrong."

"It's what I have to do," I said.

He shrugged. "Well then, you want some help packing?"

I blinked. That was it? We were done talking about it? "Ah, no. I'm already packed."

He smiled. "Figured." He pulled the stack of twenties and his credit card from his wallet and handed them to me. "I have to get going to work, anyway. You be careful. And call me when you get settled so I know you're safe. Okay?"

I hugged him. "I love you, Dad."

"I love you too."

Chapter 40

I SAT AT THE KITCHEN TABLE, looking at the blank piece of paper. I was trying to write a Dear John letter to Mason, but hadn't managed a word. The truth was that I had no idea why I was leaving him. I had a bunch of bullshit reasons, but none of them felt real. I wasn't brave enough to try and find the truth under my lies.

I gave up and went up to my room for my bags. I looked at the earrings and necklace on the bedside table. Maybe I should bring them with me. He'd want me to have them, right? But I didn't deserve them. Maybe he could return them. So I left them behind, like everything else.

The stairs looked longer than they ever had before. I made my way down them, feeling tired and sick. The front door opened, and I stopped so suddenly I almost fell down the last few steps.

Mason walked inside and smiled up at me. "Hey, I forgot my cell phone." He was going to say more, but the words died on his lips as his eyes went to my bags. Those beautiful blue eyes locked on mine, full of hurt and anger. "You weren't even going to say good-bye?" he demanded, moving toward me.

I tried to take a step back, forgetting I was on the stairs. I lost my balance and sat down hard. I didn't want to be cornered upstairs. I had to get out. I had to run away from this. I scrambled to my feet and jumped down the stairs, but he stood in front of the door, blocking me in.

"Let me go, Mason," I said, blinking back tears.

"No."

I dropped my bag to throw my hands up in the air. "I warned you. I said from Day One that I wasn't going to stay. I told you over and over. And you promised me you'd let me go. You told me you would be okay."

"I never promised I'd be okay," he snorted. "Why weren't you going to say good-bye?"

"Just let me go."

"Go where?" he asked. "And for how long?"

"What does it matter?" I asked.

"Well," he shifted his shoulders, "it's not like you're never coming back."

"As far as you're concerned, I'm not," I snapped. This was my moment. I had to make him hate me. I had to say something terrible enough that he'd want me to go.

He flinched. "Why?"

"Because a million reasons. Why doesn't matter. It's over, Mason."

"Why matters to me," he said, seeming to get bigger somehow. "And you're going to tell me."

I forced myself not to back away from him. "Don't tell me what to do."

"I've earned an explanation, Divine." He folded his arms and leaned against the door.

"Don't fucking call me that!" I yelled.

He cocked his head, apparently unmoved by my rage. "I always call you Divine."

"I never said that you could."

"You never said I couldn't."

"Well I'm saying so now."

"Too late now."

"Fuck you, Mason."

He shrugged. "If you're in the mood, sure." Some of the anger was creeping back into his tone.

"Get the fuck out of my way!" I shoved against his chest.

"You don't get to order me around, Divine." He caught my wrists, surprising me with the gentleness of his grip. "I am not a dog, no matter how many times your mother called me one. I make up my own mind. I do what I want to do. You don't get to make decisions for me."

"And you don't get to make decisions for me, either."

"I'm not. I'm only asking for an explanation. Tell me why, and I'll let you go."

"Why are you doing this?" I demanded, pulling at my hands. He released me.

"Because I love you."

I screamed. "Don't fucking say that."

"Not saying it doesn't make it not true for these past months." He shrugged. "I love you, Divine. And because I do, I feel that I deserve an explanation as to why you are leaving me."

He was being so calm and reasonable. Why wasn't he yelling and throwing things? Why wasn't he giving me an excuse to run away? To make him the bad guy? I thought of the only thing I could say that might make him back off.

"I don't love you," I snapped, but I couldn't look him in the eye when I said it.

His hand caught my chin and lifted my face so I was looking at him. "Say that again," he said.

I tried to look into his eyes and lie, but for once, I wasn't my mother's daughter. I closed my eyes and repeated it. He dropped his hand. "Liar."

The word felt like a brand. I was a liar. I was a thief and a cheater and a coward. And I had to get away from him before I ruined him. He was a good man. He deserved someone whole, someone good. Not some fuck-up con artist (turned artist), with more luck than talent. I had to save him from loving me. Nothing good had ever come of that.

"I told you, now let me go," I said.

I watched his face as the calm disappeared. I hated myself as his powerful shoulders sagged and he moved silently away from the door. I grabbed my bag and ripped the door open with too much force, almost hitting Mason with it. I ran to my bike, shoving the smaller bags into the saddlebags. Before I could get my helmet on, Mason caught my arm. I looked up to see tears in his eyes.

"Please don't go," he said.

"You said you wouldn't do this," I snapped, wiping at my own tears.

"I didn't know I'd feel like this." He didn't wipe away his tears. They ran down his face like a river of pain. "I didn't know I was going to love you this much. Divine, please, please don't leave me." He was shaking. I never could have imaged seeing him unravel like this. He was Mason: big, confident, arrogant, and powerful. He didn't cry and beg. He was like superman. Until I had broken him.

I pulled my hand out of his and put on my helmet. I got on my bike and kicked up some dirt as I left the driveway. I couldn't help but pause at the road and look back. Mason had collapsed onto the front steps. He was sobbing so hard he couldn't even watch me leave.

CHAPTER 41

I HAD NO DESTINATION. For the first time in my life, this bothered me. I'd never had anything significant to leave behind before. I was too numb to cry as I drove my bike over the bridge.

It was the right thing to do. I was never going to settle down. I couldn't be the woman Mason needed me to be. I had to end it now, to save him from years of disappointment. I hated hurting him, but saw no other way to save him. Loving me was dangerous and never ended well. Stacey was the perfect example. I should have remembered that, and told Mason to go that first night. I couldn't change the past, though. A voice in my head muttered, *but aren't you tired of running from it?* I ignored it.

I drove on autopilot, not caring what highways I took or direction I was going. But I didn't make it far. I could barely keep my eyes open. I pulled off whatever highway I was on and located a crappy motel. I paid for my room in cash and parked my bike in the space in front of it. I took my bag inside and collapsed on the bed, fully clothed. I burst into tears and cried myself to sleep.

My cell phone ringing woke me. I almost screamed, and considered actually doing that, when my body reminded me why it was a bad idea to fall asleep in leather chaps and a corset. What parts of my body weren't numb were in pain. I was going to have creases indented on my skin for days. I grabbed the phone and managed to answer on the last ring.

"Hello?" I hadn't even checked to see who was calling. Under the circumstances, that wasn't the best thing to neglect.

"What the fuck did you say to my brother?" Gage demanded.

I closed my eyes and twitched my limbs to restore circulation. "That's between me and him," I began.

"Bullshit!" he yelled. "You're bullshit. What the fuck is wrong with you, just taking off like that?"

"You knew I was leaving," I snapped.

"Yeah, but why like this?" he demanded. "We welcomed you into our lives, hell, into our family. You could have at least said good-bye. Was that really too much to ask?"

"Yes."

There was silence for a heartbeat.

"Are you coming back?" he asked.

"Yes." I flexed my right leg, the leather creaking. "Eventually," I added when he didn't say anything.

"Then why is Mason acting like you died?"

"Because I made a choice and he didn't like what I chose."

There was another silence.

"I don't give a shit what you do," he finally said. "But stay the hell away from my brother. Don't call him. Don't be all smiles when you visit next time. In fact, stay the hell away from all of us!" The phone went dead and I dropped it back on the bedside table.

I stripped out of my clothes and stumbled into the tiny little shower. Even if the shower hadn't been lined with mildew, I didn't think I would have felt clean afterward anyway. I lay back on the bed, aware that I needed to eat something, but not interested in heading down the hall to the vending machine.

I left the hotel the next morning. I wasn't sure where I was, but I was fairly sure it was still in Massachusetts. I drove around for a few minutes and found a highway. I headed south and found myself in Rhode Island. A shiver passed through me as I entered Jamestown.

I continued on to Newport. Mama loved Newport, which for some perverse reason made me feel safe there.

I was lucky enough to find a small cottage available for a reduced weekly rate, due to a sudden cancellation. It wasn't on the water or anything grand, but it had a nice backyard and garden. I parked the bike and brought all my things inside. I unpacked in less than five minutes and went outside into the garden to call Ray.

"I was starting to worry," he answered.

"Sorry, Dad," I said, taking a lot of comfort in the words. "I found a place in Newport for the week. Just got here."

"I've always wanted to see Newport," he said. "I've heard it's beautiful."

I hadn't noticed. "It's kinda like the Cape, actually."

"How are you doing?"

"That's a complicated question." I sat down in the grass. "I guess I'm okay." I had a million questions, but I knew I shouldn't ask them. I stuck to something safe. "I miss you already."

"I miss you too. But hey, that's why we have cell phones, right? And you'll be back eventually."

"Yeah." I couldn't wait any longer. "How's Mason?"

There was a long silence on the other end of the phone. I picked at the grass and waited, refusing to make any sound as I began to cry.

Ray took a deep, long breath. "I am only going to say this once, Divvy. You chose to leave like you did. You *chose* not to say goodbye, not just to Mason, but to everyone else who cares about you. I respect your choice to leave, and I support it. But I do not condone the way you left. I'm furious with you, actually. But there's nothing I can do about that. All I can do is refuse to tell you anything about what's happening here."

I stared at my phone. "You won't even tell me if Mason is okay?"

He laughed, but the sound was bitter. "It's a stupid question, anyway. Of course he's not. But that's all I'm going to say about it. You left the way you did, and I'm not going to make it any easier on you."

"Oh, come on," I began.

"No," he snapped, and I flinched. "If you really cared about anyone back here, you would have said good-bye to them. If you want to know what's happening, then come back."

"I thought you said you supported my leaving?"

"I do. But you can leave without hurting people. You chose not to do that. And honestly, I can't talk about this anymore without yelling at you. I don't want that. So I'm hanging up now."

"But, Dad . . ." The line went dead.

I stared at my phone. Why hadn't he yelled at me? Why was he being so understanding? I wanted him to yell at me, and that realization made me sick. Part of me wanted him to yell at me, so I had an excuse to get defensive and feel justified in leaving. I went back inside and tried to fall asleep again. My cell phone rang and I dove to answer it until I saw that it was Izzy calling. She had this uncanny ability to know when something was wrong. I didn't have it in me to lie to her, and I didn't want her to drop everything and come to me, so I silenced my phone. My stomach was cramping; I realized I hadn't eaten in two days. There was no food in the cottage, though I did have a small kitchen. I didn't want to eat. I didn't want to go shopping.

Nausea finally motivated me to get on my bike and go find some food. I bought a few essentials and forced myself to eat. I tried to sleep, but couldn't. I went back out and bought a bottle of tequila. I turned around halfway to the cottage and went back for a second bottle.

Chapter 42

I SPENT THE FOLLOWING day curled around the toilet, wishing I was dead. I checked the bowl twice to reassure myself I hadn't actually vomited up an organ. I vowed never to drink tequila again, but knew it was the same empty promise every hungover person has made at one time or another. There was still more than half a bottle of tequila left sitting on the kitchen counter.

I forced myself to eat toast, though I didn't have the energy to actually toast it, so it was just bread. I drank water like I was drowning, and that seemed to help a little. By six thirty at night, I was able to stand and take a shower. I considered that a great success.

I decided my balance wasn't recovered enough for the bike, so rather than go out for dinner, I microwaved some popcorn and ate a package of Pop-Tarts. I turned on the TV, which was on the Weather Channel. It always seemed like the TVs in hotels and rentals were left on that channel. "Must be a conspiracy," I muttered to myself.

I was too miserable to work up much concern over the tropical storm threatening to become a hurricane. It was on its way up the coast, and would likely hit New England full force. I thought about the fishermen I'd befriended on the Cape and hoped that none of them were caught out in the storm. I hoped that their boats survived without damage. And I felt like a shit for leaving without making solid plans for the charity art show.

I changed the channel to cartoons and proceeded to eat popcorn and drink water. I considered drinking more tequila, but passed out on the couch before I found the motivation to go get it off the counter.

The next morning, I felt physically well enough to go out. I didn't have a destination, but I almost enjoyed myself on the bike. It was a beautiful day. The tropical storm, which had become Hurricane Linda overnight, was two days away. If I didn't watch the Weather Channel, I'd have had no idea.

I went to the beach and floated in the ocean so no one would notice my tears. I couldn't seem to stop crying. Swimming was good because it kept me away from my phone. I'd almost called Mason about a hundred times. I wanted to hear his voice. I just wanted to know that he was okay, or that he was going to be okay, at least. I knew that the reason I wanted to hear it was that I didn't think he *was* going to be okay.

I called Ray that night. We talked about the hurricane and the preparations he was making to the house. He reassured me that the gallery and my studio were shut up tight, and none of my work would get damaged. He told me he was considering adopting another dog. I didn't ask about Mason or anyone else because I was too afraid he would yell at me. I needed at least one person not to hate me. I managed to call Izzy, deciding that if I ignored her third voicemail she'd panic and come find me. She'd done so once before; showing up without actually knowing where I was or why I needed her. I wasn't up to talking about the past with her, so I told her I'd broken up with Mason but that I was fine. She didn't seem convinced, but I talked her out of quitting her job and coming to find me.

I tossed and turned that night, unable to sleep. A question was plaguing me. Why had I left like that? I hadn't intended to. All summer I'd planned on giving everyone a little notice, maybe even throwing a little good-bye party. Deciding to leave Mason had changed that, but that still didn't explain why I hadn't told anyone else I was leaving. It was in my twisted nature to sneak out on Mason, trying to avoid the fight we'd had, but I'd had no reason to slink away from the others. I could have easily called Nancy and told her I was going. I didn't even have to see them in person. So why had I left like that? And the day after the show? I knew there was a reason, but I had no idea what it was.

I gave up trying to sleep around four in the morning. I dressed and went out on the bike. I hoped no cops pulled me over. Seeing as I was already crying, I doubted I'd get a ticket, but karma probably wasn't in my favor at the moment. I drove aimlessly, as I always did.

I watched the sun rise over the treeline. I blinked, wondering when I had stopped the bike, and where I was. I almost fell over when I realized I was parked on the side of the road next to a graveyard. I almost threw up when I realized which graveyard I was looking at.

And then it hit me. I knew why I'd left in such a hurry. I knew why I'd left Mason. I knew why I was at the graveyard at dawn on August 28. It was Stacey's birthday.

I took off my helmet and left it on the bike. I walked along the fence to the entrance and made my way along the path. I'd only been to the grave once, the day of the funeral, but I knew exactly where to go. Her gravestone was simple and stated:

Stacey Ann Lumen
August 28th 1990 – February 11th 2006
Beloved daughter.

I stared at the words. I'd done the same at the funeral. I was jealous of Stacey. Even though she was dead, she had been loved. I remember thinking that my tombstone wouldn't have read "beloved daughter." It wouldn't have read beloved anything. I didn't belong to anyone. I was alone. If I died, there wouldn't be anyone to handle funeral arrangements. I'd end up cremated and lost to the world, without a headstone or anything to mark that I'd lived at all. I remember thinking that this was fitting.

I stood looking at the stone for a long time. I wasn't a religious person. It wasn't that I was an outspoken atheist or anything, more that I hadn't once in my life considered spirituality, or the presence or absence of a God. I wasn't sure what I believed, but now I found myself talking:

"Happy Birthday, Stacey." I sat down on the grass in front of the stone. A morbid part of me acknowledged that I was sitting on top of her bones, but I tried not to think about it. "I should have come here before. I don't know why I didn't. Well, I did try a few times. I didn't make it inside the cemetery. I had a car and was parked on the side of the road, but couldn't come in to see you. And two years ago I tried again. Never made it past the gate. I owed you more than that. I'm sorry."

I wiped at my tears and traced the word *beloved* with my fingers. "I'm sorry for a lot of things. I've done a lot of shitty stuff in my life. I've lied, cheated, stolen, broken hearts. But none of that compares to what I did to you. I am so sorry I stole your life from you. I'm sorry I killed you. I've tried to tell myself for eight years that it was an accident and I am not a murderer, but I can't lie to myself. I feel responsible. And you're not here to forgive me. You're not here to tell me that it's okay. And you're not here because of me. And I can't take it back." I pulled my knees up against my chest and cried.

Chapter 43

I DON'T KNOW how long I cried on Stacey's grave. It felt like years, but the sun hadn't moved much above the treeline. I heard footsteps and tried to pull myself together. I wiped at my face to dry the tears and hoped the maintenance guy or whoever was approaching wasn't in the mood for a chat. I looked back over my shoulder and froze. I wanted to run, but my body wouldn't move. All I could do was sit there and watch as Colleen and Paul Lumen walked toward their daughter's grave.

Colleen hadn't changed much. She was still carelessly beautiful despite her hair going naturally gray. She had the same wide, generous mouth, and the big brown eyes Stacey had inherited. Paul had lost his beer belly and his hair was completely white, despite him being four months younger than his wife. They were dressed in their work clothes: Colleen in a pantsuit for her office manager position at a law firm; Paul in a nice but inexpensive suit for his job at the bank. They were average, hardworking, middle-class people. They looked perfectly normal, unless you looked into their eyes and saw the loss embedded in their souls.

Colleen saw me and her mouth fell open. "Divvy?" she gasped.

I scrambled to my feet, desperate to get away. The last time I had seen her, Colleen had told me she wished I was dead, and that had been one of the nicer things she'd said. The couple was here to pay their respects to their daughter. The last thing they'd needed was to see me, her killer.

"I'm sorry," I mumbled, mortified that my legs were numb; I stumbled and almost fell. If I didn't get it together in the next second I was going to drop to the ground and roll away if that was what it took. I made it two steps in the wrong direction, further into the graveyard.

"Divvy, don't go," Colleen called. I was so shocked, I stopped moving. I turned around to see her actually running to catch up to me. She didn't quite slow down as she collided with me, throwing her arms around my neck. I was too stunned to return the hug. I stood frozen as she began to cry.

She stepped back, her face flushed. "I'm sorry, I just had to do that." She grasped my hand. "I am so sorry, Divvy. I'm sorry about all of the things I said. I didn't mean them. Oh, praise Jesus, you're here. I've prayed every day for a chance to see you again, to set things right."

I blinked, my mind refusing to accept her words. "You . . . you're happy to see me?"

She patted my cheek. "Of course we are. Oh, baby girl, I regretted those words the moment I said them. I was out of my mind with grief. I prayed every day that you'd come back and I could apologize. That you'd come home, back to us."

Paul smiled at me, but didn't try to hug me. He put an arm around his wife and shook his head. "I'd about given up hope of ever seeing you again," he said. "But Colleen never doubted. She said that one day we'd find you again. That one day, we'd get a chance to mend the past."

His wording struck me. *Mend the past.* Was that why I was here? Was my past the reason I was always running? Was I really a gypsy, or was I just running from the horror of Stacey's death?

"Look at you," Colleen said, as I continued to stare at them blankly. "All grown up. Not that you were a baby or anything when you lived with us. You were pretty then and you're beautiful now."

My mind was starting to work a little. I smiled. "I've been crying and binge drinking for two days. I must look like hell."

Paul laughed. "You know I'm the honest one," he said. "So, yeah, you look a little haggard. But you're still beautiful. Gray-tinted skin, red eyes, and all."

I smiled and shook my head. "You two haven't changed at all."

Colleen rolled her eyes. "Now who's the flatterer?"

I looked from one to the other. There was still a hint of sadness in their eyes, but it wasn't the way I had remembered them. Time had obviously healed the wound and left them as whole and healthy as parents who'd lost a child could be. They had more laugh lines than frown ones, and hadn't lost that welcoming vibe.

"I've always been so afraid to see you," I admitted. "I thought you hated me."

"Oh, sweetheart." Colleen pulled me into another hug. This time, I hugged her back. "We could never hate you. We love you. We didn't take you in because we felt obligated. We welcomed you into our family because we loved you."

"I wish I'd been brave enough to come back and talk to you," I admitted, pulling back. "I've got this sinking feeling that the chaos and heartbreak of the past eight years could have been avoided if I'd just faced what happened."

"Don't be so hard on yourself." Colleen shook her head. "It took me a long time to come to terms with losing you and Stacey."

I blinked. She'd lost me? That was how she thought of it? All this time I'd feared she'd turned into a bitter, hateful woman because of what I'd taken from her. But she wasn't bitter or hateful. She was hugging me and smiling.

"I don't know what to say," I admitted.

"I've got a lot to say, actually," Colleen said. "I've got a million questions. I want to know all about your life and the years I've missed. And we've got so much to tell you."

"Do you want to call in to work?" Paul asked her. "I can try and get the day off."

"Don't do that," I said. At the horrified look on their faces I continued, "I'm staying in Newport for at least a week. And, well, probably longer now. I won't vanish without a trace, again. I promise."

"That's wonderful," Colleen said. "We could still take the day off today..."

"I actually need some time to think," I admitted. "Just a few hours to let this new world make sense to me."

"Of course," she smiled. "I'm smothering you. Here you've thought the worst for all these years, and I've had that same time to prepare for seeing you again. What about coming to dinner tonight?"

Paul made a face that worried me. "Darling," he said to Colleen, using the endearment I'd found so tacky as a teenager. "I'm not sure that's a good idea. We need to talk to the kids first."

Kids? My world was already too weird, and this new bit wasn't fitting any better than anything else. I must have had an interesting look on my face because Colleen shook her head.

"It's a long story," she said. "I'll give you the short version. After Stacey died and we lost you, well, we both felt so empty. We had this big, empty house and all this love to give, but I couldn't have any more children. I thought about you every day: alone in the world, needing a family. And it made me realize how many children were out there, just like you. So we became foster parents. And three years ago we adopted two of our foster kids. A brother and sister."

"That's wonderful," I said. "Ah, do they, well, know about me?"

"They know the whole story," Paul said. "But I think that the conversations we need to have would be easier without them there. It would be awkward for them, and you. Not that I don't want you to meet them..."

"I understand," I interrupted. "And I would prefer having some alone time with you two before I meet them."

"They are both going out tomorrow night," Colleen said. "Would you like to come over for dinner tomorrow?"

"I'd love to."

They hugged me, and I hugged them. They reluctantly went to work, and I went back to my little cottage and cried a mix of happy and sad tears.

Chapter 44

I POURED OUT the last of the tequila. I cleaned what little mess I'd managed to create in the days I'd been at the cottage. Then I was out of things to do to occupy my mind. I sat at the table and forced myself to just feel.

I thought about my life with Stacey, Colleen, and Paul. I'd been happy there, but had never felt like I really belonged. I wasn't sure why. Probably because I'd spent the first sixteen years of my life with a crazy woman who'd told me I'd never belong anywhere. My mother had worked hard to imbed serious emotional damage, the extent of which I was just starting to realize.

For the first time in my life, I questioned whether I continuously moved because I wanted to, or because Mama had told me to. No matter how much I hated her, deep down, I'd always wanted to please her. Did I actually like floating from place to place, never belonging to anyone or anywhere? Was this really the life I wanted? For years I'd told myself yes to those questions, but had I been lying to myself all these years? Was I living my vagrant life, in some unhealthy and useless attempt at getting my mother's approval?

I had her approval, I realized. She was proud of me. She had gifted me with her absence, the only thing she could give me. I knew that she'd keep watch for me in the art world, where I planned to try and make a name for myself. I knew now, for the first time in my life, that she did love me, even if she'd never said the words, and never could. She had released me, but I hadn't released myself. I was still stuck in the same pattern. If I wasn't Wanda Therese's daughter, who was I?

I'm Ray's daughter, I thought. *I'm a woman with a family and a home. I have a promising start to a career and a savvy business manager. I have a man who loves me and wants to make a life with me. At least he did before I ruined it.* I wondered how much damage I'd done by leaving like I had. Could Mason ever forgive me? Did I want him to? Did I want to go back to him? I wasn't sure of the answer yet, but at least I had acknowledged the question. I'd never once in my life contemplated going back before.

I knew that I'd always love to travel. That was part of my nature, and I assumed that even if I did settle, I'd require frequent vacations. But I didn't have to abandon everything and never return. My life didn't have to be a series of quasi-friendships and broken connections. I could just become an eccentric artist with a close group of open-minded friends and family.

But what if I can't do it? I worried. *What if I try to settle down, and can't? What if I realize that I do need out? Wouldn't that be so much worse?* I kept thinking about it, laying out the scenarios in my head:

What if I settled on the Cape, married Mason, and two years later snapped and took off? What if I had kids and then took off on them, too? I wasn't sure I could risk that. I wasn't sure I wanted children, and I knew that Mason did. I shouldn't commit myself to a man when I knew we wanted different things. But did we? I was afraid to have children, but I didn't necessarily not want them. Wasn't everyone afraid they'd fuck up their kids?

And if Mason was willing to wait awhile, and give me time to be sure I could settle, then there was nothing to fear, right? But was it fair to ask him to put his life on hold, on the off chance I could somehow keep my shit together? What if I never got over the fear, and he spent his life childless, ending up hating and resenting me?

"Thinking like this isn't helping," I admitted aloud. The sound of my voice in the empty cottage startled me. I suddenly realized,

I didn't like it empty. I wanted people around me. I missed Dad, Mason . . . the whole Tavish family. I knew now, I had to go back, and soon. Even if I decided I couldn't be with Mason, I had to go back and apologize for what I had done, and somehow try to explain myself.

But first, I had to take some time here. I couldn't wait to go back to my old home again, to sit and have dinner with Colleen and Paul like we always did. I wanted to hear about their lives, and tell them about mine. But mostly, I needed to talk about the past. I needed to talk about Stacey's death, my part in it, and its effect on our lives. I couldn't move on with my life if I didn't settle my past first.

Unfortunately, I couldn't do any settling until tomorrow night. What the hell was I supposed to do with myself until then? I'd just poured out the tequila. I glanced outside, but the weather was starting to turn. I'd completely forgotten about that approaching hurricane. I turned on the TV, which was inexplicably back on the Weather Channel. Hurricane Linda had picked up speed, but had been downgraded to a Level Two. It was likely to lose even more steam, and be downgraded to a Level One by the time it hit Rhode Island and Massachusetts. I wasn't worried about it anymore. There would be wind damage, flooding, and power outages, but a Level One hurricane was little worse than a bad nor'easter, though sometimes those normal storms did more damage than the hurricanes.

Still, I wasn't looking forward to being alone in this little cottage during Linda's fury. Maybe I could stay with Colleen and Paul? I couldn't suggest it though. Maybe they'd offer? The storm wasn't supposed to hit until the morning after I was going to have dinner with them. Maybe they'd ask me to stay. I wanted to be in someone's home.

I settled at the little kitchen table with a sketchbook and began to draw. I wasn't surprised to see Mason emerge from my pencil strokes. I looked at my cell phone. I couldn't call him. The conversation we needed to have had to be done in person. But I did want to call, even just to hear his voice for a minute. I wanted to know he was okay, despite being fairly certain he wasn't.

I called Ray, and told him about Paul and Colleen. He was supportive, but I sensed an edge of jealousy in his tone. I could understand it. That couple had been parents to me when he'd been denied the privilege. They were part of my childhood, something he'd missed. I told him some of what I'd been thinking about all day, hoping that maybe he'd give in and tell me about Mason. He didn't tell me anything, and I was too afraid to ask.

I decided to check the weather one more time before heading to Colleen and Paul's for dinner. I turned on the TV to get an update on the storm. It was due to hit Rhode Island at eight the following morning. It was downgraded to a Level One hurricane, and was shifting slightly out to sea, where the cold New England waters typically killed the power and momentum of all hurricanes.

The Weather Channel's field reporter was standing on a beach by the raging waves. The hurricane hadn't arrived yet, but the storm-surge had. The large cresting waves behind the reporter didn't look like Cape waves, which tended to be small. The reporter was talking about the dangerous rip current that was now present.

"The beaches have been closed for the past half hour," the woman said, "but that hasn't stopped everyone . . ." The camera panned over to a group of surfers. I didn't hear the rest of what she said, as I noticed something far too familiar about one of the surfers. I stared at the TV, trying to be certain, but I knew in my heart that Mason was the jackass on the white longboard.

I grabbed my phone and called him before I could think it through. Obviously, he didn't answer. I listened to his voice as he told me to leave a message and he'd call me back as soon as he could.

"Mason Tavish, what the hell are you thinking? Get off that surfboard and go the fuck home before you give your mother a heart attack." I ended the call and stared at my phone. Had I really just said that? Out of all the things I could have chosen, those were the words that came out of my mouth? Shaming a man was bad, but using his mother against him was worse.

I thought about calling again, but knew it wouldn't improve the situation. I thought about calling Ray, but didn't want to get into a fight. Right now, I didn't think Ray and I could talk about Mason without fighting. But I had to do something. I called Gage. He didn't answer, and I sat there considering leaving a message or not. At the tone I heard myself speaking, "Look, I know you hate me, but I just saw Mason on the Weather Channel surfing like a lunatic. I can't remember if you're back at school yet or not. I just wanted to make sure someone knew what he was doing, and would miss him if he didn't come home. That's all." I hung up.

There was nothing else I could do short of driving to the Cape, going to the beach, and hauling him out of the water by the cord on his wetsuit. It wasn't my place to police him anyway. I'd made that perfectly clear when I'd left him. The fact that I wanted to take it all back and scold him like a terrified girlfriend didn't change what I'd done.

Chapter 45

COLLEEN AND PAUL'S house was as I remembered it, only more cluttered than before. It was obvious that two teenagers lived there. Colleen showed me pictures of them, proud mother she was. John was nineteen and would be starting his first year at URI in a few days. His sister, Helen, was starting her junior year in high school, and was an aspiring musician.

We spent the hour before dinner talking about their kids, and the other foster children they'd had before them. I told them briefly about my travels, but mostly we talked about finding Ray, and my summer on the Cape. They asked to see pictures of my art, so I used their computer to show them the website Zach set up for me. I had more pictures on my phone and scrolled through them, but it was a mistake. I scrolled too far and ended on a picture of Mason.

"Who's that?" Colleen asked.

I stared at the picture. It had been taken on the beach. He was shirtless, with a football in one hand and a beer in the other. He was grinning at me over his sunglasses.

"That's the reason I've been binge drinking," I sighed.

"Bad breakup?" she asked.

"I left him."

She looked at the picture. "Ah, sweetheart, why? I mean, look at him. If I were a little younger . . ."

"Let me see what you girls are slobbering over," Paul said, taking my phone. He looked at Mason. "I feel a sudden need to go to a gym."

I grabbed my phone back. "So he's got a nice body. And he's a generous, hardworking, dependable, family-oriented guy."

"Okay, so then what's wrong with him?" Colleen asked.

"Nothing, and that's the problem," I sighed. I sat at the kitchen table. "I left because he's in love with me," I admitted. "As you are painfully aware, I don't respond well to attachment."

Colleen sat beside me and took my hand. "How did you leave it with him?"

"I tried to sneak away while he was at work, but he'd forgotten his cell phone and came back, just as I was carrying my bags down the stairs."

"You were living with him?" she asked.

"No. I lived with my dad, but Mason had practically moved in with me. If we weren't at my place, we were at his. He'd said he knew he only had a limited time with me and didn't want to lose out on any of it."

"So you had warned him you were leaving?" Paul asked.

"Yes. Repeatedly. He said he'd be okay. But I don't think he is. And he probably would be if I hadn't left like I did. I was so horrible to him when he caught me leaving. I did it on purpose, thinking that it would be better for him if I could make him hate me. I realized the moment I was gone how stupid it was. But I didn't understand then why I was leaving him, so how could I have explained it?"

"Why did you leave him?" Colleen asked.

"Well, I guess partly because I needed to be at Stacey's grave when you and Paul came." I smiled at them. "I didn't realize this was where I needed to be, I just knew I had to be somewhere. And at a particular time. Can't explain any of it. But there wasn't a reason to end my relationship with Mason, not when I fully intend to return to the Cape."

"So, why did you?" Paul asked.

"Because I don't think I deserve him," I said. "Because I don't know if I will ever be able to settle down. He wants a wife and children. He wants someone stable, who's not going to flake out and disappear for months at a time. I don't know if I can give him that."

"How do you know if you don't try?"

"At this point I don't know if he'd even take me back," I admitted.

"Not to sound like a broken record, but how do you know if you don't try?"

I sighed. "So, what's for dinner?"

Paul laughed gently, and turned to Colleen. "She still does that."

"Does what?" I asked.

"You mention food when you're uncomfortable with a conversation."

I rolled my eyes. "Just feed me already."

The food was gone now, and the three of us were sitting on the couch enjoying glasses of wine. The wind was picking up outside, and I could tell Colleen was getting nervous about her kids being out. I was glad they were still out. There was a very important conversation we still needed to have.

"I'm sorry I left the way I did," I said, with no preamble.

Colleen set down her wine glass carefully. "I guess we do have to talk about this."

"Yes, we do," I said. "I'm sorry that Stacey tried to follow me. I'm sorry she died. I wish I could take it back. I've wished that every day since that day. But I can't." I wiped away my tears. "She died and I can't take it back. So I just ran from it. I kept running and tried to convince myself I was a gypsy, just like Mama. But I'm not. I've just been a scared kid running from a ghost."

"Oh, sweetheart." Colleen moved to sit beside me. "You didn't think you'd have anything to come back to. The way I treated you after the accident, those horrible things I said, of course you ran away. And stayed away. I blame myself for that."

"It wasn't your fault," I began.

"Oh, yes it was," she interrupted. "I own my mistakes. I made thousands with you. And they started the day you moved in. I should have made time for you. I was just so busy with my own life, I didn't notice how much you needed me. Your mother left you, just like that. And I never talked to you about it. I didn't sit down with you and discuss how you felt. I didn't ever make it clear that you were a part of our family, not just a guest who had nowhere else to go."

"You always made me feel welcome," I protested.

"But I didn't take the time to make you feel loved," she said, "to show you that you belonged here. Guests are welcome, of course. You weren't a guest, but I never said that to you. I never told you how much I loved you. How happy I was that you were a part of our lives. I just took it for granted that you knew. But how could you? The way you'd grown up, with that awful mother of yours, it was stupid of me to expect you to recognize love and acceptance."

"I didn't ask for your attention," I countered. "I never told you I wanted to talk about Mama leaving me. I kept it all in. I didn't know how to be part of a family."

"And I believe that's why you left," Colleen said. "I think that you felt that you didn't belong. That you were an outsider."

I considered her words. I remembered seeing the easy way Colleen, Paul, and Stacey talked to each other. They'd watch movies together curled on the couch. Colleen had braided Stacey's hair. She'd never offered to do anything with mine. Paul and Stacey played tennis together. No one had offered to teach me to play. I'd always felt that I was just there, taking up space, while this happy family lived around me.

"I think that is why I left," I said. "You were all so happy, and I just felt out of place. But it's not your fault I left," I insisted. "Or if it is, it's just as much my fault. I didn't ask for the things I needed. I just withdrew, until I felt so alienated I had an excuse to run. It's what I've done ever since."

"Maybe it's time to break that cycle," Paul said. "Divvy, because I never said it before, I'll say it now: Colleen and I love you like a daughter. You will always be welcome here. This is your home, and it always will be. No matter where you go, you'll always have people who care about you, and a home to come back to."

I hugged both of them, feeling a lightness in my chest I'd never experienced before. There was no bitterness, no anger. Stacey's death had been a horrible accident. No one had blamed me, except me. And I now decided that it was Stacey who had guided me to her grave that day, so I could be found by her parents, so I could come home again, and let her spirit rest.

Colleen and Paul insisted that I stay through the storm, and I didn't protest. I had no desire to weather a hurricane alone in a rented one-room cottage. I pulled my bike into the garage between their cars, glad that it would be safe. I loved my bike, and while I could afford another one now, it had sentimental value, seeing that I'd cheated someone out of it in a poker game.

I met John and Helen when they came home from their various dates. They were wary of me, but friendly enough. I had a feeling we had a lot in common, understanding what it was like to be without a home or parents. I respected their privacy and didn't impose on their space more than I could help it. Colleen and Paul set up the pullout couch for me, although I'd told them they didn't need to go to the trouble.

I asked if I could charge my cell phone, remembering that if we lost power I wouldn't be able to for a while. When I went to plug it in I noticed I had a text message, from Gage: *Mason is home safe.* That was it, but it made me feel a lot better. He wasn't dead on the beach somewhere, and Gage didn't hate me so much that he wouldn't tell me. I thought about calling Mason. I had so many things I had to tell him. I needed to explain why I had left like I did, and to apologize. But I couldn't have that conversation on the phone. I had to face him, and I wasn't done fixing my past yet. I needed a few more days. A few more days and I'd go home and try and fix what I had broken.

Chapter 46

I SPENT THE NEXT two days with the Lumens. We went around the neighborhood, helping clean up after the storm. Paul had a chainsaw and helped some of the elderly neighbors cut up fallen braches and trees so they could be easily moved. No one had lost power, which was nice. There were outages in a few areas, the Cape in particular. Ray still had power and he said everyone had come through the storm okay. I told him I was planning on coming home in a few days, and was going to have a long talk with Mason, assuming he was willing to listen to me.

"Really?" he asked.

"Yes. I've been talking with Colleen a lot, going over the past. I can finally see my life for what it is. I see the destructive patterns I've set myself in. I don't want this anymore. I am not a gypsy like Mama. I want to have a home."

I could almost hear his smile. "I can't tell you how good it is to hear you say that."

"Do you think Mason will talk to me?" I asked.

He sighed. "He isn't doing very well," he admitted. "Seeing as you're coming back to face him, I'll tell you what's been going on."

"Why do I get the feeling I don't want to know?" I asked.

"'Cause it's not good," he said. "Mason's a wreck. He's drinking himself stupid every night, and can barely get through the workday.

He's been in three fights that I know of. Not serious ones, but the boy is pissed and looking for someone to beat on."

I sighed. "Jackass!"

"Yes, he is. But people in pain do stupid things."

"Like abandon their loved ones for no reason with no explanation?"

"Yeah. Things like that."

I sighed again. "I'm sorry, Dad. I should never have left like I did. I'm going to apologize to everyone. I'll bake a cake, grovel, whatever it takes to get forgiveness. But it starts with Mason. Do you think I should call him?"

"Honestly, I think it's worth a try. I'm scared for him, Divvy. He's falling apart."

"Okay. I'll try and call him."

"Let me know when you're coming home," he said.

"If Mason is really doing so badly, I'll come home tomorrow, or the day after."

"Okay. I'm proud of you, Divvy."

"I haven't earned that yet. I love you, Dad."

"Love you, too."

I hung up and stared at the phone. I'd changed my background picture, from Mason-and-me to something generic. I went through the pictures on my phone, knowing I was procrastinating. I relived my summer with him, feeling worse and worse about leaving him. Before I could change my mind, I called him. I had no idea what I was going to say. I still had no idea when his voicemail picked up. I couldn't leave a message. I had to talk to him. I hesitated too long before hanging up.

I went for a ride on my bike to kill time. I tried calling him again when I got home. He didn't answer. I tried again an hour later. When I tried a fourth time it went straight to voicemail. He must have shut off his phone.

I tried to call Gage, but he didn't answer either. I managed to leave him a message though. "Hey Gage. I'm coming home tomorrow or the next day. I'm sorry about everything. I'm a fuckup. I'm gonna try and fix things. I just thought you should know."

Paul put a hand on my shoulder as I hung up. "He won't answer?" he asked.

"No. And I left that message for his brother."

"The one who lives with him?"

"Yes. I'm hoping Gage will tell Mason I'm coming back."

"I know you have to go, but it's still going to be hard when you're gone," he said.

"Well this time I'm not gone-gone," I said. "We agreed that I'd call every Sunday. And I'll come and visit again, as soon as I fix what can be fixed . . . back home."

"With any luck you'll bring Mason with you."

I sighed and looked at my phone. "I'm not feeling very optimistic."

"That was never your strong suit," he admitted. "But that's what you have me and Colleen for. We're glass-half-full people."

"I'm a broken glass kind of person."

He kissed the top of my head. "Maybe Mason is superglue."

I sighed, thinking, *or he'll just get cut on the broken glass.*

I decided to put off going back to the Cape for one more day. I drove to the graveyard in the morning and sat at Stacey's grave for a while. I didn't know if I believed in heaven or God, in ghosts or spirits, or anything. I just felt that Stacey was responsible for me reuniting with Paul and Colleen.

I lay on the grass and looked at the clouds, searching for shapes.

"We used to do this a lot," I mentioned to the grave. "You liked the clouds, but I always preferred stargazing at night. Now that I look back on it, I think I related too much to the clouds. I was always moving and changing my shape. I preferred the stars because while they moved, it was in a predictable way and they never changed. I wanted to be more like the stars. Like you were."

I sighed. "I don't know if you're here, or if I'm just talking to myself. It could just be an amazing coincidence that I was here on your birthday. But it makes me feel better to think that you set that up, that you've been trying to get me to stop running for years . . .

and I just wasn't listening to you. Maybe it's self-serving, but I've decided to take this as a sign that you forgive me. I mean, hell, even if there is no afterlife and I'm just talking to a stone, what's the point in holding a grudge against myself? You wouldn't want me to be miserable my whole life. If our situations were switched, I'd want you to be happy."

I rested on her grave and watched the clouds. "I wish you were here to help me figure out how to fix my relationship with Mason. You were always so much better at that stuff than I was. I've made such a mess of it. I'm so worried about him. But I don't know if I can fix it. I'm pretty fucked up still, and I can't guarantee that he won't get hurt again. But I guess no one can guarantee that."

I listened to the gentle wind, which was the only reply to my thoughts. A dog-shaped cloud drifted across the sky overhead and I smiled. I wanted to get a dog. Ray had told me yesterday that he had been looking at local shelters. I wanted to rescue a homeless middle-aged dog, one of the ones most people would pass over for a puppy. A dog would need a home to live in, but would be up for the occasional adventure. It needed to be a big dog. Maybe I could find something bigger than Mop, if such a creature existed.

"That settles it," I said. "I'm going back to the Cape. I'm gonna do my best to get Mason back. And I'm going to rescue a big, unruly mutt, because a dog can't take care of itself and I won't allow myself to abandon it."

I wasn't sure I was making a ton of sense, but it felt good to have a plan. I wanted Mason, but I also knew that getting him back wouldn't solve all my problems. I had issues, and he wasn't the cure to them. He could help me, but I had to do most of the work myself. And even if he didn't forgive me and we were over, I'd still get a dog and stay on the Cape. If the worst happened, I'd name him Bear and let him sleep with me and become a crazy dog-lady.

CHAPTER 47

I WOKE TO MY cell phone ringing. I glanced at the time, immediately alarmed. No one I knew would call me at 7:00 a.m. without a damn good reason. Gage's picture flashed up on my phone and my heart jumped.

"Hello?" I answered.

"I can't do this," he said.

Fear shot through me at the tone of his voice. "Gage, what's wrong?" I asked.

"I can't do this. I thought I could, but I can't. I can't leave him alone."

He must have been in shock. His voice sounded hollow and was an octave too high.

"Gage," I said, firmly. "What can't you do?"

"Clean up the blood. I thought I could, but I can't touch it."

My heart skipped a few beats. "What blood? Gage, what's going on?"

"I'm gonna be sick." The phone was lowered and I heard him stumble to the bathroom and throw up. I put my phone on speaker and grabbed my open bag of clothes. I ran into the bathroom to get dressed.

"Gage?" I prompted, forcing myself to slow down enough to put on panties. (I had a long motorcycle ride to the Cape, and I wasn't about to attempt that commando.) "Gage, are you okay? Why is there blood? Is Mason okay? You're scaring the shit out of me. Please talk to me!"

"We're okay," he said. "The doctor said he's going to be fine."

"What happened?"

"I found him." Gage was barely breathing. I wanted so badly to crawl through my phone and hold him. He sounded so scared. Why was he alone? What the hell was going on?

"Found who, and where?"

"I got home, and found Mason lying in a pool of blood at the bottom of the stairs." His tone was flat, and it terrified me. "I thought he was dead. His whole face was covered in blood. I've never seen that much blood. I need to clean it up."

I forced my brain to concentrate on the key piece of information: *the doctor said he's going to be fine*. Gage was freaking out and incoherent, but I had to stay calm. Mason must have fallen down the stairs. He'd been to the doctor and was sent home. He and Gage weren't in immediate danger. The only thing I could do at the moment was calm Gage down.

"Gage, sweetheart, take a deep breath for me, okay?"

"I don't want to be here," he said, starting to cry. "I can't be here. But Mason can't be left alone."

"Gage, calm down. Listen to me."

I heard him take a long, shuddering breath. "I thought he was dead, Divvy. He was lying there so still. I just stood there like an idiot. I didn't know what to do."

I pulled on my bra and T-shirt. "But you did do something, right? You got him to the doctor?"

"I called 911. I went in the ambulance. They asked me all these questions, and I didn't know all the answers."

"You're at home now, right?" I asked.

"Yes."

"And Mason is there with you?"

"He's in his room, sleeping."

"Okay." I returned to the living room and started tossing my remaining belongings into my bag. "The doctor said Mason is going to be okay, right?"

"Yeah. But he's not supposed to be alone for a while. He has a severe concussion, and it's not safe for him to try and walk by himself." He was starting to make more sense.

"Is anyone else there with you?"

"No. They're still at the hospital with Bo."

My heart stopped again. "What's wrong with Bo?"

"Something went wrong with the baby when she found out about Mason." He was sounding hollow again.

"Are they both okay?" I tried not to shriek.

"Oh, God, Divvy, I'm sorry. Yes, they're okay."

I sat down on the couch and waited for my hands to stop shaking. "Gage, you need to snap out of this. Tell me exactly what happened."

He took a long breath. "Okay. Mason was shit-faced, and he fell down the stairs. The doctors said he must have fallen face-first. He's got eighteen stitches on his temple and he broke his arm. He's got a concussion. When Bo found out he was in the hospital, she freaked out. I don't know the details, but she started having serious contractions. The doctors admitted her because there was something wrong with the baby's heartbeat. But she's okay now. She's calmed down and the baby is perfectly fine. They're keeping her in the hospital just to be safe. Alex is past due anyway, so they're thinking about inducing labor. They kept Mason for twenty-four hours, then said he could go home. So I drove him home. And now I'm here. And I have to clean up the blood . . . and I just can't."

"Gage, I'm gonna call my dad and send him over to be with Mason. I want you to go to your parents' house. Go and take a hot shower, and try and get some sleep."

"Okay. I can do that. I'll wait for Ray to get here before I go."

"I'll be there in two and a half hours."

"You're that close?"

"I'm only in Rhode Island. For fuck's sake, I was going to come back today anyway. Didn't you get my message?"

"No. A lot happened yesterday. Or was that two days ago?"

"It doesn't matter. I'm gonna call Ray. Just sit down and try and relax."

"Okay."

I hung up and called Ray. "Do you know what's going on?"

"Divvy?" His confused tone was answer enough. I quickly filled him in on the situation, not surprised that during the chaos no one had called him. He started running over to Mason's house while I spoke.

"I'll be there as soon as I can."

"I'll be here with him till you get here."

I hung up and reached for my bag just as Paul handed it to me. Seeing as the phone had been on speaker, he'd heard the entire conversation.

"Is this everything?" he asked.

"Yes."

"Do you need any money to get home?"

"No, I'm good. Tell Colleen and the kids I said bye."

"Drive safe, Divvy," he said, pulling me into a hug. "You're no good to anyone if you get yourself killed driving like a maniac."

I knew he was right, but God help anyone who got in my way. "I'll be safe," I said.

Chapter 48

THE DRIVE FROM Rhode Island to Eastham was the longest two hours and twenty-four minutes of my life. I managed not to get pulled over, and only broke a handful of traffic laws. I roared into Mason's driveway and skidded to a stop, nearly losing control of the bike. I wrenched off my helmet and ran for the open front door.

Ray was crouched at the base of the wooden staircase, scrubbing at the floor with bleach. My stomach turned as I saw the circle of stained blood. It was mostly gone, except for where it had soaked in, between the floorboards and in the cracks of the wood. He looked up at me. I needed to get to Mason, and I didn't want to stop and talk to my dad. He moved back and pointed upstairs.

"He's still asleep."

I ran past him, my boots making enough noise on the stairs to wake the dead, or the deeply concussed. Mason's bedroom door was open. I burst into tears when I saw him on the bed. He wore only boxers, revealing countless bruises covering him from head to toe. His left arm was encased in a cast from wrist to elbow. A large bandage covered the eighteen stitches, but I could see they'd had to shave part of his head. His eyes were open, though the swelling from the wound made the right one squint.

I was afraid of hurting him, but I needed to hold him to prove to myself that he was really okay. I knelt on the bed and carefully put my arms around his neck, keeping my weight off his bruised chest. His casted arm bumped against my hip as he tried to raise it to hold me. I was crying and shaking with a combination of relief and fury. I pulled back and barely resisted the urge to slap him.

"What the fuck were you thinking?" I shouted.

He flinched. "Please don't yell right now."

I stood up. "Oh, I'm gonna yell," I snapped, though I did lower my voice as much as I could. "You are a grown fucking man. I know I did some fucked-up shit to you. I'll own that. But what the hell? Seriously? You almost killed yourself, Mason!"

"It wasn't on purpose," he said, sounding so pathetic and beaten that it stole some of my rage. "I'd never do that."

"I know that, you shithead." I threw up my hands. "You wouldn't ever try and kill yourself. You just disregard safety and good sense, and put yourself in dangerous situations. Like bar fights and surfing during fucking hurricanes!"

He flinched, and I realized he was crying. I tried to pull myself together.

"I'm sorry," he sobbed, raising his hands to cover his eyes. "I'm so, so sorry."

My anger banked and I sat on the bed, catching his arms to lower them. I wiped the tears off his face and shushed him. "Okay, okay. I'm sorry I yelled at you. You just scared the fucking shit out of me. I've spent the past week reliving Stacey's death with her parents, and finding a way to get myself enough together to come back here, and you almost go and kill yourself! Are you trying to give me a complex? I'm busting my ass trying to overcome my psychotic belief that loving me gets people killed . . . and you pull this fucking stunt?"

He blinked. "What?"

"When I left, I went to Stacey's grave. I didn't do it on purpose. I just found myself there. And Stacey's parents were there. And I found out they don't hate me like I've always thought. I realized I'm not a gypsy, and that I don't want to live my life like this anymore. I want a home, and a family, and stability, and . . . yes, a fucking white picket fence! I realized that all I wanted was to come back here and take it all back. I wanted to tell you how much I love you, and that I'm so sorry I lied and said I didn't. I wanted to fix it, to fix us, but I was afraid I'd fucked it up too badly and you wouldn't talk to me, but I was determined to try to get you to listen and then Gage called and he was freaking out and talking about blood and then I drove down here and now I'm yelling at you and making you cry and I love you so much and don't you ever fucking scare me like this again!"

He smiled at me. "Say that again."

"Don't fucking scare me like that again," I teased, knowing full well what part he wanted to hear.

He reached up with his good arm and traced my jaw with his fingers. "Please?"

"I love you!" I nuzzled my face against his hand. "But you're still a jackass."

"I know. In my defense, you were a serious bitch."

I sighed. "How are you? Really? Don't BS me."

He lay back and closed his eyes. "I'm afraid to face my family."

I took his hand as he started to cry again.

"What the hell am I going to say to Bo? She was so upset she almost lost the baby. I couldn't have lived with that."

I shushed him. "The baby is fine. So is Bo."

"Gage isn't fine," he said. "I can't imagine what it was like for him finding me like that. The poor kid is still shaking. And it was already bad enough before."

"What do you mean?" I asked.

He closed his eyes tightly. "I hit him."

"What?"

"I got in a fight with Dan at a bar. Gage tried to break it up. It was an accident. I was drunk. Hell, I can't remember it really. I think I caught him with my elbow. I knocked him down. He's got a nasty shiner."

I put the story together. "So, after you accidentally hit Gage, you went home and threw yourself a guilt party, got absolutely hammered, and fell down the stairs."

"Yes. And now the poor kid is fucked up for life because he found his big brother lying in a pool of blood."

"Gage will be fine," I said. "It's gonna take some time, but he'll be okay. They all will. You scared everyone."

"I shcared myshelf," he admitted, slurring his words. "Divine, I don't want to sleep."

I leaned over and kissed his cheek. "You need to, Bear."

"What if you're just a dream?"

"I'm not a dream. I promise."

"You'll be here when I wake up?"

"Yes."

"Promise me?"

"I promise I will be here when you wake up."

"Forever?"

He was asleep before I could think of the right thing to say.

Chapter 49

I WAS HESITANT to leave Mason's side, not wanting him to panic if I wasn't right there when he woke again. But I had a feeling he'd be out for a while. I stood at the top of the stairs, looking down. I could see where his head had hit, because there was a chunk of wood missing on one stair. I shivered as the image of him falling came unwelcome to my mind.

Ray looked up from where he was still scrubbing the floor. "How is he?"

I forced myself to walk down the stairs, skipping the step with the chunk missing. I walked into my father's open arms and blinked back fresh tears.

"He's so hurt . . ." My voice came out in a whisper.

"He's gonna be fine."

"He's extremely lucky. He could have broken his neck."

"He's lucky he has a head like a cinderblock."

"Yeah, well, it's a cracked one."

"But not broken. He'll be up and about in a day or two. The break on his arm is gonna keep him out of work for a while, though."

"He's worried about Gage. So am I."

He nodded. "He's still in shock. I almost didn't let him drive home, but it's not far. He called me when he got there, like I asked."

I pulled out my cell phone and called him. He answered on the third ring.

"Are you here?" he asked.

"Yes. I got here a little while ago."

"How's Mason?"

"He's sleeping."

"Did you talk to him?"

"Yes. He's worried about you. So am I. Is anyone home with you?"

"No."

"Do you want to come back over here? Ray and I are here. If you don't want to be alone."

"Is it cleaned up?"

"Yes. You can't see it at all anymore."

"I want to come home. I want my bed. I don't think I should be alone right now."

"Are you okay to drive?"

"Yeah. I think so."

"See you in a few."

I hung up and called Nancy. Her phone was off, likely due to being in the hospital with Bo. I left her a message. "Hey Nancy. I might be the last person on the planet you want to hear from, but I wanted you to know that Gage called me this morning. I just got back. I'm here with Mason. Gage isn't doing so well. I'm gonna keep him close to me until he calms down. Please let me know if I can do anything, and I hope Bo and the baby are doing well."

I hung up and went back inside to talk to Ray.

"Gage is coming back here," I said, inspecting the scrubbed floor. There wasn't a trace of blood left.

"He looked like hell when he left. Poor kid."

"We need to stop calling him a kid. He's twenty-one."

Ray rolled his eyes. "He's a kid. He's lived a fairly sheltered life, too. Nothing really bad has ever happened to him. He's also by far the most sensitive of the Tavish brothers. Mason and Axel are rough, physical guys. Gage tries to play tough with them, but he isn't."

I heard a moan from upstairs.

"Go sit with him. I'll see what I can do for Gage when he gets here."

I went back to Mason, but he was still asleep. I curled up on the bed with him, careful not to press against his bruises. He mumbled something, but I couldn't understand. He did it again, and I realized he was saying my name. He started to shift uncomfortably, and the mumbling got louder and more panicked.

"Mason?" I sat up and touched his face. "I'm right here. It's okay, Bear. I'm right here. Go back to sleep."

He sighed and lay back. I ran my fingers through what was left of his hair. He kept it short anyway, but he was going to have to buzz it or wear a hat while the shaved part grew back. He had three or four days of beard stubble. I ran my fingers over the roughness. I loved him so much. What had I been thinking when I left him?

There was a light knock on the door frame. I turned to see Gage. He was dressed in a pair of basketball shorts and a white tank top. Something about the way he stood made him appear years younger. I got up off the bed and walked to him. He looked fragile, and painfully vulnerable.

"How are you doing?" I asked.

He looked in at Mason and started to cry. I pulled him down the hall into his bedroom, not wanting to wake Mason. He was shaking violently and his breathing was ragged and uneven. I put my arms around him, and he started sobbing in earnest. I held him, stroking his back and soaking up his tears.

"I'm so . . . fucking . . . mad at him," he managed to get out between whimpers.

"I know."

"I keep s-s-seeing him . . . lying there. I'm afraid to c-close my eyes."

"It's okay, Gage."

"It's not okay." He held me tighter, so hard it was difficult to breathe. "I thought he was dead. I thought my brother was dead."

"I know, sweetheart. But he's okay now."

"I want to go in there and punch him."

"Trust me, I know the feeling. I yelled at him."

He pulled back, obviously fighting to get control of himself. He wiped at his face to dry his tears. I wasn't surprised to see such open emotion from Gage, but I could tell he was fighting it. He was trying to be strong and stoic like his older brothers.

"I wanted to blame you," he admitted. "But this wasn't your fault. You fucked up his head, yeah. You did some damage with whatever you said to him when you left. But everything after that was his doing. He was the one who was getting blind drunk every night. He was the one punching walls and throwing things. He's the one who hit me."

I reached out and brushed my fingers across his bruised cheek. "He cried when he told me about that."

Gage snorted. "Mason doesn't cry."

"Yes, he does," I said. "He cried, because he's terrified you won't forgive him. He thinks you're fucked up for life because you found him like that."

My comments had the desired effect. "I'm not fucked up for life," he muttered, defensively. "I'm gonna have nightmares for months, but I'll get over it."

I smiled. He'd needed to hear himself say that. "Yes, you will," I reassured him. "Trust me. I've seen some horrible things in my life. What I'm worried about is if Mason will ever forgive himself for this. For you finding him like that. For Bo ending up in the hospital."

"That's on Bo," he snorted. "She's just as bad as Mason. I mean, he had already been assessed by the doctor as okay when we told her. She totally overreacted and scared the baby, and even Zach had to be sedated."

"I tried calling your mom to check on Bo, but she didn't answer."

"They were resting comfortably when I left the hospital at six. Zach is sleeping off the sedative they gave him."

He sat on his bed. "Can you just distract me for a while?"

I sat beside him and told him about Stacey and her family. I told him all the things I'd been thinking about the past few days. I watched his eyes drooping while I talked. I shoved him down on his bed and told him funny stories about my traveling days until he was asleep.

I smiled to myself, knowing my traveling days were truly behind me.

CHAPTER 50

I STEPPED BACK from Mason and turned off the buzzer. I'd buzzed off his hair to the shortest setting, trying to blend it with the shaved patch as much as possible. He refused to shave his head, so this was the best we could do. He looked in the bathroom mirror without any enthusiasm.

"It looks okay," I said, only half lying. Mason was handsome enough he could have bad hair and no one would notice. A day of sleep had eased the swelling and bruising, and I'd removed the bandage over the stitches. He was going to have a long, thin scar, but half of it would be under his hair once it grew back.

He continued looking at himself in the mirror, but I had a feeling he wasn't paying attention to his hair. I thought he was looking *for* himself, not at it.

"I have to go talk to Gage," he said.

Gage had slept most of the past day, just as Mason had. They hadn't spoken at all since Gage had brought Mason home from the hospital, and that conversation had contained about four words and been fogged by painkillers.

I kissed Mason's cheek and squeezed his hand. "Just go talk to him. He's your brother. He loves you. Nothing could ever change that."

I shamelessly eavesdropped at the bedroom door when Mason went inside.

"Hey," Gage said.

"Hey."

There was a long silence. Eventually, Mason spoke. "How's your head?"

"A lot better than yours," Gage said, with a trace of his usual good humor.

Mason grunted a laugh. "Yeah. Think I should give up and shave the rest of it?"

"You'd look like an ass. So, yeah."

There was another silence before Mason said, "I'm sorry. I'm sorry about everything."

"It's okay . . ." Gage began.

"No, it's not okay. I'm your big brother. It's my job to keep you safe and to set a good example. I'm supposed to have my shit together."

"I said it's fine."

"It's not. I don't know what I've been thinking the past week or so."

"You were thinking that the love of your life fucked you over, and left you for no reason. You're allowed to be messed up about that."

"But that doesn't mean I get to binge drink and scare the hell out of you. I hit you, for fuck's sake!"

"It was an accident."

"So was falling down the stairs. I'm sorry you had to find me like that."

"I'm glad I did. Mason. The doctors said that if I hadn't come home when I did, if I hadn't found you so soon after you fell . . . you probably would have died. I'm gonna have nightmares, yeah. But I still have you, so I don't care. Just never ever do anything like that again. Holy shit, are you crying?"

"Why, are you surprised?"

"You don't cry. You're the tough one, remember?"

"You've been promoted to the tough one now. I'm taking a sabbatical."

I peeked around the door frame to see them hugging. Mason wasn't generally comfortable with physical displays of affection.

It was one of the primary differences between them; Gage hugged everyone. He snuggled on the couch with Bo, and occasionally had with me. He'd never had to be the tough one, which left him free to be himself. Mason, as the eldest in a relatively poor family with four kids, had taken on a particular role with his siblings. He'd taken on extra responsibility at a young age, and it had shaped who he was as an adult. Letting Gage see him cry and then hugging him was a monumental thing for him, having always felt he had to be the strong one.

Gage pulled back. "So," he said. "I saved your life. Doesn't that mean you have to be my slave, or something?"

Mason grinned. "Don't press your luck." He paused, and put his hand on his little brother's shoulder. "I love you. You know that, right?"

"Don't get all sappy on me." Gage rolled his eyes. "Of course I know."

"I just don't think I've ever said it to you."

"Well I love you too. You jackass."

I smiled and went downstairs to make them breakfast, and stopped at the broken stair. I had been jumping over it, as if not touching it made it not-have-happened. I realized that was my pattern. Something bad happened, and I jumped over it, pretending it didn't exist. So I'd ended up with so many things to jump over that I couldn't find a safe place to land. I had to break that pattern. I forced myself to walk down all the stairs, even the one that had almost killed the love of my life. I was done searching for a safe landing. I'd just put one foot in front of the other, like a normal, well-adjusted person. I had people now to catch me if I tripped.

Chapter 51

MASON AND I WALKED the hospital corridor in silence. He was anxious about seeing Bo and Zach. The doctors had decided to induce labor, after determining that the baby was healthy and there shouldn't be any complications. Bo had asked to talk to Mason before being induced.

Mason was walking stiffly due to his numerous injuries, but he refused to take more painkillers. He'd borrowed a baseball cap from Gage, seeing as he didn't like or own any hats, but wanted to hide his hair. We turned the corner and found Zach standing in the hallway outside of Bo's room. He looked at Mason with a rage I hadn't been prepared for. Zach was a big man, but I'd never once been nervous around him. Now I wanted to hide behind Mason as he shifted his weight toward us.

Mason walked slowly up to Zach, obviously bracing himself for a physical or emotional blow.

"Don't say anything," Zach said, in a tone that made the hairs on my arms stand up. "Not one word. Not to me, not right now."

Mason nodded, keeping his head down like a scolded child.

Zach rubbed at his eyes. "I'm not thinking right. I'm overreacting. But I do know that you aren't to blame for what happened to Bo and Alex. I still want to find a stairway and toss you down it right now."

Mason nodded again.

Zach sighed and shook his head. "I'll calm down. And once I do, I'll find something horrible for you to do to make this up to me. Okay?"

Mason nodded again.

"I'll give you some time with your sister," Zach said. He paused and put his hand on Mason's shoulder. "I'm glad you're okay."

I watched him walk away. "I knew he'd be mad, but that was a bit scary."

"Zach's first wife committed suicide while she was pregnant," Mason told me. "Then he almost lost this baby, too. He's allowed to want to hurt me. Hell, I kinda wish he'd have hit me."

I looked at Zach's back as he turned the corner. I never would have guessed that he'd had that much trauma in his past. Then again, maybe that was why he laughed so rarely.

We went into Bo's room. She lay on the bed in her gown, reading a trashy romance novel. She looked up and smiled, putting the book aside.

"What's with the hat, Mase?" she asked. "You hate baseball caps. And baseball."

Reluctantly, he took it off. Bo's eyes went to the stitches and his shaved and buzzed hair, and her eyes filled with tears.

"Don't fucking do that!" Mason said. "Don't get upset. If you get worked up again, Zach is going to kill me. Literally."

She sniffed. "Just come here and let me hug you so I know you're really okay."

He leaned down and she put her arms around him. He sat on the bed beside her, twisted awkwardly because of her belly. She closed her eyes and I saw her mouthing what I thought was *thank you*. "Don't you ever scare us like that again," she said to him.

"I promise, Bo. I'll never do anything like that again."

She released him and wiped at her tears. She glanced at me. "You're responsible for him now, you know. He obviously needs a keeper."

"I've accepted the job," I said. "Even though I was a bit late." I forced myself to stop wringing my hands. "I'm sorry I left like that.

I've been meaning to apologize to everyone, but things were a bit crazy and I haven't had time."

"Well, you came back." She shrugged. Then her eyes narrowed. "You are planning on staying, right?"

"Yes," I said. "I'll admit that I might have to take a little vacation now and then, but I'll always come back, and I won't abandon everyone when I go."

"Good." She lay back and closed her eyes. "I'm gonna be too busy with this kid to keep an eye on Mason. Like I said, he needs a keeper."

"Does your mom hate me?" I asked.

Bo snorted. "Of course not. We're all mad at Mason for acting like a baby and hurting himself."

"It was an accident," he muttered.

"Falling down the stairs was," Bo said. "Getting hammered drunk and acting like a total ass for a week wasn't. Do you remember calling me at 3:00 a.m.?"

He sulked. "No."

"Well, you overshared, big brother. Just so you know."

He slouched lower. "I said I'm sorry."

"Actually, you hadn't yet."

"I'll say I'm sorry for the rest of my life, okay?" he muttered, putting the hat back on as the door opened. Zach walked in, choosing the opposite side of the bed, to keep his distance from Mason.

"Doctors will be here in a minute," he said.

"I'm perfectly calm. Don't pretend you didn't come in here to check," Bo snorted.

Zach glanced at Mason.

"Stop looking at him like that." Bo slapped at his shoulder. "It was my fault for overreacting like I did. Hell, everyone told me he was fine. I just lost my fucking mind. That was my fault, Zach. Mine. Remember all those times you said stupid things and I left the house crying? Mason didn't come over and hit you with a baseball bat, now did he?"

"Only because you asked him not to," Zach muttered, but there was a hint of a smile.

"Yes. And he listened to me, because he's my brother and he loves me. And you are going to listen to me, because you are my husband and you love me."

Zach sighed and leaned down to kiss her forehead. "Okay. I won't toss his worthless ass down the nearest stairwell."

"Thank you," she smiled.

Zach glanced at me for the first time. "So, done with your disappearing act?"

"Yes. I'm sorry I left like that. And I never thanked you for the show. It was amazing and wonderful, and I never would have had any of it without you."

He shrugged. "It was fun. You need to start working on the fishing series, though. I've already been talking to the local charities. And you should keep the gallery open, now that you're going to be here. I've had tons of people call wanting to know when you were going to have another show. You've got some offers for commissioned work, as well."

I stared at him. "Seriously?"

"I'd have thought that your success at the show would have cured you of this misconception that you lack talent." He rolled his eyes, a very boyish gesture for a big, bearded man.

"I'm working on not hating myself," I admitted. I found myself telling them about my trip to Rhode Island. I talked about Stacey and her parents, and how I had come to the conclusion that I'd been a gypsy for all the wrong reasons. I reassured them that I was going to stay, for the longest periods of time that I could, until it was permanent.

When the doctors came for Bo, Mason and I headed to a waiting room. We found Nancy, Trace, and Gage lounging on couches. I hadn't expected a warm welcome, but I should have known better. Nancy jumped off the couch and ran to hug me.

"How are you?" she asked.

"I'm sorry I left without talking to you . . ."

"Don't worry about it," she said. "The important thing is that you came back when we needed you. And thank you, for taking care of

Gage. I didn't realize he was that upset. I should have known, but I was just so distracted by Bo..."

"Mom, I'm fine," Gage whined, blushing.

"None of you are fine," she snapped. "All three of you are trying to give me a heart attack. Axel is now my favorite."

Mason sulked dramatically. "I thought I was your favorite."

She narrowed her eyes at him. "You want another lecture?"

"No."

"One more word and you'll get one. Don't be mouthy to me. I've been through enough the past few days."

He caught his mother and pulled her into a hug. "I love you, Mom."

She smiled. "Good. Now start showing it by taking better care of yourself."

"You don't have to worry about me anymore. I've got a keeper now, according to Bo."

Nancy gave me a harsh look. "Gage told me you plan on staying this time."

I took the opportunity to rehash my Rhode Island trip again. I'd have to do it a few more times probably, with Axel and Maxine, and friends like Kol and Laura. We had plenty of time to kill, so I ended up talking about my childhood with the Lumens. I told them all the stories about my life, stories I'd never told anyone before. I wanted to make up for leaving, so I was going to give them as much of myself as I could.

Chapter 52

I JUMPED AS THE ALARM sounded, nearly ruining the portrait I was working on, of Kol on his boat. I set my pencil down and looked out the window to see who had pulled in the driveway. The alarm was a new feature Ray had installed once I'd opened the gallery full time. There was a strip in the driveway and when anything went over it, the alarm sounded in the house and in my studio, so I'd know I had a customer. It was turned up extremely loud, to make sure I actually heard it while I was working.

I was wearing jeans with numerous holes and worn patches, and a blue leather vest that showed off the bear on my belly-button ring. The first week I'd had the gallery open I'd tried to dress professionally; the reality was, I wasn't up to putting on that kind of show on a regular basis. If people liked my art and wanted to show up at random to see it, they were gonna see the real me, too.

I smiled at the woman, who was already inside, looking around. I'd gotten used to talking to customers, though it still felt odd to just stand there and watch them. We chatted about how it was still warm for October, and how nice it was to have the summer tourists gone. I knew I was going to miss the business from the summer crowd, but for now it was nice to be able to take a left on the highway. I wasn't that far removed from a tourist myself, but the customers didn't realize that.

The woman purchased a print of the man tying his daughter's shoes and chatted some more about her children and how much she loved my work. While she was talking, the alarm went off again. I glanced over her shoulder out the window and smiled as Ray's truck pulled into its usual spot.

I swiped the woman's credit card in the new attachment to my phone, loving that Zach had set it up for me. I had a cash register set up in the corner, but mostly I ended up using my phone for everything. Technology was amazing.

I walked to the door with the woman and waved to her, but my attention was on Mason and Ray. They were home from work. Mason walked over and kissed me. He was sweaty with a dusting of sawdust; my favorite flavor.

"How was work?" I asked.

"Fine. My arm's still bothering me a bit," he admitted, indicating the arm that had until recently been in a cast.

"Maybe we should have stayed in Maine a few more days."

"Hey, some of us have to work!"

"I'm working."

He smiled and kissed my nose. "You're always working. It would be fun to go back to Maine soon, though. Maybe for a long weekend."

"You know you don't have to go along with my travel bug," I reminded him. "You don't have to come with me every time I travel."

He nodded. "I know that. And whenever you get the itch and go for over a week again, I'll resort to calling you every day until you feel bad and come home."

I smiled. We'd enjoyed two weeks of camping in Maine while his arm was broken and he hadn't been able to work. I'd met some interesting individuals while there, and now had some striking portraits of them in the gallery. Most of my time had been occupied working on the fishing series, although the show wouldn't be until next summer. We were going to have a smaller version of the benefit in a few weeks for the locals. I figured the prints would make good Christmas gifts for the fishermen and their families.

Ray had gone inside without saying hello, which wasn't normal. I had a hunch as to why, though.

"Does Ray have a date with Laura tonight?" I asked.

"Yeah. They're doing dinner and a movie."

"So we've got the kids?" I asked.

"Not tonight. They're with Maxine."

Maxine was six months pregnant, but that hadn't slowed her down at all. She'd decided she wanted to run a day care out of the house, and was in the process of setting up the business. She was going to have two kids all the time, anyway, so why not add a few more?

"So we're kid-free?" I asked.

"Yep, 'cause we're going on a date, too."

I smiled and ran my fingers through his hair. The scar wasn't that noticeable now that it had grown back in, but I knew he was still self-conscious about it. He was also still tiptoeing around his family, especially Zach. I told him Zach was so preoccupied with baby Alex that he'd completely forgotten about the whole thing, but Mason still worried.

I took his hand. "So where are we going?"

"Wherever you want."

"That's a dangerous thing to say to me, you know."

He pulled me closer against his side. "I trust you."

I smiled as we walked into the house. The only place I wanted to go was home. And home was wherever he was.

From *Fluke Chance*, Book 3 in the Cape Cod Cadences series

I WALKED INSIDE the bar, instantly feeling at home. I wanted to head right to the pool tables, but I knew that Divvy was waiting for me at a booth. The struggle to ignore the pool tables became more difficult as I noticed the man bent over one of them. I loved a man in jeans and work boots, and he filled his out nicely. He was a big guy, broad shouldered and well muscled. He had a fantastic ass. He wore a T-shirt with Jorgenson Landscaping written on the back. I admired the muscles of his arms, noting the sleeve of black tattoos on his right one.

"Izzy!" I heard Divvy yell from a booth in the other room. I forced my eyes away from the hunk at the pool table to smile at my oldest friend. I'm ashamed to admit my gaze went right back to the guy, however.

He'd moved around to the other side and was now facing me. At first, the only thing I noticed was that he was wearing a black eye-patch. It was so bizarre that I didn't notice anything else for a couple of seconds. But even that oddity couldn't distract me from the rest of him for long. His shirt hugged more muscles in all the right places. His skin tone and features suggested Eastern European. He was unshaven and it made him look dangerous and sexy. It was dark in the bar so I couldn't be sure what color his eye was, but it was lighter in contrast to his dark hair.

He must have felt me watching him because he glanced up and met my eyes. I smiled my best inviting smile, not being the subtle type. He instantly looked down and pretended I didn't exist. I wasn't surprised. He might be trying to look like a badass, but he wasn't fooling me.

"What the hell, girl!" Divvy yelled. "What's so interesting you're keeping me waiting?"

Pull your head out of your ass, Isabella. He's just a guy. So it's been awhile since you got laid. Your best friend still comes before a hot piece of ass. I gave one last lusting glance at the pirate and wondered how good of a pool player he could be without depth perception. I'd have to find out another time.

ACKNOWLEDGMENTS

I want to say thank you to everyone who has helped me write this book. My family, friends, co-workers, and random acquaintances, who listened to me yammer on about my idea and about every little change I made. Thank you to my writing group, The Tuesday Group that Meets on Fridays: Anita, Barbara #1, Barbara #2, Carol, Iris, Jerry, Joan, Pat, and Yvonne. Though my work schedule kept much of this book from you, every word you sent my way was so encouraging and appreciated. And thank you to my team from Booktrope, for making my second book a reality!

ALSO BY NIKOLE JALBERT HOUSER

Catching Bodel (Romance) Bodel Tavish is content coasting along in life without challenges or goals until Zach Cutter inherits the Cape Cod house where she lives and changes everything.

Made in the USA
Middletown, DE
18 June 2016